FREQUENCY

The Hour of Power Has Come

HILLARY RIES SHEKINAH MA

BALBOA.PRESS

A DIVISION OF HAY HOUSE

Balboa Press books may be ordered through booksellers or by contacting:

Balboa Press
A Division of Hay House
1663 Liberty Drive
Bloomington, IN 47403
www.balboapress.com
1 (877) 407-4847

Because of the dynamic nature of the Internet, any web addresses or links contained in this book may have changed since publication and may no longer be valid. The views expressed in this work are solely those of the author and do not necessarily reflect the views of the publisher, and the publisher hereby disclaims any responsibility for them.

The author of this book does not dispense medical advice or prescribe the use of any technique as a form of treatment for physical, emotional, or medical problems without the advice of a physician, either directly or indirectly. The intent of the author is only to offer information of a general nature to help you in your quest for emotional and spiritual well-being. In the event you use any of the information in this book for yourself, which is your constitutional right, the author and the publisher assume no responsibility for your actions.

Any people depicted in stock imagery provided by Getty Images are models, and such images are being used for illustrative purposes only. Certain stock imagery © Getty Images.

Print information available on the last page.

ISBN: 978-1-9822-4805-5 (sc)
ISBN: 978-1-9822-4806-2 (e)

Library of Congress Control Number: 2020909551

Balboa Press rev. date: 05/27/2020

This book is dedicated to the Hopi Nation for their huge contribution to humanity by way of their visionary and prophetic wisdom and teachings contained within the "Hopi Prophecy," which is my main inspiration for this book.
Thank You!

Secondly, I would like to dedicate this book to all the Healers, Light Workers, Rainbow Warriors, Grid Workers, Star Seeds, Shamans, and to all the Protectors of Life … to the Water, Land, Sky, Children, Elder, and Animals Protectors.
Thank you!

Finally, I would like to dedicate this book to you, the reader, for having the audacity to read something out there on the fringe. Your support in my coming out as I share my message of hope to humanity, means the world to me.
Thank You!

Thank you to my children Ambrosia and Rhiannon, who I have laboured to share this message in honour of and for the seven generations to come. Be the change you want to see in the world. Thank you to my lover and to my friends who believed I could complete this project and write this book even though I have never written a book before. Believe in yourself, anything is possible!
Thank You!

I do hope that you my beloved reader enjoy my message to humanity. While this book is considered a Sci-Fi Fantasy there are many points of truth that can be investigated, and I do urge you to do so. For you may find that the truth in regards to life is in fact a Science Fiction based Fantasy story indeed.

Blessings,
Aho!

**For
Soul
Entertainment
Purposes
Only**

CONTENTS

OPENING PRAYER CALL TO THE FOUR DIRECTIONS

Please take a moment to sit inside the sacred space of awareness
with me as we tune now into the Circle of Life and to our Breath
of Life. Pray with me as we begin this conscious journey that we
may have eyes to see, ears to hear, and a heart that is wide open.
Placing your hands now on your heart
center, please repeat after me ...

To the East, to the Place of the Rising Sun
To the Winged Ones, Bird Tribe, Angels, and Fay
To the Bringers of Life of Prana and of Chi
To the Element of Air and Sacred Eagle Vision
Be with Us We Welcome You Here Now
Aho
To the South to the Place of the Peaking Sun
To the Dragon Nation
To the Purifiers, Protectors, and Passionate Ones
To the Element of Fire
To the Great Rainbow Serpent Who Sheds
Old Skins and Transforms All Things
Please Assist Us in Shedding the Old Templates
and Timelines of Lack and Limitation
Please Help Open Us to Our Divine Potential Now
Aho
To the West to the Place of the Setting Sun
To the Merfolk Mermaids and Mermen
To the Element of Water
The Sacred Waters of Life, Our Blood Sweat
and Tears, Rivers, Seas, and Oceans
To the Ancient Mother and Grandmother of the Sea
You Who are the Keeper of Ancient Mysteries

Please Assist us in Remembering Who We Are Why
We Are Here and From Whence We Have Come
Aho
To the North the Place of the Setting Sun
White Haired Man White Haired Woman
To the Sasquatch Beloved Guides and Guardians of Life and Truth
To the Element of Earth
Help Us to Rebirth
Please Assist Us in Raising Our Vibrations Up to 5D
and Help Us to Usher In the 5th Age of Peace
Aho
Mitak Oyasin
All my Relations

THE HOPI PROPHECY

You have been telling people that this is the Eleventh Hour,
now you must go back and tell the people that this is the Hour.
And there are things to be considered... Where are you living?
What are you doing?
What are your relationships?
Are you in right relation?
Where is your water?
Know your garden.
It is time to speak your truth.
Create your community.
Be good to each other.
And do not look outside yourself for your leader.
"This could be a good time! There is a river flowing now
very fast. It is so great and swift that there are those who
will be afraid. They will try to hold on to the shore. They
will feel they are being torn apart and will suffer greatly.
Know the river has its destination. The elders say we must
let go of the shore, push off into the middle of the river,
keep our eyes open, and our heads above the water.
And I say, see who is in there with you and celebrate. At
this time in history, we are to take nothing personally,
least of all ourselves. For the moment that we do, our
spiritual growth and journey come to a halt.
The time of the lone wolf is over. Gather yourselves! Banish the
word 'struggle' from your attitude and your vocabulary. All that
we do now must be done in a sacred manner and in celebration.
We are the ones we have been waiting for.
--Hopi Elders' Prophecy, June 8, 2000

MESSAGES FROM THE "WISE ONES"

Understanding the Times

"The caterpillar-me is history, my metamorphosis, a mystery, and today... today is a present, my struggle gifted me."
Manali Oak

Beginning disclosure statement, this book may make you want to question everything you think you know, but take it from me that is a good thing! I invite you now to open your mind and your heart to what lies beyond your perceived understanding of life itself. For what lies beyond the boundaries of your conditioned thought constructs is freedom and authenticity. Before getting started I suggest you grab yourself a cozy blanket, a pot of warm herbal tea, and have your medicine bag on hand... here we go ... prepare for lift off!

The "Wise Ones" have spoken and would like to get their message heard for it is a message to humanity. I come to you now as their messenger to share with you their wisdom upon understanding the times we all find ourselves in today. The first section of this book is a collection of messages from the "Wise Ones," whom are a team of "Spirit Guides" that seek to share their message to help guide us all through what is to come in this time we are finding ourselves in where there is great change and transformation afoot.

Let me start by introducing myself to you, my name is Sophia Star Water, and this is my story. "Her-Story" you can call it rather than his, lol. Now I do not mean to sound divisive for I know that we are all in fact equal and at one as is defined by the "Law of Oneness" which states ... "Everything is connected to everything else. What we think, say, do and believe will have a corresponding effect on others and the world around us. All of humanity and God are one. We are always connected to the Source of God because the energy of God is everywhere at once, and permeates through all things living or material, as well as the knowledge of God which is infinite and always available to us. Each soul is part of God's energy. Everything that exists seen and unseen is connected to each other, inseparable from each other and to the field of divine oneness." With that being said, "Her-Story" is a story based on a holistic holographic awareness of "The Circle of Life." Not a linear story but a story that speaks to and introduces you to a round table of high conscious beings and their understanding of the "Law of Onesness." Her-story is a story that speaks of the wisdom of the ages and sages and their message they offer to us all as we reconnect to higher consciousness.

The message that is being offered asks for us to stop pretending that pain feels good, that wrong is right. It offers the guidance to stop living in illusions of separation giving us some misguided perception that we can go on and continue to hurt one another and not have to feel the pain. To stop pretending that the way we are living is sustainable or even humane when clearly it is not as we look out into the world around us and see the many crises' breaking out. This is why the "Wise Ones" have come to share their message, for they want us to wake up and remember who and what we are, that we were made in God's image and that we have a Divine purpose to fulfil!

The question to ask one's self the "Wise Ones" say is ... how can I, how can we as the human race collectively continue to live in disharmony, imbalance, or dis-ease one more day knowing that what we do to the web of life we do to ourselves? Honestly, how can we carry on pretending that what we are doing to the world and one another is appropriate when it is clearly smacking us in the face with repercussions for our actions and consequences for our behaviour?

Again, this is why the "Wise Ones" have come forward for they understand that we have been led astray by very deceptive forces and they offer to us their help. They want to reveal to us now the secret that has been hidden, kept safe in Mystery Schools around the world since the beginning of time. They come to enlighten us, to share with us all that they know. For they want us to know that there is an absolute reason as to why everything is the way that it is. That it is all a part of a Divine plan engineered by them and they ask us to trust in the process.

Our modern ways of living which have disconnected us from what is real and what is sacred has been making it very difficult to maintain or even sustain life on our great Mother. Mother Earth, the "Wise Ones" say has taken our misuse of her and abuse of her for far too long now and they have said enough is enough. Once again as the "Law of Oneness" states, "everything is connected to everything else." With that known and even confirmed through Quantum Physics I invite you to listen to what the "Wise Ones" have come to say because Mama is calling for you, she is saying "time to get up dear children, wake up from your dream state and remember who you are!" This is what the "Wise Ones" want you to know. They come to let us know that they have called for the return to the "Law of Oneness" from the broken sphere of duality that we have all been held bound to throughout our collective past.

The "Wise Ones," say that as we return to "Oneness" and to the "Unified Field of Consciousness" itself, that we will mend the "Sacred Hoop of Life" from where it had been broken long, long ago. The "Wise Ones" have also said that as we mend the "Sacred Hoop of Life" as was taught by the Hopi Nation, that we will make our way full circle back to truth like a miraculous return to innocence thus moving us into a New Age called the 5th Age of Peace as was long prophesized.

What the "Wise Ones" say about truth for this is very important to them and it is the medicine of the Sasquatch guides I work with directly; they say that the truth can appear real even while being absolutely false or even fake. That the real actual and factual truth resides within the sacred space and place where the curtains have been brought down and the wizards behind them revealed. It is the place where the veils have been lifted and where there is no longer any need for secrets or lies. This is simply because there is no ability to have secrets and lies while existing in a high conscious, high vibrational field as the "Law of Oneness" expresses.

Real or true authentic high conscious energy and information is transparent, it is not clouded by opinions and perceived ideas or judgements; it just simply is! This is because in the "Law of Oneness" which is the operating field of the "Wise Ones," all is shared in truth and in honesty, nothing is done in the darkness for all is known and shared by felt presence within the light! This realization between what is done in the darkness in comparison to what is done in the light is how you will be able to discern and determine what is real and what is not. This information is accessed through the Totem and teachings of the Sasquatch Nation, for they are the Guardians of Truth and their medicine is Honesty!

These messages and teachings that have come from the Sasquatch Nation is good medicine for you all right now to ponder and apply for there are many demons in Angel's clothing deceiving people each day. Selling people into limiting beliefs, thought constructs, and false information that appears real. The "False Shepherds" as Sasquatch likes to call them, get off through their egoist pride as they trap the innocent in illusions and delusions while then pursuing their own greedy quest for power capitalizing all the way off the innocent through their false Luciferic New Age movements and their other active Psy Ops running.

If you want to speak with Sasquatch or any other interdimensional being they want me to tell you that all you need to do is to invite them to connect with you, that it is entirely up to you and your free will. It is crucial however if you would like to do so, to have a decalcified pineal gland that can still speak in pictures. We call this area of inner communication, dialogue, and channeling the third eye or Ajna Chakra which is connected to one's soul. The soul consciousness is focused through this center as the pineal gland is considered to be the seat of the soul within the Yogic tradition. This is also the way "Animal Communicators" speak to animals it is what the "Wise Ones" call the language of love. The language of love is the ability to speak in pictures, showing rather than telling a message to another. I, Sophia Star Water call this dream spell speak. This is how all interdimensional beings Star Nations and Fay speak, they speak through the heart and third eye. It is also essential if you would like to begin connecting with the "Wise Ones" to come in a good way when inviting connection to these great majestic beings. You can also make offerings to them, build altars, and make sure to come forward with no force or agenda. They can feel you see you, all of you, and they read your heart like a book. For them there is no illusion or delusion that they are under, they have ascended from that state of consciousness and live in truth by law.

Now the Sasquatch guides that I am connected to who are a part of the "Wise Ones" but have their own council as well, refer to themselves as the "Great Council of Elders" or the "Elders" in short, and it is they who have taught me the picture or symbol of the Luciferic New Age movement which they are wanting us to be very cautious of. The picture they send is of an inverted web of life. This inverted web of life draws you to it as it is made from fool's gold and appears to be like pure gold shimmering in the light of the sun. They have conveyed to me that it is a trap, which draws you to its glamour or magical illusion shimmering in the morning dew just like a spider's web draws the fly. For in truth not all things that glitter are gold! Once you become stuck in this sticky web, the "Elders" say the next thing to happen is that a poisonous spider creeps right up to you and anesthetizes you with its venom putting you to sleep. While you than sleep in an inertia and amnesiac like state, it then sucks the essence right from your soul. Stay mindful the "Elders" say for these times are like the days of Christ when he walked into the temple of his father's house yelling ... "you have turned my father's house into a harlot!" Yes the wicked, so in need of prey the "Elders" say, will defile any and everything including the sacred and consciousness itself to feed upon.

The "Wise Ones" want us all to realize our Mother Earth is in distress. It is true currently right now Mother Earth, Pacha Mama, is sending out her SOS to the world and I bet she sure hopes that someone out there gets her message in the bottle! Let it be known, as in please "go tell it on the mountain over the hills and far away" as the Gospel song says, that we are at an end of an age the "Wise Ones" say. Yes, we are at the end of the fourth age to be specific as the Hopi people have taught and this is what the "Wise Ones" really want you to know. Now I know how you must feel, that is a very big horse pill to swallow! So, let us just take a pause now for the cause and have a moment of silence to allow for that all to settle in..... Cue the solfeggio high vibrational music xo

Now after a deep breath lets go on, the "Wise Ones" have also come to say that there is a very important realization that we must all make (and they say real eyes instead of realize, which I love). We must collectively real eyes they say that there is quite a lot of convoluted misinformation and disinformation being produced intentionally by our media and authorities. Yes, they are doing their best the "Wise Ones" say to intentionally confuse and disorient humanities consciousness because if we were to wake up, we would not participate for one moment further in their petty evil war games that are being played out daily against each and every one of us around the world. No, the wicked do not want to lose us, we are their host. They need us way more then we need them. That is why the "Wise Ones" say with a laugh, and they do have quite a sense of humor, that we all have got to check ourselves before we wreck ourselves, hence the message of this book.

You see the "Wise Ones" and I want you to know; despite all that I have brought up already, that this is not just a time of doom and gloom. It is a very sacred time now that we are all in. Whether you can acknowledge this time as sacred or not does not matter as much as how important it is how you will respond to all that is coming ahead of you. For it will become more and more essential as the years go by that we the people help one another wake up from the dream, the spell, and the trance that humanity has been under for thousands and thousands of years now.

What is this dream you may wonder, this dream that humanity has been under the spell of for time immemorial? Well, that is what this whole book is about, and it will be revealed through the pages yet to come. Now I know some of you may be like, what is this lady talking about? I am not dreaming; I am wide awake! Sorry but I have got to ask, are you? Are you awake? I ask that because this dream or spell has put the majority of humanity in its trance for so long now that the dream has become considered real and the real … a dream.

The beauty however is that the dream spell is wearing off and people by the thousands are waking up each day all over. The "Wise Ones" say that this is a sacred time that we are all finding ourselves in even though there is much we have to detach from and an enormous amount of sorrow to heal. But the truth is, the age of chaos and illusion known as Kali Yug is over. The dreamtime is coming to an end, spells are being dispelled, and the trances we have been under through mind controlling affects are no longer effective!

In the words of the "Elders," "This is a sacred time for all you humans, even as you are reading these words right now wherever you are whoever you are. Know you are collectively ascending from the lower densities rising back up from the fall from grace so long ago. Come rise back up little brothers, little seastars, rise to 5D beyond duality. All you need do is to open your minds hearts eyes and ears to the truth that is coming for you as you are being released out of the cage of 4D consciousness! This is why it is a sacred time, a good time. Please humble yourselves to the roots of grass oh human, send your ego to the back seat where it belongs, let your soul drive your ship from now on. As you do this we welcome you our brothers and seastars, we welcome you home to oneness!"

The "Wise Ones" say that it is the mission of those who keep us in bondage to thwart our ascension and keep us ensnared into their prison planet so that we can continue to be their slaves and host. The "Wise Ones" have had to become very creative to be able to help us given the level of infiltration that corruption has made. The "Wise Ones" speak to this corruptive force as a parasitic force. They say that the parasitic force has employed their corruption against the will or consent of humanity which is in direct violation to sacred law. They have done this the "Wise Ones" say through technologies and mind control agencies that are being delivered to us through genetic modification of our food, water, air, and medicine. Sounds terrible I know, but just have a look around you, just study your history even a bit and you will find that the "Wise Ones" are not wrong.

The good news though as it is always important to acknowledge that there is good news the "Wise Ones" say that the parasitic corruptive forces have had their time and the knowledge of good and evil is now complete. To quote the "Pleiadian Star Mother Council" who are also deeply connected to the "Wise Ones," they say that "resistance is futile, ascension is unavoidable. Prepare now by raising your frequency your vibratory capacity, for this is key to return hOMe dear children."

While the light and various allies of truth whom I refer to as the "Wise Ones" are working to reveal the wizards or lizards, lol, behind their curtains and veils of deception; we see that the parasitic forces have grown quite powerful; indeed, just take inventory of what they own … everything! However on the other hand of this false sense of power that they hold, there also exists a vast and unlimited team of beloved benign and benevolent Guides and Guardians of Creation that I have come to call the "Wise Ones" as I have mentioned before. It is they who are working around the clock tirelessly behind the scenes putting out the fires of the dark ones or the parasitic forces. They are sending in their messengers, healers, and technicians by the fleets and in legions to help us all along the way. Perhaps you have made contact already with a few of your own team. Perhaps you yourself are a Star Seed. Regardless of whom you are or from where you originate from, I encourage you to open your heart to the "Wise Ones" for they are your family and your allies, here to help you no matter what. All you have to do is ask.

Now call the parasitic forces or dark lords what you want … vampires, pedophiles, psychopaths, sociopaths … the "Wise Ones" say they are guilty of all your worst accusations. This despairing truth that most have been blind to for so long will continue to now be revealed and unfold in your current reality as painful as it may be to realize that you had been deceived. Yes, the feeling of being violated or deceived is a sensation indeed that you will all have to come to peace with as you watch the wicked get called out and cast out for the demons that they are in one grand spiritual exorcism ritual that is going on now behind the scenes.

The silver lining in all of this on a positive note is that the "Wise Ones" have officially called for the return to the "Law of Oneness" which will cancel and nullify all that lives in darkness, deceit, corruption, and wickedness. This you will come to see was always the plan, for yes there is a great plan underway, one that is quickly wrapping up to its conclusion.

The "Wise Ones" want you to know that they have elected to have me, yours truly Sophia Star Water, along with many other time travellers from the future to come back from 5D where we dwell now, to share with you our stories and our teachings for we know exactly what the plan is and how it all ends. The "Wise Ones" have asked me to do this as they feel that my story is imbued with the light of hope and that by sharing it, it has the power to bring a seed of hope to each person who reads it. For as the world turns and burns and yearns for salvation, the only thing at the end of a day that I had found when I walked 4D which allowed for me to keep waking up and carrying on despite the shit show erupting, was hope. As Desmond Tutu said and I quote, "hope is being able to see that there is light despite all of the darkness."

Apart of the "Wise Ones" are also the Merfolk; the mermaids and the mermen, and it is they who have taught me the next lesson I would like to share with you. Now you know how we all spell the word, right? Therefor our word is our spell. This is because we and all life are made primarily up of water. Now water the Merfolk teach is the receiving, grounding, imprinting, and conducting element which allows for us to become that what we speak. This is the great power and medicine of all Merfolk. It is in the science of Cymatics, and was taught to humans recently by one of their own great mermen who had come to the Earth as a man to reveal the secret life and magic of water.

Because of this great teaching, I have wrote very specific words as spells within this book to awaken your consciousness to the bigger picture of what is really going on and to seed within you hope as medicine. For when the dark days that are yet to come covers the light up in shadow, through hope you will know in your heart that once the storm passes, there will be light again, and no doubt a rainbow to boot. This is what the Merfolk remember and speak of when Lemuria and Atlantis were taken down and the mighty floods covered the Earth for they were witnesses to these times and to the great signs of wonder that appeared after when the first rainbow appeared.

Now by no means am I the first messenger that the "Wise Ones" and the Guides and Guardians, also known as the Galactic Confederation and Councils of Light, have sent to Earth. They have always sent in their messengers and prophets throughout the ages to help guide and direct consciousness. For consciousness you see, is really where the real battles are taking place between the forces of evil and the sources of goodness.

Hence, the coined term by one Graham Hancock stating that there is a "war on consciousness."

Be very aware and discerning the "Wise Ones" say for there are those who will seek to hack into your consciousness and even leave mind viruses there! I highly recommend you guard your consciousness with mindfulness from the pirates that will rob thy and sell you to their merchant ships. For consciousness you see is not an object, it is not a visible thing per se, it is an energetic beingness. It exists in the causal plane which then translates into form as physical. So while you may not see this direct war on consciousness now; once you become woke and have gained the eyes to see and the ears to hear as in from the unconscious to subconscious to conscious even super conscious, you will find that the unseen is far more powerful and profound then what is seen, especially since a typical human being only sees .0035% of the entire visible light spectrum. It is in this unseen yet very real world where all the Guides and Guardians or "Wise Ones" exists and where we are all destined to return in the 5th Age of Peace that is beginning.

This is the truth that you will one day ultimately real eyes as it is the necessary awakening requirement to see what is beyond the veils of illusion when one becomes self-realized. This is the same realization one has when they die and are no longer under the spell of third and fourth density. However there is another truth which must also be realized and that is that hidden in plain sight agenda right there in front of you this whole time. This agenda is being broadcasted through subliminal programming and it is in everything and everywhere you go. This programming and conditioning is for keeping your consciousness locked into the servant and slave archetypal mind control, shackling you to a ball and chain, tying you against your free will to a false reality. Also right there hidden in plain sight within human flesh suits has been the Dark Lords of the parasitic clans who in truth are the Archons or Architects of the Matrix, so saith the "Wise Ones." They are made up of the Dracos, the Reptilians, the Greys and other corrupted entities disguised throughout history.

Think of consciousness as the sunglasses from in the movie by John Carpenter called "They Live," one of Sasquatches favourite movies. In the movie "They Live" a man finds these sunglasses and puts them on, once he began wearing them he could see quite a different world then what he had previously been aware of. He could see that hidden in plain sight all around him in billboards and ads there had been all along subliminal messaging and programming feeding into people's subconscious minds to buy buy buy consume be slaves and do what they were told. This was all going on while their conscious minds had no idea! Also there were aliens inside the so called flesh suits of the political leaders and news broadcasters all hidden in plain sight as they controlled the people and governed their consciousness by making all the rules.

This is why the Indigenous people of the world have taught that it is necessary to be in truth and at oneness with Great Spirit so that one can have what is called "sacred sight." With sacred sight you are no longer blind nor unconscious to truth, for the truth is only hidden in plain sight everywhere for those who cannot see, but for those with sacred sight, it is clear as day. Hence "Amazing Grace how sweet the sound that saved a soul like me, I once was lost but now am found, was blind but now I see!"

The "Wise Ones" teach by example, and the example they would like to share with you is the NEWS. If you break down the word NEWS ... you will find that it stands for N. North, E. East, S. South, W. West! Now what you may not know is that the NEWS is used to cast a circle and then to program consciousness; as in tell us a vision "television" "programming" found on different "channels," all words used in magic and the craft.

So yes, I am afraid to say to you that the NEWS is used to program your consciousness and that is why it casts a circle using the four directions when they say, "this is the NEWS." Not to mention the fact that the NEWS is also almost entirely fake, or illusion. This is why you will find it casts spells of fear and continuously draws your attention to all that is wrong in the world, for they are perpetuating that through their casting of a circle and ritual of performance and of course the spells that they speak. Just have a look at "Project Mockingbird!" That is quite an eye opener.

If you do your research and I implore you to do so, you will find that what is at the root of all this deception and corruption is magic itself. Yes, magic. For magic is working within media, music, television programming, you're NEWS, your religions, your politics, your money, your daily life rituals; everything is governed by magic. This was illustrated in the Bible's first book in Genesis where it stated "in the beginning was the word and the word was made flesh," sure sounds a lot like magic to me. Also, if you spell the word then the word is your spell as I have mentioned before, is that not what Abracadabra really means? Yes, Abracadabra translates as "I will create as I speak." So, in other words everything being spoken is being created. How is that for a game changer!

This is why the "Wise Ones" felt that it would be helpful for me to share with you my story as we feel that in 2020 it is time now more than ever to balance the records and to reveal that which has been hidden and held secret within the occult societies throughout the ages. 2020 is 20 / 20 hindsight, end game for shadow play. Our greatest hope in sharing this information that we present to you here throughout this book is for us all to be able to change the outcome within the templates and timelines through this next decade to come, for the "Wise Ones" want you all to know that we can change the way things go when we are aware. We have the opportunity if we can only but wake up and take back our power, to quicken the process of our transition period as we move into this next new age called the 5th Age of Peace and ascend to 5D.

Consider me if you will to be a messenger for you from the other side of the great morph you are all consciously or unconsciously in now, come to deliver to you a higher message then that of the one you will find within the narrative of your "handlers," #mkultra. You see, I have already lived through where you are finding yourself at right now, trippy hey. I have been there, done that, and burned that artificial t-shirt made from petroleum none the less in the Matrix's plastic paradise! Yes, I have already been through what you are about to go through and since I am alive and well, truth to be told feeling better than ever, I offer to you not only my insight but literally the light of hope that really everything is going to be ok and can even be better than what I went through if only you could wake up and help make a difference.

No matter what, those of you who are in resonance to 5D, where I am coming from now, this is where you are all about to break on through to get to like Jim Morrison sang when he invited you to break on through to the other side. Yes, that is right you are about to break on through to the other side and get yourself to freedom, to 5D and the 5th Age of Peace as was long prophesized. So the "Wise Ones" say "keep vibrating in love, keep praying, keep your eyes on that which is above you, and never give up!" This is the real yoga of our times, when all the teachings and lessons all must be applied.

Before we go down this rabbit hole any further I want you to know that for every demon there is an Angel. For every illness there is a cure. For every wrong there is a right and for every sin there is a virtue. Just like Michael Franti from Spearhead sings, "all the shit you feeding us is fertilizer!" Yes, that is the secret that is the truth that I want to share with you. That is the existential big black cat that I have come to let out of the hypothetical proverbial bag. That you are way more powerful then you realize! #alchemistmuscle .... Use it!

The "Wise Ones" want you to know that I was elected and invited to share with you my story by the High Council of Guides and Guardians within the Galactic Confederation so that you will have an idea of what is taking place behind the scenes. My prayer is that you will find inspiration here in these pages now bound into this book and blessed by many Star Nation beings that have transmitted their energies into the paper and ink used to make this very book just for you and ultimately empower yourself and others along the way to the 5th Age of Peace by helping rather than hindering what must be done.

The High Council of the "Wise Ones" feel that by sharing my story with you, it will help you understand what is coming and that it will give to you the guidance you will need on how to best prepare and thus respond when the Hour of Power does come. That is why I have chosen to name this book "Frequency The Hour of Power Has Come," for the Hour of Power will come through frequency through energy and vibrational atonement.

I have also named it "Frequency The Hour of Power has Come" because of all the frequencies vibration and energies that this book holds even though they may be invisible to the naked eye, trust me they are here. They are transmitting power to you even now just like radio waves which deliver messages by completely invisible means. So, feel into my words and the messages of the "Wise Ones," allow them to work their good magic upon you, for the power of feeling is where the healing can take place so we can start dealing with the issues at hand.

Now when the Hour of Power does come, the "Wise Ones" want you to know, it will deliver its frequencies power and vibrations triggering a purification process that will begin to reset humanity and creation from the 4th world to the 5th Age of Peace as was foretold on "Prophecy Rock" by way of the Hopi people. I invite you to begin creating harmonic resonance to 5D vibrations as my book and story will lie out, for that will be the key for you to ascend and evolve into the blessed New Age that is coming.

Since so many of the old oral passed down traditional stories have been lost and replaced by "his-story," history, the story of the patriarch that is; the "Wise Ones" have had to become very creative in finding ways to deliver truth to you. Therefore, they have had to use science fiction and fantasy as well as to drop their seeds of enlightenment in movies, anime, and comic books all to spread their messages and teachings secretly to help the human race wake up.

Now personally, I have always thought that women were juicy storytellers not just because I am a woman but because women are life givers, we are nurturers, and we have been telling stories since the beginning of time to our children and in our red tents. That is why when I was asked to come and share with all of you my message I came with the idea to share my message as "her-story," to speak to "his-story" and then well, edit the outcome.

You see, I have wondered in long hours of the night, where has "her story" been? And you know the shocking truth that I have found is that it has been muted just as the Indigenous voice has been muted and all who have been oppressed by the victors of genocide by way of the colonialists. Yes, it is sad but true; "his-story" is infamous for writing history in the favor of those who have conquered the people who had gone before them while simultaneously erasing their culture, their language, and ultimately their truths along the way. It is no coincidence that as genocide ensued and the colonialist took over, that the world turned from a predominant matrilineal story and celebration of life, to a patrilineal and destructive story of life.

With the voices of our women and our Indigenous tribal people muted and choked nearly right out, so have their stories been silenced and almost forgotten. As the Native Americans have said, how the west was won or lost depends on if you are a settler or native, for each side will tell you quite a different story indeed.

Let it be known that I Sophia Star Water and the "Wise Ones" that I commune with come to you now to tell you the story that you were never meant to hear. For this story as "her story," really is "our story," a story of a people with amnesia. The story of a near about conquered people who never truly gave up even though they had forgotten who they were, why they were here, or even from where they had even come from.

This story is a story about how despite the manifold of attacks by the parasitic forces who sought to consume and control everything, how we as a people were able to rise up and overthrow our oppressors by way of a great plot or an engineered plan that had been designed an eternity ago called "The Great Reset." Maybe now in 2020, now more than ever as the world is falling apart around you, you are ready to hear this story, for it is long overdue.

Looking back now upon it all from the other side of the "Great Reset" here in 5D as a recap or review; history with its whole fear-based action thriller porn laced series of episodes, had been for sure at times a great rush! But let me just say, it is a living dream come true indeed once you get past the eye of the needle and sew yourself into the 5th Age of Peace where I now call home.

It is indeed a wish come true transcending beyond the adrenaline and adrenochrome based vibe of the patriarch's story, and the 4th Age of the Archons in 4D, which is peaking now in your current timeline and finally cueing "The End" at last. I hope you can get that, that you can put that in your peace pipe and smoke that truth in, realizing that everything you must go through will all be worth it once you make it to the other side of the dreamcatcher as I call "The Great Reset" to be. That nothing you have suffered through is in vain for once you real eyes (realize) the big plan; the truth really does set you free.

Like a soap opera, these days of your lives on planet Earth are about to be catapulted into a wild drama trauma reality TV series resembling something more akin to the Twilight Zone. Do not say that you were not warned. Like all things in matter and nature however, everything has a time and a season, a rhyme, and a reason. With every end there is a new beginning. It is the circle of life spinning around and around into infinity and beyond just like the infinity symbol. Like that of an egg becoming a caterpillar only to morph into a butterfly, this is the wisdom the "Wise Ones" have come to share.

The "Wise Ones" say that you as humanity are an egg, as each one of you is conceived from an egg that had started off in your mother's womb. You are a cosmic egg that had become a precious baby which grew as far as you could into a man or woman and that you are now ready to enter into your own destined chrysalis that quarantine offers. Yes, you are being forced to go within to get out of the Maya or illusion and delusion that we have all been held under.

The Wise Ones" say that we are currently transforming into our next evolutionary upgrade. We are being called, forced even to go inside ourselves now to separate from the illusions of the parasitic forces and their constructs known as Babylon so that we can morph into beautiful Superhuman beings'. As Superhuman beings' we will rise with our newfound wings and fly high into 5D and the 5th Age of Peace. The symbol for this which the Fay or Faeries have taught me is a diamond. For it is only under great pressure the Faeries say that a diamond is formed. Our Superhuman upgrade is very much akin to our Diamond Bodies of light, thus we have this incredible opportunity happening hidden through the lens of a Pandemic. The Faeries say, "Only under great pressure can diamonds form. This is why beloved humans you are under such great pressure; it is the only way for you to get the necessary fuel to ignite your Merkabas', or diamond bodies of light."

Yes, we are becoming Superhuman! That is what all of the "Wise Ones" want you to download upload and hold space for within your mind's eye and sacred hearts as we roll into our next evolutionary upgrade. But first we must let go of our attachment to our Homo Sapien body and the material plane. Just like the caterpillar must let go of its body to then transform into its butterfly evolution, we humans must also let go of our attachment to our caterpillar like 3D bodies and undergo the necessary shape shift transformation to attain our 5D bodies of light. As we allow for this necessary process to occur, we hold space for our beings to be able to go through the necessary shifts and changes needed to allow for us all to emerge into our next evolutionary upgrade as Homo Luminous, the illuminated human.

Now if we are all in a story, we must all have an archetype, right? If that is true, then I have always seen myself in the "Book of Life" as a character very close to that of "Alice in Wonderland." Much like Alice, I too was on a grand adventure or a journey to find the truth about what life was all about, back on my last Earth walk that is. I too became surrounded by fantastical characters and I too had discovered that by gazing through the looking glass of my third eye, I could get the answers that I needed to return to where I belonged and so can you!

But first, before I could return to the world above metaphorically speaking, I had to find out the answer to the most important question that life could ever dish out, who am I? That question right there, who am I, is the most important question the "Wise Ones" say we must all ask ourselves. Just as the caterpillar in the book of "Alice in Wonderland" said when he asks Alice … "Whhoooooooooo arreeee yoouuuu," I too had to find out who I was as so do you, to solve the riddle of the dream. For reality is like a dream, perhaps nightmare at times where you find yourself chasing time, following the white rabbit further and further down into its never-ending black hole, always watching out for the Red Queen who wants nothing but to sacrifice anyone who gets in her way. While that all may be true, once you unlock the blocks and solve the riddle to the combination code to life, you can than morph from the archetype of one who is lost and victimized by life to one who is found, and thus becomes a Hero for others.

The truth is that what you refer to as reality is like a wave of information. It is a wave of information carried through energy which is about to peak now in your timeline and come crashing down. You may have already begun to notice as the whitewash of the crashing economy, crashing freedoms, and crashing privacy laws sprays you in the face so to speak.

"Mark me," says a beautiful regal Andromedan who just now has walked through as I write this, "blessed ones in your timeline of 2020; society will enter an end game episode to the hunger game sitcom that you have all unwittingly been a participant in your whole entire lives. Prepare yourselves now for your whole world and lives are about to change. Raise your vibration; stop feeding the parasitic force of the old dying paradigm, for a New Age is coming! Open your hearts and surrender to the One!"

You see it is due to the critical time in history that you find yourself smack dab in the middle of now, and to the unfoldment of prophecy occurring, that has triggered these "Wise Ones" to come forward and share their messages with you. To send me back through the looking glass from 5D to your present time to share with you what is really going on, as most people they say have not quite figured out the riddle yet. Our point in doing this is to inspire you and to give you the gift of hope, something you will need to hold onto like a lifeline in the times that are to come.

You see coming to you all now in this next decade is an ultimatum and ultimate reset of all the ages in one grand cycle of purification which consciously or not you are now quickly moving right into. I humbly give to you my story so that you, yes you, will have the strength and courage to let go of the shore of your .0035% visibility of the entire electromagnetic light spectrum and push off into the river of life and truly then be like water as Bruce Lee said and flow. Flow in trust and surrender to the plan that the "Wise Ones" have set into place long long ago.

The Hopi people are very sacred to the "Wise Ones" and it was they who taught all who would listen about the two paths and two destinies of man coming in now through divergent evolution which is the baseline to the "Great Reset" that is coming. They spoke of how there is the path of the materialist with all their greed, lust, temptation, and narcissist ways always seeking more never sated always hungry. Much like a parasite if not entirely a parasitic behaviour. Then of course there is the spiritual path known as "The Good Red Road." It is on this path where you will find people who walk and talk in a good way in an honest way and in a loving way. It is this path where people maintain a connection with spirit, with life, truth, and their humility, their heart that will go on to 5D and the 5th Age of Peace.

I must warn you that the parasitic forces that have had dominion over the materialistic path since the beginning of time will begin to struggle like never before to maintain their power and control over all that they have built. They will kick and fight and scream like little children relentlessly refusing to give up their empire and will do anything and everything to maintain control. There will many who will try to sell you doom and gloom, to play upon your fears and capitalize off them; chose not to participate say the "Wise Ones." There will also be those who are fakes, who are pseudo spiritualists who will try to sell you the sacred, remember the sacred is not for sale!

Let this be a good time as the Hopi Prophecy says; "This could be a good time! There is a river flowing now very fast. It is so great and swift that there are those who will be afraid. They will try to hold on to the shore. They will feel they are being torn apart and will suffer greatly. Know the river has its destination. The elders say we must let go of the shore, push off into the middle of the river, keep our eyes open, and our heads above the water. And I say, see who is in there with you and celebrate. Currently in history, we are to take nothing personally, least of all ourselves. For the moment that we do, our spiritual growth and journey come to a halt. The time of the lone wolf is over. Gather yourselves! Banish the word 'struggle' from your attitude and your vocabulary. All that we do now must be done in a sacred manner and in celebration."

So in a good way, in a sacred manner let us all reflect right now upon the fundamental truth within nature that the rise and fall of life on Earth is nothing new and that it has been going on for time immemorial. Like the inhalation and exhalation process of the breath of life, we have risen and fallen lifetime after lifetime age after age. This just has always been the way. Through each age and era within the 1st world, 2nd world, 3rd world, and again now presently in the 4th world of life … we have all fallen only to rise again, pumped and dumped like the economy micro and macrocosmically in a fractal like succession of ways, as all things are fractal in nature.

Truly each age of realization has been like a life form of its own born in its infancy then aging maturing till it peaks and then fades again unto death. This journey has been mirrored in each age of realization, born in its own way in its own infancy maturing until its peaked and thus concluded by coming down to its end only to then be born again and arise in a new age of evolution once more. This is the procession of the equinoxes and the grand cycles within cycles of seasons and lifetimes held through reincarnation. Truly this procession and cyclical ascension within the sacred spiral of time known as the "Golden Means" is a sacred geometry of pure energy, a sacred mandala for time and space and it is this that is the Galactic Confederation's ship's wheel that has been steering creation since forever.

As you are reading this now currently in your present timeline humanity and the 4th age are ripe and ready once again to birth a new Earth the "Elders" say. As the Hopi have taught there will be 9 signs to the coming end of the fourth age of man. These signs will start first with the coming of the white man to Turtle Island. Secondly, the land will see spinning wheels filled with voices, or in other words, the wagons with all the pioneers and settlers who came and took over Native America. Third there will be a strange beast like a buffalo that will come and over run the land … something like our cattle ranches you could say. Fourth the land will come to be crossed by snakes of iron, or trains tracks. Fifth, the lands will become criss - crossed by giant spider webs, the grid of electricity. The sixth sign would see the lands crossed by rivers of stones; freeways. The seventh sign would see the oceans and seas turn black with many animal die offs; oil (see also for you good students out there, the black snake prophecies too of the Hopi Nation). The eight sign would bring many people wearing their hair long like the natives; hence the hippies (check the Rainbow Warriors specifically). The ninth and final sign would be the "Blue Star Katchina," described as a dwelling place in the heavens that falls to Earth in a great crash and thus begins the time of the purification process for the then Fifth Age of Peace to begin. When the purification process is complete the Hopi say, we will then be heralded by a "Red Star Kachina" as a sign and signal announcing the completion of this transitional time.

To quote the First Nations music group called "A Tribe Called Red," let me share what their reflection of this time is for I feel it pretty much sums up the whole two paths of the Hopi Prophecy pretty crystal clear ... "We are the Halluci Nation, the human beings, the people that see the spiritual in the natural, through sense and feeling, everything is related, all the things of earth and in the sky have spirit. Everything is sacred, confronted by the alienation, the subjects and the citizens see the material religions through trauma and numb, where nothing is related, all the things of the earth and in the sky have energy to be exploited, even themselves, mining their spirits into souls, sold Into nothing is sacred not even their self ...The A Lie Nation, the alienation." There you have it the spiritual path and the materialist path if you will, shared through the lyrics of The A Lie Nation by Tribe Called Red, a great song for all you who love to dance!

So, with all that in your mind's eye to see I come to say to all of you who will listen, who have the eyes to see inside my words and can actually feel into the messages of the "Wise Ones" that are encoded into them, that it is time to get grounded right now and tune into Mama Gaia for she is peaking in her ring of fire. Can you not feel her shuddering? She is in full heavy labor! Taste her sweat hear her cries as her contractions rip through her body even now from deep within. Just have a look at the Schumann Resonance which is the heartbeat of our Mother Earth, right now her heart is activating huge as it is ramping up higher and higher from her usual 7.83 hertz. Remember as the "Law of Oneness" states, we are all connected so what happens to our Mother Earth is also happening to us and all creation. If you are feeling heart palpitations and all sorts of crazy physical, emotional, mental, and spiritual phenomenon, know these feelings and experiences may also be related to "ascension symptoms."

Within your time frame these contractions will become quicker and quicker all the time as if in a cadence or rhythm. As these contractions quicken so does the time of the tribulation quicken to come to a necessary end. As the phrase goes, "where one door closes another one opens," this is true for all who are ready to finally birth this new Earth, this New Age of Peace and return once again to unified consciousness.

"His-story" is coming to an end the "Wise Ones" say and with it all the programming of pain and suffering. While this paradigm closes what opens in its stead is the realm of our Divine Souls, which the Egyptians referred to as "The Dimension of the Blessed." We must all prepare to close the door to illusion as it is the gateway to the lower astral hell which contains all knowledge of evil and suffering and will soon be wiped away as the great sand paintings done by the Tibetan Monks in their great Mandala art meditations.

It has been foretold by many great shamans and prophets throughout time and space and the "Wise Ones" themselves that there will be needed many midwifes' for ascension to help hold space for this great shapeshift to occur. This great shapeshift as an analogy, just to give you a picture to work with gifted to me by the Dragon Nation, is a lot like how Diana Prince becomes Wonder Woman. Do you remember her and how she spins into her higher self? For this is exactly what is about to happen to all life on Earth as we complete our journey into the underworld and the lower densities of our lower chakras and thus recalibrate ourselves by activating our bodies of light. This process is what is meant from the verse, "As it was in the beginning, so shall it be in the end." For we are made in the image of God just as Jesus had taught in his lesson when he said "ye are Gods, yet ye know it not." I say it is time to remember and better yet embody our Divine Legacy and Inheritance for at this turning point we will be than given the "Keys to Creation" and become masters of our own right!

The "Wise Ones" want you to remember that you are spiritual beings. You are a star enclosed into a body of form made from the Earth. The Earth, she is your body. Her water, is your blood. Her air that is your breath and her fire that is your spirit! Since the fall from grace from whence we fell like shooting stars from the higher spheres of the higher densities to these lower vibrational fields of materialism and matter; we have been on a sacred journey. A journey to find out who we are despite all the lies deception and conditioning we have been programmed with so that we can "ouroboros," or snake eats it tail, or in other words return to "As it was in the beginning" for that truly shall be how it will be in the end, only we will have earned our rights as "Masters." This whole journey is much like getting one's Master's Degree for we are in for sure a school of life.

As you dip your toe into all my words that I share with you in these first pages just to get you primed for what's coming, I invite you to now get ready to take the big plunge with me into the deep end of my stories' waters. Let me invite you to now dive deep into the potential and possibilities brewing up for you already as you go beyond the 4D box of consciousness that you may have previously been subscribed to. Allow me to remind you that you all will be asked to make the ultimate decision to either rise in love or to fall into fear.

Remember that F.E.A.R. really is just False Evidence Appearing Real and that you cannot serve two masters. So, you will have to choose whether you are you going to serve love or fear. It is a lot like the quote "To be or not to be that is the question," because fear and the lower world ... that is about to get recycled back to pure energy ... as in no longer exist. Just saying, choose wisely as love will be exalted in the 5th Age of Peace and restore sacredness to the world and wholeness to the great "Hoop" or "Circle of Life!"

Now while there are for sure parasitic forces that you will come to learn about who create fear and harvest fear feeding off of it through their endless hunger games; remember that there is an even more powerful energy alive known as "Source." The Source has the power to transcend all force and eventually will zero point the parasitic forces recycling them to pure energy. This zero-point process will occur at the very end of the plan known as "The Great Reset," and will return all those who align themselves to it through resonance and entrainment to the Source yet again full circle. This will mark the birthing of the 5th Age of Peace.

Just as a sweet little note, I always use to like to say, "May the source be with you," something my homeboys and I came up with, for true power does not have to force! Instead it honors free will. Free will is a sacred law respect it or not. The truth is the parasitic forces are in violation for about a gazillion infinite ways as they have violated our "Free Will" time and time again. That is why "The Great Reset" plan was conceived engineered and designed to deliver us all in resonance to the "Source" once again and to bring us home to the "Promised Land."

The Source is known within the Galactic Confederation as the Naturix. I want you now to consider that there is a map of consciousness and on the lowest end of the map there lays the parasitic forces breeding hatred, enslavement, greed, lust, and the need for pain to feed off known as loosh. Now on the other end of the map that is where your destination or destiny awaits you … if you choose and that is where the 5th Age of Peace begins as the new template and timeline for humanity.

Already in the higher spheres of life existing within the higher vibrational densities there is a great celebration going on for success has been achieved within "The Great Reset" plan above. Now as you may or may not know that which happens above translates in only a matter of rippling time to that which is below and in the same respect, everything that happens within us happens without and vice versa. So the good news is that above us, all the parasitic forces have officially been drawn out from all of creation and focalized right to the host of Earth's body via her iron core crystal magnetic beacon. That is why we must now complete our end of the bargain down here on the lowest densities of creation in 1, 2, 3, 4D.

Sounds terrible, I know. But this process has been necessary to be able to draw out all the parasitic forces from the whole of creation to be able to be cleared once and for all. This has always been the plan, the great riddle, the secret that I have come to let you in on. For the time has come for the combination lock upon the quarantine of Earth to be finally unlocked and unblocked, allowing for the healing of the nations and for the liberation and emancipation of all sentient beings! As the

Hopi say, this could be a good time; it just depends where on the map you find yourself in resonance to.

Currently in your day and age of 2020, there are great changes underway as the necessary purification programs have been completed in the higher densities and dimensions and are trickling now down to yours. This purification process is trickling down layer by layer within the lotus of life all the way down to the core, to 1D, to the iron core crystal which is magnetically drawing out all the parasitic forces from all of the galaxies and universes right down to it. That is why it feels so darn heavy and maddening here on Earth in 2020, I remember.

Just like the Shiva Shakti energies within the Kundalini fire, the purification programs designed by our Guides and Guardians with the Galactic Confederation have had to fully attract all the parasitic forces from Creation and bring them down to hit rock bottom within 1D or the root chakra. That is what the first age was all about. After the first age we had the second, the sacral chakra age of 2D, followed then by the third and solar plexus age, 3D. Now we are presently in the fourth age and fourth chakra or heart chakra and 4D; where all the magic of alchemy can finally take place.

The heart chakra is the center of the great Alchemist that is why the heart lives inside of the treasured "chest". The heart chakra or "Anahata," which translates as "unstruck" or "unhurt" even "unbeaten," is the great and mighty morph agent, for the heart chakra has the power of zero-point technology. It is the Heart Chakra the "Wise Ones" say that we have had to reach energetically to be able to trigger the "Great Reset" and they feel that enough of humanity has been able to activate their heart chakra successfully and that the turning point was reached in 1987 during the "Global Harmonic Convergence."

Now Zero point energy according to Wikipedia and its explanation of the Etymology and terminology of the concept states that; "the term zero-point energy (ZPE) is a translation from the German Nullpunktsenergie. The term zero-point field (ZPF) can be used when referring to a specific vacuum field, for instance the QED vacuum which specifically deals with quantum electrodynamics (e.g., electromagnetic interactions between photons, electrons and the vacuum) or the QCD vacuum which deals with quantum chromodynamics (e.g., color charge interactions between quarks, gluons and the vacuum). A vacuum can be viewed not as empty space but as the combination of all zero-point fields. In quantum field theory this combination of fields is called the vacuum state, its associated zero-point energy is called the vacuum energy and the average energy value is called the vacuum expectation value (VEV) also called its condensate." Now that is a lot to take in I know but let me explain, it is in the heart chakra where the higher and lower worlds meet as one and whereby the vacuum or zero pointing of all parasitic energies can be eliminated once and for all, so that a new world and a new age that is governed by peace may begin.

The process of the attractant and descent of all the parasitic forces to the iron core crystal beacon of Pacha Mama is now complete the "Wise Ones" say and that is why the higher vibrational spheres are celebrating. At this time our collective ascent is what is allowing for an alternating currency of AC energy to trigger the great reset plan and activate ascension; exactly like that of a Tesla Tower and that of the kundalini serpents of light which move up and down the scales of the chakras creating the kundalini energy bringing pure Source energy which clears all obstructions and detoxifies the body bringing in light. As this AC energy is generating the power to employ the zero point process within us and without, we complete the groundwork from below to this great master plan allowing for us all to return back up to where we belong.

Now as these two serpents of light known as the lunar serpent called "Ida" and solar serpent called "Pingala," intertwine themselves igniting each chakra with pure Source energy, they fuel the ascension process and ignite the zero point technology of our sacred hearts which have been engineered within us. Remember "As within so without, as above so below." As these serpents of light create this AC energy and call for the conducted power of transformation to happen inside of us, there is a reciprocating feedback inter-loop which feeds the as within and so without law of resonance. This is the basic science within the engineered plan called "The Great Reset." The plan to draw all energy down to the roots, to the iron core crystal of the Earth itself, then reset it through the transcending fires of Shakti Kundalini which is thee primordial "Source" power that has the power to transcend any and everything.

This overall reset plan engineered by the "Wise Ones" that has been drawing all the parasitic forces to 1D has now made it all the way to 4D and it is "go time" the "Wise Ones" say. "Time for the green lights of the heart chakras of the world to unite, time to Zero point no need to fight. Activate your crystal oscillators inside of your sacred hearts, Zero- point any and all dissonance and parasitic forces now!" Says my Sasquatch guide Keera Anna. She is a real bad ass!

Know that all of you out there who are reading this book right now are already ascending back up to love where you belong as promised through prophecy. Yes, the "Wise Ones" want you to know that as you may find it hard to believe given your current state of conditions, that Earth or Gaia has completed her mission. The mission to provide not only a body to be a host for all the parasitic forces, but also to be a school for all who would attend to learn of the knowledge of good and evil and thus choose which either force or source you would of your own free will serve thus graduating as a Master to join the ascended ones who have already graduated or simply return to pure energy through the Zero-point process, again it is entirely up to you, you are the one you are waiting for. This is what the "Wise Ones" have come to share and illuminate within us as their message stands clear … to be or not to be that is the question of the "Wise Ones."

Like the Hopi Prophecy says, "You have been telling people it is the eleventh hour, now you must go back and tell the people that this is the hour!" The hour of power is coming, the tick tock is getting closer to the time where the alarm bells will ring … time to wake up! While the Earth School experiment has been underway on the micro plane, on a macro plane there has also been a higher mission occurring which as I have mentioned is called "The Great Reset." As the one in the many and the many in the one, there has been the above parallel to that which is below, as well as that which is within … also been manifesting without.

This whole reset program, though it may appear to be cruel and harsh, has been a necessary distillation process. I am not going to lie to you at first even I was like whhhaaaaaat? No kidding seriously how can you not be like wtf? However, now that I see from heaven's eyes, now that I have gotten beyond Maya, beyond the illusion; I realize that the whole time the true Earth and all our relations have been just fine. That this carbon copy that I will explain more in detail soon, has been the grandest illusion of them all. I have learned that not only are the Dark Lords or parasitic race ... masters of deception and disguise, but so are the Guides and Guardians of Light that is why I have come to call them the "Wise Ones!" And of course the sacred coyote or "Heyokah" spirit has struck again! This time deserving an academy award or golden globe statue for sure!

I bow to you oh sacred "Wise Ones" and salute you for your brilliant master plan and thank you for your teachings!
Sophia Star Water

"HER - STORY" BEGINS

A Message from Sophia Star Water
"Hope...which is whispered from Pandora's box only after
all the other plagues and sorrows had escaped, is the best
and last of all things. Without it, there is only time. And
time pushes at our backs like a centrifuge, forcing us
outward and away, until it nudges us into oblivion."
Ian Caldwell, <u>The Rule of Four</u>

Greetings, may the source be with you! I am Sophia Star Water and this is my story, Her-story that I have come to share with you. My message that I weave into the words within the pages of this book is the story of my life, my tribe, and our journey as we ascended to 5D and the 5th Age of Peace. It is a story I wished I could tell you all around a sacred fire while we roasted vegan marshmallows. But alas, I have been tasked to share with you my story by the "Wise Ones" and so here it is channeled just for you from 5D with love.

I come to you now to be your white butterfly of hope for that is my, Sophia Star Water's signature medicine and totem, hope. Now hope of course was the last thing to leave good ol' Pandora's Box, do you remember that story? Pandora's Box is an old Greek mythos, a story of how and when all the sorrows and evils of the world were released upon us. These sorrows and evils of the world had been previously held inside a box that had been given for safe keeping to a man and his wife whose name was Pandora. The box was supposed to be held closed shut tight and kept secure by protection of this man and his wife. This box had been left to their charge by some Angels, don't ask me why. Now curiosity got the better of Pandora and she of course opened the box as she wanted to see what it held inside. When Pandora opened that box which she had been forbidden to open, she accidentally released then all of the chaos of creation, all the evil and suffering possible right into our world. Goddess Mia you got to love the old stories. Good old Pandora.

Sounds a lot like the forbidden fruit and the apple saga or story of Genesis whereas within the Garden of Eden there was yet another woman, this one named Eve, who had been tempted to eat of the fruit from the tree of knowledge by a serpent; remember that one, how could you forget right? Yet again another classic example of a story wrote by a man whether it was Moses or any other of the Patriarchs from the Bible who had depicted yet another wanton woman this time named Eve messing it up for everybody. Now Eve as you may remember was just like Pandora, warned to never eat of the tree of knowledge, just as Pandora was warned to never open that darn box, but of course, she did. Little did she know I am sure that, that one bite of that one apple would have her and her man Adam cast out, evicted from the Garden of Eden and that the two of them would fall from grace!

It is not a coincidence that the first card in the Tarot deck is the "Fool" for the Fool card depicts a person who is beginning on a journey. It shows a youth walking joyfully into the world, taking his or her first steps. It shows them as being exuberant, joyful, excited. They carry nothing with them except a small sack, caring nothing for the possible dangers that lie ahead on the path. Indeed, the fool is soon to encounter the first of possible dangers, for as she takes another step that she is blindly walking, she topples right over a cliff. Now "Tarot" in the ancient Kemetic language of Egypt means "Royal Path" and indeed it has been a royal path that we fools have all been walking for we have all been on the fool's journey.

After ages of dealing with all that had been unleashed, all that we have dropped into; it is time now to have that one last thing exit Pandora's Box; cue Sophia Star Water as I now make my grand entrance.

Yes I, Sophia Star Water offer myself to you now and introduce myself to you formally as the white butterfly named "Hope." I come now to you to offer myself as that one last thing to leave good ol' Pandora's Box. You can say we have been taken down by women, but I dare say … it is by woman that you shall be lifted up, for as many with a good mama know … it is mama you run to when your hurt or in despair. It is the mother consciousness that is the comforter and counsellor. It is the Mother Earth who has laid down her life for you so that you could learn the knowledge of good and evil, and it is she who has made the ultimate sacrifice to be the host for all of the parasitic forces. Fools that we may all have been, the Divine Mother of Grace comes to us all and offers to us her unconditional love and forgiveness. It is she who helps us reach the last card within the Major Arcana of the Tarot which brings us fools on our royal path to Mastery.

I want you to know that through hope all darkness is illuminated for hope is the fuel that powers faith and trust. Hope like the Hopi people have kept the sacred fire lit within humanity and has kept the teachings alive of how to reach this next new age that is coming, The Fifth Age of Peace. I discovered that for myself long ago and am called now to share my story with you so that you can relax, like a lot, and let go of the shore of your perceived understanding. Let the river of life take you to this new age and new world. Let yourself surrender knowing that the river has a destination, and that seriously all that you need to do is keep your head above the water.

Consider this book if you will and the message within it, a rite of passage, a call to action, a sign, and an omen from the future planted within these pages to help guide you on your way to that which is coming. This book is a story of both "his story" and "her story" for it is of both the past and of the future and what will come to be. I share this with you now to seed within your consciousness a golden ticked to true freedom, an invitation to the ascent to 5D, and for the attainment of the 5th Age of Peace as the Hopi have taught and prophesised.

So, who am I and why was I chosen to be a messenger you may now be wondering ... I was born in 2012 when the end of the world was predicted by way of the end of the Mayan calendar. Talk about an intense day to be born as I was born on that exact day of the winter solstice, the exact day of the supposed end.

My parents had later told me when they were being taken away by the officials, by the agents of the Matrix, that it was not the end of the world that heralded my birth but the end of Maya. Now the word Maya is the Sanskrit word for illusion and it was my parents who had told me that awful day as they were being ripped from my arms, taken because they knew too much and had become a threat to the establishment; that the day I was born was not the end of the world, but the end of Maya. That my birthday marked the end of all illusion, and that I must now learn how to see through the illusion to know the truth which would set me free.

My parents told me that the Mayans were the keepers of time which is illusion and that they as the keepers of time were on a higher level also the keepers of the great illusion or Maya itself. Hence, these sacred timekeepers called themselves the Mayans. My parents told me that humanity had fallen into Maya back at the time of the great fall of Atlantis, and that at that time we also fell from our Avatar selves down into illusory selves. This by the way is expressed through the animal totem medicine of the Dragonfly and the story of how Great Spirit turned the mighty Dragon into the mere Dragonfly to teach humility. Yes, that is the same truth that applies to us humans as well.

My parents had also told me that as the darkest hour always comes right before the dawn, that in these ever darkening days that we too were just about to break through to the other side and into the dawning of the Age of Aquarius. They told me that we would meet again one day in the New Age of the 5th Age of Peace and that they would find me in 5D out of the dust and ashes of this illusory world. They spoke of how we were rising back to the higher densities' of the quantum fields of life from the lowest and that the Mayan calendar ended heralding the time of the great return to truth like a Dragonfly returning to its all-powerful Dragon form. They also told me that as I was born on this epic symbolic day for a reason and that that reason was because I wielded and yielded the great power of truth as my super-power. I was a conduit they had taught me for the great transformation coming and that I was to always remember that I was not born of illusion but born of truth.

My parents told me that I would help others one day find the truth in them as well and that was why I was being taken away for I was to be trained like a soldier in boot camp … trained to become a warrior for truth and liberation and that ultimately my training was to begin that awful day. My parent's last words to me were "beloved daughter, beloved

Sophia, keeper of wisdom as you were named for, we are so sorry we must leave you far too young to fend on your own in a circus of clowns (they knew I hated clowns)… know that we will see each other again … this is not the end but only the beginning, (crying more like wailing my mother said) … be strong child you are born of truth. We will meet again in the 5th world with all our kin in heaven. Now go and save as many souls as you can…" The last image I have of my parents in the 4th world was that of them walking off into their fate; heads held high, eyes looking up to the sky, walking towards their freedom out of all the lies.

So, you see for me the truth bomb hit early, way too early, for a child. For a child should never have to grow up in fear. But the truth bomb was to be dropped regardless of one's age sex or religion and it would come to hit hard upon the head of humanity by 2020 and then intensify every year after until the great reset would sonically go boom.

Yes, from 2020 to 2024 all denial like a river dries up in the consciousness of man and the so-called conspiracy theories as was coined by the CIA, shall become authenticated as time will tell. By 2024 there will be nowhere left to run to and nowhere left to hide in the illusion in the Maya which is being dissipated now like a fog.

Looking back, I must declare in all honesty we all did of our own free will take that bite of the proverbial apple after all invoking in the knowledge of good and evil …. Right? Just ask yourself if you have an apple phone? It is the apple in our eye! It is the A.I. in our eye, the all-seeing eye which is watching all of us all the time with its artificial intelligence profiling each of us, programming each of us tracking our every move; and we were the ones who paid for it! We consented by purchasing and operating the proverbial mark of the beast giving it permission to take over us as it was always designed to do, unwittingly.

As I share with you my story and my truth, I cannot help but to remember when Jack Nicholson said in a movie once, "you can't handle the truth." Now, my observation growing up was that in fact people indeed could not handle the truth and instead of seeing through the illusion to be able to even grasp the truth; would instead turn a blind eye, a deaf ear to the cries, and walk on past all of the injustices and lies and that is exactly what my parents had done before they get woke to the agenda.

You see my parents tried to warn people about what they saw coming and eventually were taken from me because of their felt duty to warn the masses and try to stop the crime being waged against humanity and life itself. They were taken from me just because they would not vaccinate me nor would they consent to micro-chip me or themselves. They were taken for standing up for free will, for not going along like good sheeple, and specifically for not doing what they were told defying the Dark Lords.

Bear with me now, I know that this is a heavy load to take and perhaps right away you are wondering do I really want to subject myself to this crazy sounding story. I do not blame you. I am not going to lie to you; this is not a fairy tale but if you feel you can handle the truth, read on.

For I have come from the future, chosen because of the strength of my will and devotion to the sacred, to tell you all of what I have been told and about what have I witnessed. You see, The Matrix, which is the artificial version of the Naturix, and I know this is going to sound crazy but, in all seriousness, the Matrix started out originally as Black Goo, yes Black Goo. Black Goo that had started off as a particle then transformed into a spore, then to a fungus which spread throughout the cosmos and fell to Earth on an asteroid thousands of years ago in the time of Atlantis. When it had fallen to the Earth at the end of the Atlantis epoch it then infected the Earth and her ecosystem taking over life itself like a cancer. Just check out Edgar Cayce's readings on it and for sure just so you know that I am not crazy do check out Harold Kautz Vella's work on the Black Goo particles for I know that most of you all have to have your facts and that is good, you should question what you are told. You should use critical thinking and investigate the truth!

For those of you who are good students, who are seekers of truth, I do recommend some homework at this point now so that you can get some real education upon this matter as I really am not kidding! This present moment right now, if it has not happened for you already, is going to have to be the point in existence where you will begin to realize that reality is far more of a science fiction fantasy thriller than what you may have wanted to believe! Please find this link as a beginner entry level ticket into some deep dive research. I would like to thank with all my heart one of my heroes, Harold Kautz Vella and the work he has done in his research and science on Black Goo and honor him by sharing his work with you: https://www.youtube.com/watch?v=6g9h5GwoEFo

Yes, the Black Goo is a particle a molecule that was able to multiply and spread like a mold. This black mold eventually spread successfully throughout all of creation contaminating the elements until it became a force of darkness and the origin of all black magic. This black magic force like Darth Vader then waged a war on creation killing many all over the Universe even blowing up whole planets just like in Star Wars with the Death Star.

Not everyone however is given the Shaman sight to see this truth and that is why others must share information. Let us not forget the story of the ships at sea and the Shaman who was able to see these colonialist's ships, while the villagers were not. For the villager only could see what they had been trained and conditioned to see while the Shamans, they see beyond the constructs of their conditioned reality.

Now over time this force of darkness evolved mastering the hunt, the harvest, medicine, religion, banking, governments, and overall reality itself as they became the masters of the universe or our so-called fallen Angels and Demi-Gods known to us as "our leaders." We know them on the Earth as the cabal, the elite, or the 1% who own, operate, and control everything.

To understand how the Dark Lords of the Matrix took over everything and where the Dark Lords plan is all going think of a tool becoming a weapon for everything that has been created to be a tool, they then copycat and reengineer to be a weapon. The Dark Lords greatest weapon is mirror magic which is a magic trick that allows for them to create a double, a copy, an illusion of the Naturix and everything that the Naturix is by inverting and perverting it all until it eventually over the last 4th age has become a complete carbon copy cat form of the Naturix just artificially manifesting as the Matrix.

This is where you are all now entering now, the Matrix. To fully be uploaded into the Matrix you first will be inserted via the chip as the mark of the beast to be entered into a superficial artificial world. Yes, that is the plan to upload your personality as a character into a cloud within the 8th sphere, as was taught by one Rudolph Steiner of the Theosophical and Anthroposophical Society or Mystery Schools. In this artificial world known as the Matrix you will be sold into thinking that you will have everything your frozen heart desires, but you will not. You will be a battery in a plastic womb feeding an endless supply of loosh to the parasitic force of the Dark Lords, and that has been all along what they have been ushering us towards. This time you are finding yourself in now, is a riddle. It is a proverbial fork in the road that you all must now chose now which direction you will go. You can advance or recede, but I recommend you do not hesitate. It is either the red pill or blue pill … The Naturix or The Matrix, Source energy or Force energy.

Through each age and through each war the Dark Lords have been guiding us, corralling us all into this great epicenter point which is ushering us into their artificial 8th sphere or Matrix. Yes, they have enslaved all of us Earthlings through their colonialization and corporatization practices worldwide just as they had done through many other spheres and planets through the galaxies throughout the previous ages and stages of Creation. The Dark Lords of the Black Goo Black Magic cults have successfully engineered their looming design for total take-over of all creation by way of corruption and destruction and now they have us right where they want us. Therefore the "Source," through its vast intelligences operating in the Galactic Confederation and the many Councils of Guides and Guardians who I refer to as the "Wise Ones" has responded by engineering "The Great Reset" and it is this great truth that will set all the true hearts that hold fast to love and light free!

The "Wise Ones" taught me that the original sin or first egoic emanation that had occurred within the infinite continuum of life by Lucifer himself ignited an error response in the Naturix itself forming a crack or a cavity within the sacred hoop of life. This crack or cavity if you will created the first separation within the field of oneness. This crack or fracture than became infected over time thus allowing the cell

1

of creation to divide light into a seed of darkness. This fracture split the field of oneness into a systematic response which had never happened before. This incident as I have said took light and broke it into division away from the cause of the fracture. The reaction to this incidence rather than response to the situation, which again had never prior occurred, allowed for the fracture or crack to fester without the attention and loving energy of the light all the way until the first Black Goo particle was born.

This Black Goo particle quickly than began to spawn itself into a mass, it replicated itself repeatedly feeding off the life source of creation like a parasite. It than like a cancer spread through all the regulatory systems of creation. This festering wound or cancer grew until it became a living entity, an actual intelligence of its own which gave rise to the Dark Lords themselves whom then waged war on creation.

The dark forces after successfully attacking many different star systems, planetary bodies, dimensions, and interdimensional beings were thus then drawn to Earth via a planted core iron crystal magnet. This magnetic core iron crystal was placed inside of the Earth by the Galactic Confederation and Council of Guides and Guardians. These great benign and benevolent ones had over a vast amount of contemplation investigation and council planning engineered a plan for this "Great Reset" to once and for all time and space clear the Black Goo parasitic forces forever and the fuel for this whole plan would be found in the essence of humility to antidote the original sin which was egoic in principle.

This is how Earth came to be the greatest show in all creation and this is how and why we have all fallen; dropped from our higher and more advanced selves and civilizations to be of service to this cause to correct the parasitic culture and restore Oneness again.

I remember when I was young I devoured my families' library for even at a young age I knew realized knowledge is power! Since my extended family whom were all scholars and historians had at one point all lived with my parents and I in our mansion up in Beverly Hills, I had access to one of the greatest libraries any child ever had access to. The history it offered of ancient worlds and stories never told by the enslavers of the time was intoxicating. I learned and read all about the Bhagavad Gita, the Popul Vuh, the Torah, The Kabbalah, The Sumerian texts, the Dead Sea Scrolls, the Nag Hamadi library, the Book of the Dead, and so many countless texts on the mud floods, Tartaria itself as well as so many other lost and forgotten ancient worlds no school would ever teach you about. It blew my mind that the Buddhists alone counted a manifold of different worlds and galaxies and mapped them out with no telescope nor any technology like that of what our present astronomers of our current reality have in our observatories, not even "Lucifer," the observatory owned by the Vatican itself.

The literature, novels, varying forms of the Bible, as well as many different Indigenous prophecies which I lapped hungrily gave me the understanding of why my parents were the way they were, why they were in such opposition of the beast system which they called the government. The beast system had its many tentacles like a devil fish hooked into the education system, the medical system, the banking system, farming and food productions, water, electricity, and well every aspect of life on Earth my parents had taught me. As I began to learn what my parents knew it helped me understand the truth that I so desperately sought. You see I was Heaven bent on seeking truth so that I could understand what my parents had fought for and what they had fought against as they went from highly reputable scholars and lawyers to being cast out as rejects from the high-end elite society of LA.

You see, just before my parents were taken by the dark lords of the Black Goo complex (as my parents began referring to the elites and their agents as) through their advancing technocracy, employed a vast network which upgraded all our power stations and electrical grids to their so called "safe grids." This update fully unleashed their Pentagram of 5G or Penta as 5 and Gram as G upon the world. It was released everywhere running through the so-called "safe grids" and began to convert people's consciousness to a synthesized neural network artificially fed to humans and life by way of Nano-bots and A.I. These Nano-bots had been sprayed in the air for years completely infecting all biological life so that all living beings by 2020 had been 100% infected through their smart dust. My uncle who was a doctor discovered this as well as he found weird little wiry red and blue things he called Morgellons in his patients. My family then tied together that these Morgellons and Nano bots were already beginning to convert human consciousness and biology into the agenda of the elite which was a trans-humanistic future world agenda manifesting through a New World Order.

The Nano-bots had been created and programmed to feed off human energy while simultaneously through the acquired life source energy like a battery, then program existence into an assimilated virtual hive mind template called the singularity ... and that was just the beginning. For next would be the forced mandatory vaccines and Matrix Micro-chip. The chip would then usher in the way for an inner neural implant placed inside our brains to advance interface with the A.I. or artificial intelligence of the Matrix. This A.I. hive mind singularity assimilation plot gathered in its victims into a deceptive glamorous world of light or in other words a false New Age enlightenment where all would be enhanced, designer augmented trans-humans. This New Age was then sold to people promising them that they could have anything they wanted; that they could be anyone they wanted and it was all possible through their virtual world. The Dark Lords virtual world would be hyperlinked into us all by 2030 as this was their plan for a brave new world, their New World Order.

I watched growing up as 3D and 4D Earth existence opened wide up like Pandora's Box to a range of frequencies which brought forth the Apocalypse. Yes, Armageddon was to be delivered by Nano-bots, biological warfare, 5G, 6G, and even 7G frequencies. The combination of all of these threats were then activated all under an ionized weaponized sky by Space X, which monitored and regulated reality with its thousands of satellites orbiting Earth in one large assimilated singular A.I. "Safe Grid. Yup, that is where again, it is like you cannot handle the truth, right. Why would you want to? Pretty much is as Sci-Fi and horror show as it gets.

But, I can tell you if you will listen that what is coming is not only an issue of domination, control, surveillance, and nanotechnologies; but that there also is an energetic reset planned as well that is underway as the "Wise Ones" have mentioned. This reset plan triumphantly transcends all The Black Goo nightmare that is to come so eyes open no fear. But to get to this transcendent flame I must also tell you that you will become infected in your beings by way of "Morgellons," the tiny threads of fibers that 100% of the population has already been infected with. These thread-like fibers have already been routinely sprayed in our skies for decades through chem –trails. These Morgellons as they have been called will become entwined and entangled with everything and they feedback inter-loop directly with the Matrix itself. The point of these Morgellons is to create within you a bio feedback connection to the Matrix and its algorithms. It will be used to overall create your virtual body and create your so called "Being of Light" so that you can be fully inserted into the Matrix or 8th Sphere as it has been called in the Cloud.

I can also tell you that there will be the issue of the release of man-made biological warfare in the guise of viruses and infections that will spread around the world in pandemics which will of course be answered by mandatory vaccinations to sterilize the masses and have control of the DNA and RNA codex of your beautiful bodies ushering all who choose to be injected with that under the "beast system" hence "the mark of the beast."

No, it will not be missiles that kill millions in the future, but microbes created to cull a serious percentage of the population on Earth and force sterilization activated by way of vibrational manipulation through the so called "safe grid" Matrix. Truth is Orwellian law is just about to be fully unleashed into your unsuspecting world and that after 2020 everything is going to get real hot real fast. This heat is the sacred flame; it is the purifying fire that will eventually burn like a wildfire everything up to the great "Reset" the great "Morph" and our collective rise to 5D and to the beginning of the next age, the 5th Age of Peace.

After being taken from my family and sold out to the shelter houses and foster system time and time again, literally being assaulted by what my parents had tried to fight; I at thirteen than met my beloved and my beloved kin. With them and through them I met my spiritual guides and together we all helped turn the tides and outcome to the story of the Book of Life.

This is what I have come to share with you, my story of how I joined forces with a group of nobodies just like me left lost and forgotten and how together we rose up from the streets of LA, from Babylon itself, and emerged from the New Age Matrix all glamorous and deceptive to herald its demise. My story is about how we, this group of nobodies and I like orphan Annie, despite all of our misfortunes, successfully helped usher in the 5th Age of Peace for all life.

Since traditionally history tells a story, not necessarily the truth but a story of how things went before the present time, I want you to consider now that this too is a story about how the fourth age of man came and then passed away and with it all the suffering and sickness it bared witness to just as the previous three worlds had all come and passed away as sands through the hourglass. These ages, eras, and epochs are all scribed into scrolls etched onto walls and rocks, just as the Hopi Prophecy was etched into "Prophecy Rock" and left to be pieces of the grand puzzle of life. The Hopi pieced together this puzzle and the picture that they hold is of as a great web of life, not made of pyrite but of true gold. Their web tells a story which had also been scribed into my soul as truth. For when I came to the teachings of the Hopi, I found all the answers my soul had been crying for all my life.

So this, the story I share with you, this is a story of love and heroic actions taken by those who were meant to give up, but never did, and instead despite the aggressive attempt to conqueror the soul and spirit of man; instead rose up like a phoenix in a fire. You too may feel like you want to give up or perhaps one day you will want to… but I want you to know that you are here for a reason and that everything has a season and that this too shall pass.

So, this is my story, Sophia Star Water's story and the story of "The Apocalypsos," my band. This is a story of how we bent the world towards evolution and how we helped build the momentum to make the mighty morphic jump, the quantum leap towards ascension to 5D and the 5th Age of Peace it would bring with it. My hope is that you will find my story both empowering and inspiring if nothing else and perhaps find your own tribe and your own calling to help raise humanity back to 5D out of duality and bring in the 5th Age of Peace with as much ease as possible.

Know that hidden like a jewel in the lotus of life there is a great teaching, a great truth that has been hidden in the heart of every religion and in the heart of every sentient being. This great teaching and truth has been taught by all the great teachers of time. In Christianity we learned about this great teaching from Jesus or Yeshua by way of his example of dying to be reborn and arise again by way of the resurrected being and the "Christ Body" or "Light Body." The Buddhists teach of this same process of awakening to one's higher self and refer to it as the "Rainbow Light Body," and the Egyptians laid it all out through their "Book of the Dead" and their teachings of the Merkaba in their ancient Mystery Schools. These few examples illustrate just like in the show Wonder Woman as I had said before, the transformation of a being as they morph into their bodies of light or Avatar selves. This is the promise of what is to come and the promise that I have come back to fill you in on, the promise that there is life beyond the illusion of Maya and that even if you begin to spin out of control as the world will; that truly we are all just spinning into our "Rainbow Bodies of Light!"

The Rainbow Light Body activation is a process whereby the spark of light from the "Source" that has been planted like a seed in the flower of your heart, once activated, allows for your rapturous Christed Body of Light to spin itself into being. Hence the great "rapture."

I Sophia Star Water, come now to you bearing my message not only of hope but also of truth to you who is reading this right now ... that there shall come a day when those who have learned to entrain their beings with resonance to the higher spheres of light and frequency; overall the vibrations that make up the Naturix, the pure existence of creation ... that they will be raptured and reunited with our galactic family at last once "The Hour of Power Has Come." When the "Hour of Power" delivers it frequencies, it will activate our collective morph into the 5th density or 5D and that is when the quarantine will be lifted off us at last.

When the quarantine lifts we will be allowed to rise back up to where we belong completing this sacred task we have been tasked to and live as Avatars, as the Masters that we were created to be. As we do this process, so do the Mother Earth and all Creation simultaneously for once again ... "As above so below, as within so without."

Yes there is much to share for many people in your present time have no idea what is playing out right before their very eyes; that is why it has always been said, "blessed are those with eyes to see and ears to hear." May you have eyes to see and ears to hear what I have come to share with you, that is all that I hope for.

So, now sit back cozy up. Open your mind and your heart... know that we storytellers are key masters who wield the power to open doorways to higher consciousness, something essential as an ingredient to the morph that awaits thee. Fasten your seat belts, here we go!

CHAPTER ONE

"THE APOCALYPSOS"

**"If you want to find the secrets of the universe, think
in terms of energy, frequency, and vibration."
Nikola Tesla**

As I meditate and reflect back upon my Earth walk during the timeline
of the 4th world, I can remember the absolute wheel of emotions and
experiences that I went through. The sensations flood me and draw
tears to my eyes. It all seems like a fairy tale now complete with heroes
and villains, exciting adventures, and magical beings. I offer to you my
story, Her-story and welcome you to the roller coaster ride of memories
and messages regarding the exciting tale of my journey to the 5th Age of
Peace. My story begins on my bearthday night when I turned eighteen
but felt like I was going on eighty.

"Huddle in huddle in my peeps, grab the hand of the person next
to you and listen up! Magnum Opus times my sistas' and my brothers,
Carpe freaking Diem! Tonight, we celebrate the completion of our
year-long pilgrimage across the 4 corners of the globe. Each one of you
knows what we have gone through to save as many souls as possible
from them dirty Draco's, them gangster reptilians, and the soulless
ones; them greys ... Come on my peeps liven up yo selves we got this
one last time to transmit the 5D frequencies ... raise your hands up
to our guides and guardians for keeping us safe as we have galactically
battled our way through the darkness and took part in the healing of the
Nations ... Here's to the Black Snakes and Black Goo ... know we be
anti-doting you ... tonight lets alchemize synergize harmonize, override
all the nasty nasty! Look in my eyes, let's take some big breaths family;
deep breath in receive the power catch the transmissions! Breath in love,
breath in light, exhale and let go ... let go of all the pain, all the shame,

all the evil … let it all go and be washed cleaned and cleared. We have been through so much together Gaias and I really got to say I love you peeps with all my heart. You are my sistas' and my brothers from the Divine Mother hahah …let's dedicate this last session to Poppa D, to our Guides and our Guardians, and to all who will rise together with us tonight to get free! Aroooooooooooooooo"

Avatar, our band's leader and our Alpha dog had pulled our crew together in a circle just before we all came out on stage that night inside The Revolutionaries Gallery for our last performance celebrating the end to our year-long tour across the world spreading our galactivating message about humanities ascension to 5D and the 5th Age of Peace that we were entering. Avatar was trying in his own way to be our cheerleader and give us the necessary pep talk we all needed, because damn times were thick and heavy, and we were just plain exhausted from travelling for the whole past year straight.

You could say Avatar's style was straight out of the comic books for his personality was that of an Avatar for real, seriously he was a modern-day superhero! He was a master of the Matrix and like Neo he had learned a long time ago how to make it past the lady in the red dress and ultimately say "No!" For Avatar it was all video game coding in his mind; everything in his genius was connected and interconnected in so many ways that his consciousness was like a web and he had access to all kinds of information. He knew how to tap into the connections of not only the Matrix and read the codes that were creating reality like a human A.I. but he could also connect to the Naturix and the intelligences of Creation via Nature. Avatar you see, he had natural intelligence, organic intelligence, S.I. or Source Intelligence … that was what my crew and I ended up calling it anyways. We believed Avatar was an example of what we were all like at one time when we existed in advanced civilizations like Atlantis or Lemuria. In different cultures he would have been called a Shaman or Holy Person or even Guru but to us he was Avatar our brother and best friend.

My favourite memory of Avatar was of him teaching us, that is my crew and I "The Apocalypsos" as we called ourselves in those days, how to ride the waves of electricity of plasma, and how to access the living libraries of creation; the Akash. He would channel from its vast archives like Nikola Tesla in his dreams. Like Rudolph Steiner he just got the bigger picture for he could tap into the interconnectivity of true power, love, and its undying message.

Reflecting back upon that night of my eighteenth birthday I remember Avatar had wanted so badly and tried so hard to rally our forces and our spirits together and give it a mega boost for it was the winter solstice and like the sun our energy was diminishing. He knew we were so tired, so done delivering performance after performance. But that was Avatar he was infamous for lighting a light in darkness, as well as for lighting a fire under our asses when necessary, which it certainly was at that moment.

"This is it Gaia's ... we may never perform again. The agents are everywhere trying to shut us down ... tonight we must rise ouroboros style. As it was in the beginning one year ago today when we started this thing... lets end it now, let us full circle and stand victorious! Let's do our breath of fire together so that we can go out with a bang, a big bang (we all did breath of fire together upon his command for like 3 minutes straight). Alright now SSSSSSoul rebels time to mount up let us do this, lets tango, lets party ... cuz it is our sistas bearthday .... Miss Sophia Star Water it's your bearthday and we gonna party! Come on everybody let's get into this ... time to step up on the stage and represent; I know you hear the crowds calling for us. Apocalypsos lets do this!!!!!"

I was turning eighteen and the night was a big bang indeed for when we got going, we got it going on, strong! We entered onto the stage to all sorts of hooting and hollering, people were crying and laughing and so ready to raise the cone of power. People came to see us from all over just for the fact that we could deliver frequency, that's what we were known for, for being able to raise the cone of power like a coven making magic and bring 5D to the world.

That night I felt like I was Gem and my band members were the Holograms synergizing optimizing the field of life all around us. We actually loved to amplify each other's auric and magnetic fields, it was like heartgasming as our own heart's bio electric field got activated it would elevate our crew and just continued to rise up everyone in our crew higher and higher. We referred to this process of getting psyched up to perform like literally pumping up the volume to an energetic stereo. We did this not only for ourselves but for our audience as people would flock to our performances because our band "The Apocalypsos" were famous for being able to generate source energy like a Tesla Tower delivering frequencies in rippling waves of ecstasy to everyone who tuned in. These waves of bliss would fan out into concentric circles far and wide; igniting kundalini like a contagion and that was what people were starving for in our times, was true Source energy.

My crew and I, "The Apocalypsos", we were a calypso reggae hip hop crew from Los Angeles, and we had become over the past year, a living force of fuel and power gone viral in the world. A viral cure that is … which served as an antidote to all the hate, pain, and violence raging out of control in our beloved world, our beloved Earth. You see Mother Earth in 2030; she had begun to go mad like a mother dog ridden with fleas desperately trying to shake them off. She was agitated being cooked by radiation and had had enough. So had the masses of people left and that is why our band and our message had become like food and spiritual water for the hungry and thirsty.

The stage where my band and I were performing that night soon transformed into an epicenter, a nucleus within a cell and the people around it became protons and neutrons entraining the body of the world into enlightenment as they danced to our music and drank from the spiritual waters of our message. It was truly a vision that could bring tears to one's eyes for people would wail, they would crack open like a chick from an egg breaking free from the shell that bound them. They would hear our music and just come back to life almost resuscitated like.

But tonight was special, it was December 21, 2030, my bearthday and closing night after an epic yearlong tour with my band and spirit clan. We were being described on the news as a band of misfits, a band of rebels by the media; they always wanted to diminish light in the world as we saw it. Truth was, we were a band of wild horses running towards freedom and we were on spiritual fire you could say. Literal violet flames on stage burning it up like smudge; like sweetgrass sage and copal all mixed up together; ya you could say we were clearing the bad vibes of the times.

Thomas, my man's best friend (more like brother) grabbed the microphone and with his base begun to strum some chords while he spoke, "in the words of John Denver, my late mother's favorite musician of her time, (may Great Spirit bless her soul he said in a whisper) who was an old school singer song writer and inspired me greatly wrote and I quote … To sail on a dream on a crystal-clear ocean. To ride on the crest of a wild raging storm. To work in the service of life and living. In search of the answers to the questions unknown. To be part of the movement and part of the growing. Part of beginning to understand. Aye, Calypso the places you have been to. The things that you have shown us. The stories you tell. Aye Calypso, I sing to your spirit. The men who have served you so long and so well. Like the dolphin who guides you, you bring us beside you. To light up the darkness and show us the way. For though we are strangers in your silent world. To live on the land, we must learn from the sea. To be true as the tide and free as a wind swell. Joyful and loving in letting it be. Aye Calypso the places…John Denver, Word brother! Yes, the places that we "The Apocalypsos" have been, what we have seen, and what we have accomplished literally is the reason we all gather here tonight and celebrate together. We celebrate the victory of nature, the victory of spirit, Aho! We want to thank each and every one of you for coming tonight, for showing up and for spreading the message of love and spirit and the transformation taking place around the world. Tonight, we not only celebrate the success and completion of our yearlong tour … we celebrate our seastar Lady Sophia Star Water, let us all wish her a happy bearthday!"

I felt like I was birthing, I felt like I was the Earth birthing yet again another solar return another age another lifetime and I was exhausted from the labor of love that was required. I looked over at Thomas as he gave me the microphone and I said, "thank you thank you everybody yes, the places we have been and seen, the truth which has haunted us in our dreams is all culminating now in this present moment and we love and thank each one of you for showing up. The potency of our collective power is palpable … can you all feel that? This is our,

"The Apocalypsos" final show completing our life changing journey spreading our galactivating message to the world. We come together tonight to celebrate and to give thanks for the coming full circle of this tour and our safe return back home which is the best present, the best gift I could ask for on my bearthday … we are stoked that we get to celebrate this great joy with all of you …. thank you thank you all of you whom have supported us … we love you so!"

Many did love us but many hated us too, for we had come to be called "The Horsemen of The Apocalypse." You see we, "The Apocalypsos," were a threat to the establishment. I guess we were just a little too high, a little too positive and empowered for their liking. So, we were deemed a bunch of hooligans, a menace to society, a threat to civil obedience; whatever.

To others though who still could feel, whom still could make conscious connection, for them we were a salve on a throbbing wound. When once asked in an interview by some grey steely reporter, "what is your message to the world?" I responded by saying with my tribe surrounding me like bodyguards, "our message to humanity is simple and sweet, rise in love or fall in fear. We are all going to have to make a choice to live in resonance or in dissonance. The fork in the road is imminent between the Matrix and the Naturix, divergent evolution is real time to feel to deal to heal get real for there is no going back once you make the choice to either serve the light and love or darkness and fear. Know that you cannot serve two masters." Let us just say the reporter did not like that … and it was taken off air immediately!

My lover Jacob, he was our lead vocalist and the most dynamic poetically handsome singer song writer I had ever met. Truth to be told, I am balls deep in love with him and had been since first sight when I had seen him at the shelter I was moved to several years ago! Jacob wrote most of our songs and played percussion, funny enough he was like our Yoda, for he was always super stable super calm and held space like a master.

His crystal green blue eyes would dance in dreams beyond reality in worlds of magic as he played upon his conga drums singing to the world his sweet songs of freedom. Lets just say he had just about every girl and gay guy around the world totally swooned by his raw electric beauty, including me. Looking out into the crowd from on stage I could see all the eyes of all the faces there totally captivated by him, moving to his voice to his rhythms, opening their hearts to him as he sang directly to their souls. …

"Rise up in love
Children!
Come along and see,
What has been prepared
In Jah's garden for thee
Oh yaaa Oh yaaaa
Rise up in love
Children!
Rise to 5D
Come along with me
Oh ya oh ya
For we are Calypso
Apocalypso
Sing along
With us The Apocalypsos
Singing Calypso
For we be
The Apocalypsos
Singing Calypso
Singing
The hour of power is coming
Time to be getting free,
Yes
Bless
While our souls be put to the test
And be sold to slavery
What a mess
Yes
As ol' pirates yes they rob I

Selling us to the merchants of the beast
Yet
Hear me as I say
Fear not children
Come what may
Just
Listen to what the prophets have to say
For
Now is the hour
Time we be getting free
From our dark history
Don't ya know life it is a mystery
Oh ya oh ya oh ya ya
Calypso
Apocalypso
Sing
With us The Apocalypsos
Singing Calypso
Singing
The hour of power is coming
Time to be getting free,
The Apocalypsos singing Calypso till infinity
Singing
Come shake your body
Everybody
Let's get a little higher
Stand by the sacred fire
Jump in the line
For now is the time.
Purify your heart and your mind
For this can be a good time
Oh ya oh ya oh ya ya
Calypso
Apocalypso
Sing along with me

Singing Calypso
Singing once again
The hour of power is coming
Time to be getting free
Come now and join us as we rise up to 5D
Yes
The star gates are now open to
Eternity
So, sing your songs of freedom
So mote it be
Oh ya oh ya oh ya ya
Calypso
Apocalypso."

That night Jacob's shirt was unbuttoned down to his heart chakra and his beautiful amulet I had made him beat upon his chest like a drumstick banging on a sacred drum while his whole body went into the music he made. His voice, ahhhhh his voice, it was like crystalline liquid light delivering ecstasy; erasing grief like nobody. For just to see him made you smile. His radiant joy was tangible, his spirit emblazoned like the sun. Ahhhhh even now after all that we have been through just looking back at those times when I would see him singing to the world and how he could make me want to caress his tanned magnetic body and make love to him right there forever. Woh girl chill! Sorry, he just always got me so good! Just looking at him made me sweat, made me feel the swirling twirling sensation that only true love can make you feel. Our kind of love is like where life gets symbiotic and synergized by the battery of our union, the combination of his positive energy with my negative energy created a yin and yang only like the power that two twin souls can create.

I could not believe he had fallen in love with me to be honest, me Sophia Star Water. I was such a little shit, standing five foot three inches of pure Diva. Latent with a massive head of dread locks woven in with shells and crystals from around the world; I was like a temple Chihuahua, little with a big mouth. My shrew opalescent face apparently made people stare as I had been told my beauty was striking and my eyes, those of an Egyptian Queen. I was not exactly full of myself or anything egoic like, but I was intense. I did not know how to have small talk, or how to be normal you could say.

Equipped with a mind that got off on digging deep and standing under life in every way; I devoured history, legends, mythos, and literature from around the world as a hobby since I was very young. I was what you would call an autodidact, a self-taught genius as my parents described me, which is why they tried to protect me from going to school; no they let my grandmother and grandfather teach me for they were adept scholars, masters of antiquity. The public schools my parents' thought was where you sent kids to be broken like a wild horse and groomed to be a slave for an elite master who would only come to use and abuse you then throw you away after they had sucked all of the essence of your spirit and strength out of you; you could say my parents had a way with words, most likely were I got my gift for spoken word from though truth to be told.

You see in my last life I grew up as the daughter of a long line of Jewish people who were all great scholars, Rabbis, doctors, and professors of history and antiquity. My father he was a lawyer and my mother a doctor and they were both very steeped in the Kabbalah teachings since they were children, how could they not their own parents had been as well as well as many, many generations before them dating all the way back to the Essenes. Although they had once been considered of a higher class of respectable citizens since they were such successful and accomplished beings, my parents had decided to take on the fight for freedom and sovereignty. Just like the old days of the Jews when they were in Egypt. Really it all started when my parents realized when I was born what was in the vaccinations that we were all supposed to take, and they forbid our doctor to give me those shots. That was just the beginning, after that my father who was a lawyer right and my mother who was a doctor worked together and dove deep into research regarding these vaccinations and the growing levels of health issues as a response to them. They then began to connect a lot of horrific dots which came together to create an evil like sigil upon humanity much like the pentagram that is over Washington D.C. My grandfather who was a Rabbi and my grandmother who was a mystic of the Torah and Kabbalah confirmed this as well to be all a part of an ancient prophecy that was being revealed via these abominations. That is when my parents started a revolution and thus were both taken from me many moons ago.

My grandparents had when they were younger with other great scholars cracked the code of the Torah and discovered the God Code hidden within it. It was from this that they were able to determine a hidden message and had realized that we were all being corralled into a prison planet warned about ages ago. They wrote books about what they called the beast system, as they referred to it as, and how it was about to wage war on our souls, for they had already taken ownership over everything else. My parents under the guidance and tutelage of my grandparents began to see through the illusions that were being programmed into our consciousness via the media's predictive programming. Just as in prophecy, there they discovered indeed there was a spiritual battle on for our souls.

We were all getting duped! Duped by a fake God, duped by a fake currency, duped by fake medicines, duped by the chip, duped by the A.I., and ultimately duped by a fake new age city of light that would be virtual and where all who lived there would be made perfect. Yes, as they were designed, augmented, and enhanced by A.I. and the transhumanist's vision for a technocratic world.

This is when my parents started a revolution and began to speak out and to warn people creating movements worldwide. They went on air getting interviewed on podcasts by a whole bunch of different journalists and "truthers." My parents had gone on to making several websites documenting everything they discovered, they had a you tube channel and all the media platforms they could upload to while trying to wake people up! That is when they became targeted individuals. That is when they reached a point of no turning back. By 2019 my parents had become authors of several best-selling books that proved how we were all going to be sold into a fake reality via the internet of things and the A.I. that runs it.

My parents were then taken down! They got hacked completely; their bank accounts, their records, their computers everything got hacked. Then they became audited and falsely accused of laundering money which of course they did not do and could prove, but they were never given a chance. They were left broke and taken as for a joke as they were photo shopped into scandalous affairs in fake videos that got prime time air on the news just to discredit them and make them look like crazy drug trafficking criminals.

Then the real bomb dropped … and not just any bomb, a nuke. That was the day when I had come home to find my grandparents were dead, just lying there dead in their bed mysteriously right after my parents had just been charged with laundering and trafficking of drugs and it was at that point, I realized my world as I knew it was over. I remember the cold chill of evil that had ran through my body that dark day when I found my grandparents laying there dead in our Hollywood home. I will never forget the look on my grandparent's face when I found them lying there after calling for them running around looking for them in all their usual places yelling Savta, Saba (Hebrew for grandmother and grandfather) for I had just come home from the park and it was in the middle of the day. Then bam, the nuke dropped as I saw them there dead all of a sudden when just the night before they had promised me my next lessons in the God Code, Geomatria, and the mysteries of the Kabbalah. I knew they had been murdered for they were as healthy as a horse and they never broke their promises never corrupted their word; it was there honor! I knew in my heart my grandparents were killed; their lips were so blue, their bodies so cold, and as I stared at them in shock, it was as if they whispered to me "avenge us little one!"

I at that point went mute; I was in a state of shock. I simply just watched silently as everything precious in my life was then taken from me, everything that was sacred and that I loved stolen. Eventually my parents were forced to surrender me to the system that they had fought against most my life.

Everything done to my family was all a complete breech against our constitutional rights and it was at this moment when I was just a child as my parents screamed "honor our rights honor the constitution, we call upon our constitutional rights, habeas corpus habeas corpus!!!" That I realized everything I had been taught growing up, which in all seriousness up to that point all felt like a crazy bedtime story, was in fact real!

I can remember long ago my father David and my mother Anath deciding to homeschool me even though I hated it. I remember missing having friends when I was little, and it made me awkward you could say as all my friends were old people. But they had decided to take me out of the system so that they would not have to vaccinate me nor pollute my perfect mind; well that was what they said. But because of my parent's choice, I had been able to save my perfect mind to educate it with true knowledge and by the age of eight use it as a tool and as a weapon against the system, against the agents that had taken my whole family away.

For later as I grew up in the system tossed around in the shelter houses for children and sold out to different foster homes I cultivated my power. I used the pain that the agents of the Matrix had inflicted upon my family and I used it as fuel to blaze my message's fire to bring light unto the darkness and help awaken people from the dream, from the fog that their own minds were enveloped in causing them to be blinded and stuck in the maze of illusions created by the beast system clueless as to which way to go.

That is why my band "The Apocalypsos" became so important to me, for they were not just a band to me but my spiritual family. They had become my brothers and sisters filling in the void from whence my parents and extended family had once been. My spirit family or band consisted of my man the love of my life Jacob, Avatar, Mill Boy, King, and Thomas who were all like my older brothers. Thomas was Jacob's longest and closest best friend as they had become like brothers raised in the system together. We also had in our band our ladies, my seastars … Mercy, Rebekah, and Queen who were our back-up vocalists to our crew and who played flutes and trumpet. They were for real like trumpet swans, graceful and sleek. These goddesses were also the girlfriends of my brothers, convenient hey. We all had met a long time ago in the foster system all orphans, all seeking love in a mad and bitter world.

That is why we became a family, self-chosen as we adopted each other and took care of each other even after all graduating from the hell we had been taken into through the shelters and foster houses.

Our motto and "The Apocalypsos" official creed, which literally helped us survive the nightmare of our childhood was …"Be a transfusion of spirit like blood to the masses, lift up the hearts of the living as yeast is leaven in the bread of life, we are the ones we are waiting for, we come to stop the sacrifice, we come to raise creation back up to paradise to 5D to ever lasting peace, so mote it be."

I remember as I stood up there on stage that night of my eighteenth birthday that all these visions of my future self and all these fleeting memories of my past were floating around in my mind as if I was in a kaleidoscope and time was spinning in a fractal all around and around me. It was as if the past present and even future had begun to compress into a coexistence of time and space and that the secret to it all was in the energy, the frequency, and the vibration. Yes that was it, the mystery that I had sought out my whole life to understand was all beyond words, for the mystery wasn't a spell as much as a feeling, an essence. It was frequency, energy, and vibration these were the literal keys that could take you anywhere. These keys could open the door to the past, to all throughout the present via remote viewing, and even to the future. Even just from the scent like the smell of a rose, my mother's favorite … which was wafting through the gallery could take me back to her arms. Or even like the sound of the voices of my brothers and sisters singing in harmony through our music which was taking me back to the memories of when we first all had first met us "The Apocalypsos."

It was right there and then in that very moment when I realized that the mystery and the secret to life really was just in the energy resonance and vibration of all things through the "Law of Oneness!" That through the frequencies and vibrations when one was in resonance to any one thing that you could attract that thing to you just like it was taught in the law of attraction. You could also magnetize anything you wanted to you while simultaneously repelling just like a magnet anything you did not want coming at you. Like inhaling or exhaling we could bring in to us what we needed and expel from us through our exhalation anything that did not serve us or what was no longer in service to us. I realized on stage that night that we as beings of energy were conductors, transmitters and that through resonance or dissonance we could become or fall apart, that we all had to make a choice to literally rise in love and resonate with Source or fall in fear and become dissonant through force. To become the change we wanted to see in the world we had to consciously choose to rise in love for if we fell into fear or our reptilian brain we would continue to feed the beast of the A.I. system and for us that was not an option. We were the ones we were waiting for, none but ourselves could free our minds as Bob Marley said.

CHAPTER TWO

AWAKENING TO HIGHER CONSCIOUSNESS

**"Your solar system, your planet, and your sun in particular
are all working to bring you into these higher frequencies.
Now, on top of all that, you have the summoning of energy
you have done in all of your previous lifetimes and in every
moment, you have lived in this lifetime. You also have helpers
like us in the higher dimensional planes who are assisting. We
are helping to bring this about for you because it is time."
The 9th Arcturian Council**

Looking back through the looking glass at myself inside The
Revolutionaries Gallery I remember that I kept thinking as I gazed
out upon all the lovely faces in the crowd that night on my bearthday,
that this night was different than any of our other performances up to
that point. That this night was more like a giant collective revival that
we were hosting for the world. A resuscitation of the sacred and that
everything felt super surreal. It was as if we were all in a candid lucid
dream. You know like a dream where one awakens to an enchanted
fantasy world all lit up and sparkling in Technicolor. Like when you
are tripping on good acid peyote or magic mushrooms and you find
yourself suddenly in a river of energy where the walls are breathing,
and everything is melting into oneness. Where there is no separation no
ending nor beginning just as it is in the pure omnipotent omniscience;
yep that was where my mind and heart was at that night and I was as
sober as Sunday.

It all just felt so ecstatic from where I stood up on the stage. Perhaps,
I was just delirious from exhaustion or perhaps it was because we really
were fulfilling the prophecies and that the hour of power was coming at
last. As I looked out unto the faces of my kin and out into the crowds

I could see the diminishing dense heaviness of people's hearts were being alleviated and returned to as light. Light as that of a feather, as the feather of the Goddess Maat of Egypt who uses a feather to weigh us as she puts our hearts upon her scales and judges each human who has died weighing our hearts on her balancing scale with a feather to see how heavy we are for one has to be light as a feather to travel beyond the low densities of the underworld.

The power of revelation flooded me as I began to understand whole heartedly that we humans had to rise up and out of our collective darkness and the heaviness of our plight to become as light as a feather so that we could fly on past the crumbling matter of Earth and 4D and make our way to the 5th Age of Peace and 5D. Just as the Goddess Maat tests us to see if we have been able to alchemize our karmas and learn the lessons needed to attain our "Ka" bodies, to activate our "Merkaba" our bodies of light so that we may be able to rise to higher spheres of life. Revelation after revelation birthed epiphanies in my mind's eye that night as I looked out into the crowds and saw that each person there was a star like that of the sun upon the hour of the rising sun, rising out of the darkest hour just before the sacred dawn of the 5th Age of Peace I so longed to attain. Yes people were illuminating right there before our eyes, lighting up like fireflies for everything in that gallery right before all of our very eyes was turning into living light; it was the most beautiful thing I had ever witnessed! I could not help but to tear up and realize what good work we had accomplished over this past year even through all our trials and tribulations.

While all the memories of the past year like a time review raced through my mind that night; memories of us travelling around the whole world sharing our performances and our message right from our hearts to the good people of the world, I couldn't help but to feel the immense gratitude of deliverance wash over me. We were home again, and I felt so grateful to all that is for all that we had learned along the way and for all the wondrous souls we had met and communed with.

As wave after wave of gratitude and awe washed over me, I became aware of a sensation, a feeling that was spreading through me. This feeling that spread through me was a bit unnerving at first, yet exciting all at the same time as I knew in every facet of my being that the veils between the worlds were lifting. As though the barriers of time and space began dissolving and that where I ended and began was losing its definition. The constructs of life in the concrete jungles of time and space were dissolving into oneness and there was no more separation from me to all that is. It was as if a whole other level to the concept of as within, so without was taking hold of me and deconstructing all my walls and all my boundaries releasing me from an invisible cage and allowing for my spirit wings to unfold from the locked up position.

There I was on stage (and I say this with a giggle) flying like an Eagle like a bird like a plane; flying, yet completely rooted to the ground all at the same time. Was it me? Or was it my superhuman self, my own Avatar, my own Supergirl coming through? I stood there up on the stage tripping out or more like tripping through a portal of awareness. I realized then right there up on stage that I was held in animation, hovering like a hummingbird. It as if I were in some sort of dream, some sort of suspension of time and space, and that all I could do was transmit my power and my light to everyone and everything in all the directions like a lighthouse or beacon guiding people to a safe shore from a tumultuous sea of stormy waters and jagged rocks.

I could feel myself surrendering to the need to just allow myself to give into whatever it was that was happening to me and through me although I knew not what I did. It felt like hours went by as I transmitted my frequency like a care bear stare to the crowd. But as I gazed around the gallery taking inventory of reactions from the people there which was difficult given the depth of the trance that I was in, I realized that the people there were discovering they too had wings and could fly and that they too were beginning to glow to shine as if they were diamonds all within a blink of the eye.

It was if we were all simultaneously beginning to realize that we all had been under an illusion, where we had believed that our wings had been clipped, and that since we had all been stuck in a cage for so long that we had forgotten we had wings at all. As the light grew all around us and as the transmitting frequencies of raw electric plasma like energy came beaming through my heart to all the others there, our hearts all collectively found total coherence and as it did it was like, Biiiiiiing!!!!

Bam, there we were all flying, all finding our wings that came right out of our hearts. We all flew for the first time in our lives together as one flock of beautiful doves riding the waves of currency channeling our peace to the world. Not physically but spiritually, we had all successfully escaped the soul cage and this great awakening caused us all to go super nova.

I could feel the world lift, to lift right up and out of the hell it had become while all our collective love through our combined heart magic restored heaven on Earth. Our collective power surged as it combined causing star gates to open wide up all round the world, opening us all up to the stars and to the Galactic Confederation itself cuing "Go Time." This is what I was seeing in visions while simultaneously I rejoiced in the sweet songs of freedom which kept rolling out like thunder from my band. Everyone there was a part of this incredible informal ritual or ceremony that was taking place and we all just kept getting higher and higher blissed right out in the ecstasy of its effects. As much as I wanted to stay grounded, I could not help but to slip in and out of the interdimensional spheres where I could see a great celebration was taking place there.

Seriously just beyond 4D, just beyond the box of perceived reality, I could see Sasquatches dancing stomping the grounds as Dragons flew around clapping their wings in beat to our music. Faeries were fluttering like hummingbirds darting here and there leaving behind them a trail of sparkling golden dust. Mermaids lifted their seashell chalices up to me for a toast and Unicorns frolicked in fields of emerald grass. Star Nation brothers and sisters of all kinds and colors appeared in and out like pulsating stars; Pleiadians, Lyrians, Syrians, Arcturians, and so many other Star Nation kin showed up to raise their cup to the completion of our long race to this finish line we were arriving at.

It was as if all these beings that were gathering with us had come to celebrate our coronation, our apotheosization, our realization that we the everyday people were truly the princes and princesses; the kings and queens of our own beloved realms and that we truly were the ones we had been waiting for all along. We the people, the sons and daughters of the God's that we had been made in the image of once upon a time, we were waking up to this higher awareness, this higher consciousness and to all that exists in those higher spheres. It was high time that the end of the great illusion, the illusion that we were mere slaves or indentured servants to the Dark Lords, was truly ending, expiring, resetting. Game over!

Yes, the keys to creation were being passed out upon the chords and tones of our instruments, through the spells and harmonies of our words and songs. We, the people, were being called forth from our lower selves to finally remember what we had come here to do and to reconnect with our higher selves so that we could complete our oaths and ascend! Just about everyone there that night inside The Revolutionary Gallery and all around the world were remembering collectively together that we were all here to put the keys of creation, which one could only attain by coming into resonance to that key just like in music and resonate, and upon attainment of that key to put it inside the keyhole of our hearts to open wide the treasure of our chest so that we could enter into the kingdom of heaven at last! Just as the Gospel of Thomas had said, "The Kingdom of Heaven is within thee, and all around," yes, we were manifesting it, the Kingdom of Heaven was manifesting right before our eyes! Right there right then, manifesting the gate to the Gods through our hearts finally allowing us the access to our true selves and our true home in the heavens, 5D baby.

It was time now; I knew it in my heart that we were returning to our truth, to our original blueprints and that we were being reconnected and reunited at last to all of our Galactic family and ancestors. We were being lifted from the quarantine of Earth and sweetly being welcomed back to the Garden of the Gods once again! Truly it is so that the truth does set us free and that the Age of Truth was crowning now like a baby going through the birth canal. "The Hour of Power is coming" … I heard whispered in my ear by the voice of my beloved Shima, my beloved spirit guide one of the "Wise Ones" who had been contacting me just before I got a hold of a major check in look from my man which snapped me back into my physical body and back on the stage real fast!

Returning to the present moment out of the kaleidoscope of time and space I became aware again that it was this time the here and the now and upon the cue of my man, who was like "WTF Soph, come back…"I began allowing the stream of light to pour through my crown again and out of my throat chakra … trusting that the messages would come through me like a waterfall and that I could surrender to the flow even while tears rolled down my face.

I retrieved the microphone from my man as he stretched out his delicious arm to me and said "I love you Soph, I know your tripping, but you got this babe, we got you, we are holding down the crystal grid, it is time for you honey to channel your nectar sweet … go deep" There I was surrendering to the flow of the great source of power that began streaming through my crown chakra from above and there it was that I began throwing down words weaving a tapestry of spells.

"As you know we all spell the word, therefor our word is our spell and as the passage goes, in the beginning was the word and the word was made flesh … just as it says in Genesis, right? Now in 2030 here we all are hundreds, thousands or even millions of years who knows after Genesis and we "The Apocalypsos" we come to say that it is lucidly evident that we all need to spell a new world and spell it fast. For with all the things going on around the world these days we, yes all you out there who still got a conscious heart beat and eyes to see, you know that we the soul rebels, those who live in the sacred, we know we sure are not going to last past the culls and martial law coming down upon our ass. But ya know as my Spirit Brother King always says in his deep and charismatic voice (which I went deep and mimicked) we know as we are told from the words of the Bible that in the beginning was the word and the word was made flesh, so we got to make flesh a new world my brothers and my sisters, a new world … and that's just what we have come here on Earth to do, for we be on assignment my peeps for reals; we gots to rise up and SPEAK! Chant down Babylon and create the world that we all seek. Let's give it up tonight to all who call themselves the Warriors of the Rainbow for we be going home my friends home to 5D, we be bringing in a new age my seastars and brothers yes the new age of peace!"

While I went off King was playing his saxophone and beat boxing all the while circle breathing like the Aborigines do when playing their Didgeridoo. I went on saying "you all know I must say, that is exactly what we all are doing here this night, yes my peeps I have been given the visions, I have been witnessing it happening right before my very eyes; we are building a new world with the cornerstones of light of love of truth of that which is sacred. Truly we are the ones we have been waiting for, yes, us … you and me; we are here bringing back the sacred, making sacred the new sexy the new black. While the world be under attack, here we are sending alchemy back!"

With my words which reverberated round after round, kind of like a beautiful machine gun spitting out sacred sounds, they then turned into poetry in motion as indeed my words were made flesh. With my crew, "The Apocalypsos," who knew what they were doing mixing my words up with some fresh conga beats, mind blowing trumpets ohhhh what a treat, and aaaah my goodness a little base like some agave to pour in the nectar as a special treat; we were complete. Some saxophone and me channeling through the microphone, a little Stevie Wonder in his hit song Ebony and Ivory … it was like keyboards oh Lord why don't we … through the frequency vibration and energy get free so mote it be … hollering out like a Wolf to the full moon I cried out with all that I had…

"Give up the violence
Give up the hate
Don't segregate
It's not too late
Come Unity
Sacred Community
*

Come together
Come gather round
Sacred Sisters
Sacred Brothers
Heed the call hear the sound

For we don't need no more violence
We don't need no more wars
Come Jah Children
And
Open up Jah doors
*

Come Unity
Sacred Community
*

Come to where our love overflows
Where sacred magic grows
For Jah conscious ones know
How to be reaping what they sew
Now ya feeling the intensity
As light be streaming in immensity
Singing
No mo density
Calling
*

Come Unity
Sacred Community
*

For we be The Apocalypsos
And we have come to say
Brothers and Sisters there is another way
Within the final hours within the final days
Open up your heart and pray
I say
*

Come Unity
Sacred Community
*

Rise up from the lies
Time to say your goodbyes
Time to choose life

Calling out those who sacrifice
*

Now
The hour of power is coming
The frequencies are rising
Timelines be colliding
So
Listen to our words
Let them be shared let them be heard
*

Come Unity
Sacred Community
*

Now love is the answer to this prophetic test
And
We The Apocalypsos
We have come to bless
Yes
And profess
Children of the Sun
Time to clean up your mess
Be the Angels guest
Don't digress nor regress
For we all got to past this test
Hollering
*

Come Unity
Sacred Community
*

Take back your power
Take back your Soul
Take back Mother Gaia
Our
Sacred World
Praying

*

Come unity
Sacred Community
*

With our fortune in our future
Time to be like water and …
Flow
Open our Spirits
And Go
For its time don't ya know
To
*

Come Unity
Sacred Community
*

Arise to 5D out of all the misery
Come with me
To Infinity
For morality is the key to your immortality
Can't you see
Can't you feel the Frequency
Now
The Hour of Power has come
It is time we be getting free
Sing along with me
*

Come unity
Sacred Community"

Tears welled up in my eyes as I scanned the room and all the lives that were there, lending up their hearts to the Heavens to be receivers of the magic that was taking place that night. I then bowed and began to introduce to the crowd my tribe, my kin, "The Apocalypsos."

"Let me introduce my love my partner Jacob on the conga drums and main vocals, we also got Brother King on Saxophone coupled by his delivering of beat boxing champion blows oooohhhhh, now here be Mill Boy running the keyboards, and we got the digital D.J. Master Avatar in the House, now here is po' boy Thomas on Base, and we got these lovely Divas on flutes and horns and back-up vocals …. Take a bow Goddesses Mercy, Queen, and Rebekah and of course here is I, Miss Sophia Star Water in the house as spoken word linguist and hip-hop speller … We are "The Apocalypsos" and we are so glad you are here. We welcome you to the other side of the nightmare of illusions going on out there and through the dreamcatcher, through the spider's web we be crawling out of danger, harm, and instead dropping the beats that lift up the streets. We are proud to announce we are also live streaming across the planet tonight … Thank you Revolutionary Radio and Rebel TV we also would like to thank Team Go Pro for their help in broadcasting this out on the world wide web. Sisters and Brothers of the four corners we humbly ask that you help us form a grid tonight of sacred love light magic and power to override the corruption and dark forces and to pull the plug on the Matrix as we come together in this sacred way to usher in a new day and the resurrection of the Naturixxxxxxx! You see people, we "The Apocalypsos" have been called to bring forth spoken word and have it be made into flesh, to midwife the birth of a new Earth template and timeline and that is exactly what we are all doing tonight together, it is what we have been doing for the past whole year through our music manifesting as medicine, our message which delivers the necessary recalibrations and activations, and the collective energy that we are able to generate as fuel to lift us all up to 5D … and tonight it is on, it is coming strong, we got it going on like King Kong; ascending back up to where we belong! So with that we just want to thank you all so very much for showing up and representing! Hope ya all have a real good time getting sublime!"

Judging by the response of the crowd, I was saying the words that were needed to be heard, weaving spells in my spoken word, and "The Apocalypso" Lions; the men and women of my tribe they were bringing the beats tones and frequencies alive, raising matter from 3D to 5.

"We have always loved singing Bob Marley's songs, us "The Apocalypsos," Jacob my love spoke out to the crowd, "he was like a teacher, a preacher, and a guiding light in our lives as we struggled through darkness deception and lies. I would like to share with all of you our vision, a vision of a future where we don't need no more struggle, we don't need no more war, where we are free body mind and soul, where we all come together to live in love and peace ….. so please Come Unity Sacred Community in the words of Bob Marley, Emancipate yourselves from mental slavery, for none but ourselves can free our minds! Aho!"

As Jacob was sharing our vision we was live on television; yes we were literally telling our vision to the world all while a virtual show of the living templates for 5D, or the Dimension of the Blessed as the Egyptian mysteries would call it, The 5th Age of Peace as the Hopi called it were animated by a holographic show that I had digitally designed and with the help of the computer programming genius of Avatar, Mill Boy, and King who were able to create it into a 3D virtual reality, ohhh ya baby it was all live streaming. Yes, we were broadcasting to the world in real time on Rebel TV a picture of the gateway to 5D and what was waiting for peeps on the other side of misery. Yes, we were imprinting the world with the images and the codex for 5D sharing with humanity the keys that would help open the door within their mind's eye to the new age. As some people say the image is the key like a mandala as to what will be for it imprints the picture that says a thousand words in its imagery, well that was what our images were doing, they were imprinting in the image of 5D where peeps be living in peace and true ecstasy.

Yup, we had millions and millions of viewers watching that night live across the globe. It was a miracle that we had done it we had gone global! We had reached critical mass! Some broadcasters out there were saying that we were like a viral cure an antidote for all the wickedness that like a cancer was killing everything good in the hood. People were crying laughing meditating all over the four directions. They were being called to their knees praying tuning in dancing hugging one another and coming together all over the Earth … Goddess mia, I could feel it in my bones, they were hearing us, feeling us, and most importantly of all they were being elevated by us!

Like a secret finally being revealed the energy our show was creating was unlocking and unblocking people's hearts around the world bringing them out of the collective entrainment to negativity powerlessness and fear and instead ushering them all to a higher experience beyond the super imposed state of nothingness, the literal void that society offered. The nothingness, the void, the zombie state was just too much and we, my crew, we had called quits on it long ago. Now people everywhere were joining us, uhhh what a rush! We were fulfilling our dream, we were manifesting our goals, we were completing our mission our destiny, and it was all viral!

My partners and I, not in crime but in sublime or pure life source energy, we sewed a needle pulling thread by getting each person's head through to the other side of that eye of the proverbial needle on the record of time and space. We could feel the shift as it was hitting the fan, we could see with tears in our eyes that the human rat race was at the finish line, for we had successfully wove them into the tapestry of the 5D templates and timelines.

It was so true, the teachings we had been entraining ourselves to that consciousness, vibration, frequency, and resonance to the "Higher Man" vibration inside us all was the golden ticket out of dissonance. The resonance that was going on that night to us and through us to sacred law and love began creating collectively through the grids, the ley lines, and our own meridians a harmony that was so pure that peeps all began to ascend into fifth density right then and there.

One could just feel the ascension happening as literally my band all confirmed via dream spell speak (speaking psychically to one another without need for words) that we all felt like we were levitating as people were waking up everywhere! It was like one of those connects the dot games but instead it was real and we were forming a crystal grid made up from the crystal oscillators within all of the hearts of the people who were participating in our show beating together as one. As our hearts became enlivened, they created within the field of life and ether a gateway to 5D and a stairway to heaven. As each person's heart was activated, their heart would begin to add exponentially to the power and to the frequency of this living grid which had begun reverberating throughout the web of life re-establishing true order out of chaos. Every time a new heart came online, the power surged allowing for us to emerge step by step from this stairway up into heaven.

The strange thing was that we all had noticed at the same time, that is my crew and I, for we all had mastered that hive mind thing after years of meditating together which we called dream spell speaking, that it was as if we had all been asleep; the collective consciousness of humanity... stuck in a trance and that the music and imagery was like energetic pulses that were clearing out the dross and confusion of the illusion played upon humanities minds from the MK Ultra or mind control programming of the times.

What had unified us shy awkward broken open souls we saw ourselves to be and put us up on the stage, my crew "The Apocalypsos" and I that is, was that we had discovered long ago that we each as individuals couldn't just hide away in closets to become skeletons starved from life and love and die. We could not just turn our cheeks either and let the system keep slapping us in the face. Nor could we cast a blind eye or deaf ear to the cries for help ... nah our eyes were wide open, all three of them and we could remember what we had been sent here for; to overthrow and override all evil by turning on all of the heart lights in the world as one giant supernova like event zero-pointing through our energetic vacuums all corruption and evil. So as we stood up there on stage that night with that realization hitting the nail on the head to our unified focus and mission, people couldn't help but align and ally to our cause and jump aboard our ship taking flight that night right out of Babylon's tight hold upon us and breaking free.

You see, by 2025 life on Earth becomes a reality T.V. show, a Sci-Fi horror story of biblical proportions. That is why I agreed to come and share my story with all of you, in the effort and attempt to see if you can change the timelines and not have to suffer as much as we had. To see if there was a way that you all could be seeded here and now with the 5D codex so that you all can fast forward through the bullshit and just get home safe. For it is all a frequency a formula of energy, a vibration; remember! But in the timeline that I lived upon when we, "The Apocalypsos" were born it was 2025 and Armageddon! Since we had met in the shelter house downtown in Los Angeles we had become our own version of the Avengers.

That was when we decided to answer the call to help humanity since no one had up to that point come and helped us any we knew what it was like to suffer, to live without, and ultimately what it was like to live inside the agenda of our superiors for as orphans you know nothing else. So, we surrendered ourselves to the only things we did know how to do which was our music art and dance. We dedicated ourselves to perfecting our music, our dance, and our art, and dedicated it all to the healing of the nations!

Avatar, King, and Mill Boy they also dedicated their time to hacking and leaking out information, and to building free energy technologies as well as developing healing vibrational tools to help heal people who had become sick from the mandatory injections. But I will get into that later.

For now, let me just say it was all because of the absolute tyranny that was being run within our society by martial law that caused us soul rebels to respond like a group of Shaolin monks and take the world by tour. We mounted up on our spiritual steeds fearless with nothing to lose for we had already lost everything else to spread our galactivating message to the world and awaken the hearts and minds of all the people who would heed our call, "The Apocalypsos call." It was due to the psychological manipulation of consciousness that we witnessed day after day night after night and the fact that everyone who existed within the system didn't not even realize that they were being pushed into a soul prison, that we knew we had to set the captives free!

It was then and there in the summer of 2025 that we were born "The Apocalypsos." Now here just five years later in the winter of 2030 as we were performing on my bearthday that we checked in via our hive mind connection, affirming and confirming that in fact we had completed our mission. For all around us people were getting free from their soul cages which had been invisibly constructed all around them digitally detaining them into the Matrix. Through the power of the Naturix though as it were channeling through us that night, boom ..... bazinga the Rubik's cube all came together intact and presto the cuckoo clock was just about to sing ... Cuckoo Cuckoo Cuckoo!

CHAPTER THREE

THE LIZARD WIZARDS
BEHIND THE CURTAINS

**The ultimate tyranny in a society is not control by martial law.
It is control by the psychological manipulation of consciousness,
through which reality is defined so that those who exist within
it do not even realize that they are in prison. They do not even
realize that there is something outside of where they exist."
Barbara Marciniak**

W hen I was a child when I last had my Earth walk, I had always
been drawn to Lemuria and to Atlantis. There was something about
the ancient worlds that intrigued me as I felt there was a phantom
mystery about who and what we were as human beings from an early
age. I read book after book about ancient civilizations that I had learned
about from my family's great library. You see I had been put to sleep
by bedtime stories read to me by my grandparents all about Atlantis,
Lemuria and the ancient worlds. I was able to read all by myself by
four and I didn't just read books about ponies and princesses, I read
the Torah. I read book after book hungry for the truth as if the words
that were in these books I read were food and that I could never sate the
hunger that lived inside my soul. I learned about where and when people
according to Socrates and Plato and other great sages of the past lived
supposedly as high and noble groups. Contrary to what mainstream
history taught my grandparents had always said, our ancestors lived
in abundant and advanced civilizations like Tartaria, Egypt, Greece,
Sumer, and Ireland where people possessed amazing personal power,
sacred vision, certain abilities to communicate with spirit, and were able
to work in harmony with other interdimensional beings that possessed

33

advanced technologies and taught the humans how to prosper on the Earth by using their advanced technologies and abilities.

People, according to the forbidden archeology documented within certain manuscripts which my family had archived in our library were more evolved rather than devolved as the Darwinians proclaimed and our education system taught. My family had all sorts of historical documents and scrolls that had been almost snuffed out completely by history that talked about how people were at one time way more like the Gods themselves then apes and monkeys. There was so much evidence in just my family's library alone that was literally the opposite of the history I was force fed when taken hostage and sent to public school.

I couldn't understand how when I was forced to eventually go to the matrix run school system once my parents had been taken, how the story was so different from the one I had been taught by my family! How contrary history was to what my grandparents and extended family knew for it taught us children that people came from savages and primitive folk, cave men rather than the sons and daughters of the most high God which is what my family believed. I felt robbed when I was sent to public school, for they did not mention anything about the advanced civilizations or technology or any of the "Siddhis" or abilities, powers that I had been raised to believe I possessed and should be inspired by.

I remember as a child that I had believed in my heart and even remembered in my soul of times when I had lived in Mu, the Mother Land of ancient Lemuria or Dwarka in India and that the Gods like Krishna or Hanuman were real. I fantasized that at one time we were all beautiful beings of love and wisdom living in our ethereal light bodies. I day dreamed after reading the Bhagavad Gita and The Book of the Dead and other Kabbalah esoteric teachings plus countless other scrolls and old texts that I was a princess of Mu and that I had lived in the ancient thriving advanced civilizations when people lived as noble beings serving the "Law of Onesness" in their many rituals and traditional culture.

I knew in my heart that I was a princess of the stars, a mermaid, and a healer and that I had reincarnated time and time again through the ages coming to share in the magic of the mystery schools which spread across Mother Earth. I could almost remote view like a movie into lifetimes when everyone was using advanced technologies that operated grids bringing electricity to the ancient worlds but also the ability to fly ships based on crystal technology. I remembered fantasizing about how I would fly in my own crystal ship and travel with my crew just like the crew in Star Wars, which apparently my parents believed was a documentary as was the Matrix movie which they also thought of as a documentary.

My fondest memories growing up was when I would lay in my sun bed like a cat reading texts about Edgar Cayce and other enlightened folk's stories about the "Tuaoi Stone" which was the operating power source for the technology known as the fire crystals which operated Atlantis's advanced empire. These visions I would have made me feel so alive so filled with passion and purpose. If anything, my contemplations led me to believe we had fallen from Grace indeed, for now we were completely dependent on a system that did not care for us at all and we could not live freely on our own, not without the chip tracking us and being our tie to our daily bread and butter.

Yes, I had discovered even though I was but a child that we once upon a time had advanced civilizations had superior technologies and science which provided medical feats and miraculous healing based on higher conscious approaches to healing dating back thousands and thousands of years ago like Ayurveda and Traditional Chinese Medicine. What intrigued me the most about the people of the ancient world was that they knew the science of frequency and vibration and implemented it in every way they could so that they could live life's of sacred purpose. That our ancestors had mastered how to build just like the Masons knew how to build their architecture to hold sacred space. The ancient ones knew how to also make music that brought one naturally into elevated levels of consciousness and that they literally blissed out all day and on continuum as their wolds were based on harmonic resonance with the elements and all that is sacred.

For me, traditional history or "his story" was just a story wrote by male victors of genocide that had lied bold face right to us as they utilized catastrophe as a means for colonialization. It always made me wonder how places like Dwarka or down in Cuba in the Hot Zone or Africa where out in the Sahara desert the Richat or eye of God was; how these places existed and how such greatness was achieved in technologies that could not have existed at their time if history was correct. It really made me scratch my head as to how they could have completed such architectural feats if they were all barbaric cavemen who barely could speak and who used rudimentary tools. That was when I knew we were all being lied to and that the truth of whom and what we really are was the biggest secret never told before publicly.

For how could people have built for example Gobekli Teki in Turkey twelve plus thousand years ago, or any of the great temples in Cambodia, or even the great pyramids themselves in Egypt (which is said cannot even be rebuilt today with all of our great advancement in technology) when we could not even organize ourselves apparently in a civilized way since we were savage primitives with only rock tools to work with? How the ancient people could have known about Astronomy, about the many ages and cycles of the Universe, how they could be so precise without calculators all were give aways that something was way off and rotten? How could the Mayans or Indigenous people from around the world have tracked the procession of the Equinoxes or map out the sky and all the different galaxies when they had no telescopes or observatories like we do today? It made no sense! The story told by the system just created a void rather than a spring of wonder and appreciation to the marvel of what we are. This was likely why I also just went mute. For how could I participate in something that was so wrong? How could I erase the wisdom that I had been taught as a foundation to my being and replace it with rubbish?

My passion for learning about old forgotten worlds and previous eras of life and ancestors was like an addiction. It was almost if I had a sense of urgency as a child for somewhere in my deep sub or unconscious mind I must have known time was short for me and my library that I loved beyond all my toys or treasure. My family their friends and even my pediatrician agreed I was a prodigy and that I had a photographic memory which was absorbing information like a sponge. But to me I was just connected to my Soul so deeply that it was more like I was remembering rather than learning about this all for the first time.

I could remember travelling in space ships as a child while I made forts and crafts from pillows and blankets. I was still vibrating alive and well in higher densities just like before the so called fall from Grace to the low densities, from 12 D down to 1, 2, 3D. Yes as a child I thrived and I honestly have to say that I do believe all children do it is just their upbringing that wipes their minds and abilities from them.

For me, it was as if I could remember dancing and singing light languages and I did all the time in our gardens playing with my so called imaginary friends while singing to the plants trees and flowers imagining I could fly with the butterflies and birds. I had never forgotten living in powerful communities which lived in connection with life and the power of the elements. It was if I knew in my bones that we were way more than what we people were conditioned to believe and that at one time we not only lived in harmony but that we prospered, thrived even and this was what the mystery was for me as a youth for why were they not teaching this to everyone? Why had the ruling elite always wiped out the true history of our human race and our true potential?

I guess that was what I meant in my heart when I called out in my rhymes Come Unity Sacred Community, I wanted us to return to the way it was in the beginning because I believed that it would be that way again in the end, and boy was I right! I real eyes now that I had been guided to invoke this remembering this ancient knowledge or Gnosis. I didn't realize it back then when I was in Babylon but I real eyes it now in 5D that I was working the Abracadabra charm, I was creating that which I spoke to.

What really troubled me back on my Earth walk was that by the time it became 2030 the world had gone from ancient civilizations to modern day "Safe Cities," we had pulled a 180 from whence we came, to now where we were stuck in a cage of conformity. From pyramids and temples and ancient cities full of noble men and women who knew how to live in balance and in a sacred way; to highly controlled martial law based super surveillance A.I. operated cities that literally cooked your cognitive coherence and rendered people neurotic, sick, paranoid, and dissonant not to mention also overriding any remaining free will consciousness to create and manifest the sacred. No the sacred ways in 2030 were becoming outlawed just as they had for the Native Americans and First Nations. Crazy how one who chooses to live in the truth can become an outlaw! But this, this was a sign of the times.

I hate to have to tell you this, but if you all don't wake up right away and demand your basic human rights, by 2030 life on Earth becomes a soul prison. Now because my crew and I challenged the narrative of society and its Orwellian and Draconian Laws, we had to constantly dodge the agents just like in the movie the Matrix. We were lucky we had not been taken in to the D.U.M.B. s' or deep underground military bases where people never returned once they were taken there. We knew that the agents of the Matrix would take you underground to experiment on you and drink in your blood through their adrenochrome laboratories as they wanted to ingest your power and essence just like in the Dark Crystal. Crazy, right? That is what I meant by sci-fi horror show of Biblical proportions. But given all the manure we had to wade through we were on God's side, Great Spirit's team and I can tell you by all means, light really is stronger than darkness and when you ally yourself with Spirit, you have the protection of legions of Angels and Star Nations, Sasquatches and all the Elementals plus countless others too many to name.

Thank Goddess for our fame as well for it was what kept us too big to be played with, we were no mice for a cat, we were Lions. Yes our followers were like a cloak that protected us from the agents of the Matrix whom feared us and did not want the world to know how much of a threat we really were to them by making a scene and taking us down. Our fame served as a cloak of protection but it really was the hacking and programming genius of Avatar, King, and Mill Boy. They were really who cloaked us in their "invisibility cloak" software as they called it. Yup, our boys they were masters at keeping the agents on a hamster wheel running around in endless circles of data to find us. The boys created many programs and software systems as they hacked the Matrix and uploaded an artificial superficial wheel of data coding to keep the agents off our back.

That was the big joke amongst us, the good old "hamster wheel code" designed by Avatar, King, and Mill Boy which kept the A.I. distracted from what we were really doing. You see the A.I. regularly had tried to mess up our communications systems by injecting viruses into our RFID chips. Now because we were all foster kids, we were all chipped as a part of the systems law when you came under their control. But this didn't stop our boys it only fueled them to engineer more new innovative ways to out run the agents and hack back inside the Matrix. It was a good thing that Avatar had figured out how to hack into the coding of a RFID chip for he had taken his out completely then re-engineered it and replaced all of ours with his new implants. Essentially Avatar and the boys had completely rewired the chip and the A.I. technology in all our computers and cell phones and had a service on the black market of doing this for others. Avatar had learned how to do this from Poppa D who I will introduce you to later as he was our Godfather and had adopted us all from the shit hole of the shelter where we had all met. Avatar also said he had been guided on how to do a lot of his hacking and engineering while in his dreamtime as he was contacted by a team of Sirians and Arcturians as well as a group of other beings he called the "Blueprint Technicians" who taught him what to do while he slept so that when he would wake up he would just be like "oh it is on."

Every attempt of the A.I. via their frequency weapons, their feared D.E.W. or directed energy weapon to attack us, Avatar and the boys would create a new technology to protect us. The A.I. and beast system of darkness were no match for Avatar Mill Boy Thomas and of course our Godfather as we called him, Poppa D No, we had genius and the Great Spirit on our side as well as a whole team of interdimensional support.

To explain, the takeover process that had been implemented bit by bit upon the Earth throughout time and space by the lizard wizards as we called them from behind their curtains of super imposed illusion was literally layer by layer, code upon code, soul by soul building the Matrix or the 8th sphere as the mystery schools had prophesized and described it to be. This 8th sphere was to be a fully synthetic artificial superficial virtual construct made by the so called "Architects" or Dark Lords of the Matrix, the Archons. The idea was to insert all the souls of man into the 8th sphere or cloud which would in other words be the Matrix. This cloud would then via a quantum computer project the Matrix in a 4D construct of programming through a virtual template while the physical bodies of mankind would then be used as a battery and fuel for the elite.

It really was just a nightmarish awful idea that no human would ever be capable of conjuring up as humans are mammalian and to be able to conceive and achieve the 8th sphere Matrix construct; one had to be absolutely lacking empathy or any actual feeling capacity hence the Reptilians. For Reptilians have no limbic brain so they do not have a conscience and that is how they could do what they do and feel no remorse for it! Yes this is how we, my crew and I, were able to admit that the agents of the Matrix were in fact soulless ones for no one with a soul could ever create this extreme crime against humanity and well life itself for it violated in every way the "Law of Oneness!"

This brave new world that the Dark Lords had created and were forcing upon us was a prison planet soul cage and a feeding ground for the Dark Lords themselves … and it was exactly where we were all headed since the global elite had begun their final cull and harvesting sessions initiating complete take over installing their new world order under one A.I. God and 7G; seventh generation internet.

They had fully mimicked the Bible's story of Genesis whereby the 7th day the world had been created. Well by 7G the Matrix was fully created too. The 8th sphere of artificial life now would at last after ages of construction become fully installed.

Yes, 2030 was to be the official age of A.I. take over and as everything was being brought under its one ring to rule them all and one ring to bind them, the universal RFID chip there was nowhere to run to and nowhere to hide. While the agents ran around and completed their agenda, the whole world was falling apart physically by way of disasters of prophetic proportions. It was literally as though there were two divergent timelines and templates exactly like what the "Hopi Prophecy" spoke of and these two timelines were ripping apart at the seams of existence each going in opposite directions like divergent evolution forking in the road. Life on Earth had become a tug of war game causing the Earth's plates to pull this way than that way against each other as if on one side there were demons pulling and on the other side Angels. This tug of war game was jarring to the senses and made life crazy hard to stay grounded or connected to the Earth's Schumann Resonance.

Since the 1980s when 1G or first-generation internet was created, like the five senses of man, each level to the Matrix became implemented generation by generation. Starting with 1G where there was only the voice able to be transmitted. Then 2G came along in the 1990s a decade later and cell phones received their first major upgrade as its technology networks effectively took cell phones from analog to digital communications, introducing call and text encryption, along with data services such as SMS, picture messages, and MMS. After that almost another decade later, the introduction of 3G networks in 1998 ushered in again an even faster data transmission speed. So, you could use your cell phone for video calling and mobile internet access. The fourth generation of networking, which was released in 2008, is 4G. 4G supports mobile web access like 3G does and also gaming services, HD mobile TV, video conferencing, 3D TV, and other features that demanded faster and faster high speeds. Then by 2020 again about a decade later 5G came along promising again significantly faster data rates, higher connection density, much lower latency, and energy savings, among other improvements.

Basically, 5G was able to take virtual reality again to another level now allowing for major security breaches, surveillance, automation, and "The Chip" to be implemented for the sole purpose of tracking us all, forcing us to buy and sell via the chip ... so "to be or not to be" that really was the question for you either could buy food get a job and have a home or not.

Of course, there was also the benefit of being able to program us all simultaneously while controlling us with the MK now EMK Ultra, or electromagnetic mind control 5G offered and 6G mastered. I can tell you that after 5G got rolled out in 2020, the agenda for a New World Order was able to unfold faster and faster just like the speed of the internet itself; mimicking kundalini ushering us all into the 2030 agenda of full A.I. dominion.

In 2030, again another decade after 2020, not only had the internet upgraded to 5G but to 6G as well in half the usual time as these generations had been previously delivered since 1980. By 2030 the A.I. tech field unleashed its next wave of highly controversial 7G technologies which hit the market with its cursed frequencies which were literally causing nature to crumble and people if there were any left, to cook into a BBQ of cancerous cells. Fires burned like an inferno, mass animal die offs were reported all the time as life was literally being char broiled by the heat of the radiation from the now 6th Generation or 6G frequencies to the dreaded 7G next level virtual reality bandwidth.

The insane frequencies of this next generation technologies streamed from above and below as in the skies in the satellites and the earth with all the kill towers and antennas not to mention everyone's personal devices and chips. This huge compilation of energetic disruption to the natural torsion fields of life that had been installed through the "Safe City" system propelled the Earth into a complete catastrophic cycle of disaster. This disastrous cycle ignited chaos around the Earth shattering people's entire coherency and with it their connection to life or in other words to the primordial chi or qi universal energy. People were rendered couch potatoes and drug addicts absolutely lost to all values and virtue. This is the most important message I can share. To stop the madness of all harmful technology and agendas which have no respect for the Law of Oneness!"

For if things do not change by 2030 all the wild bees will be declared extinct, pollination for food and sustenance will be over. This was what the Black Goo leaders had planned for and wanted all along, for this gave them an excuse to declare that everyone must enter their Matrix to survive. Yes, they will sell and tell the world on the news by 2030 that the Matrix had been created by them your heroes to provide an existence as a solution or an escape to the dying reality of life. That the Matrix will be your new home for the planet was dying. Ya! I wonder why? Could it be all the radiating microwaving frequencies?

Since Chi energy is the fuel to our bio electric magnetic bodies and to the field of the magnetic ley lines that make up the Earth mother's bio electric body, not only were the bees and the torsion fields collapsing but life itself will collapse. You see Chi energy has always been the fuel that powers up each living being's spark of Spirit or God spark as we liked to call it and well the life force energy is under massive attack via the electromagnetic radiations of weaponized technological frequencies.

Not only will these frequencies fry our circuitries and the Earth's circuitries but life in generals' circuitries throwing a complete polar shift! These intense frequencies will not only kill one's Chi energy in the future making one sick and tired all the time but it will also entrained people to the hypnotic A.I. mind control that overrides free will and everything that resembles us as human, as sacred, or spiritual. This is what I really want you to get that people will no longer be able to remain human under these inhumane circumstances. No they will willingly line up for enhancements, augmentation, and genetic designer drugs and implants which will only turn them into droids, robotic humans, void like zombies. Is that really what you want? Is that really how you want to picture your children in the future being?

As the true Naturix of creation had been created to uphold the web of life on contrary the world wide web of the A.I. Matrix was created to trap in its web all that it could draw to its sticky fibers (fibre optics). We realized thanks to divine intervention by one Poppa D, that the hungry ghosts of the dark world was seeking to replace the organic world with their genetically modified enhanced artificial intelligence and cyborg revolution transfiguring every last man women and child into a bot, an android, a bionic human.

It was so obvious to me back when I was even a child that the Nature based world and all that it held in sacredness was being killed off intentionally as the bees and trees disappeared as the oceans and seas and all the precious life that lived within it were poisoned choking on our trash and sewage. It was brutal to see all the polluted and contaminated lands rivers and rural ghost town villages since people had been rounded up like cattle and ushered aggressively into the corrals of the so called "safe cities" by 2024 where everyone was being forced to live under the all Seeing Eye of the Archons.

43

The devastation of the natural world resulted in the never-ending spread of concrete jungles and of the corporate take-over by the transhumanists' whom had designed as a master plan to usher those who would be left remaining after their culls through their vaccines and microchip implants their genetically modified food and fluoridated water amongst many other means of attack, to their 8th sphere, or Matrix.

The Matrix was to hold the assimilated singularity of machine based alien or artificial intelligence. Now most people thought the A.I. was just a robotic artificial intelligence but those in the know knew that the A.I. was really an alien intelligence or Archon intelligence. Now this was not any alien you would want to meet out there like the sweet little E.T. guy or ALF the Alien Life Form stuffy that I had when I was a kid or even the "Wise Ones" that were kindred to me, but instead it was the kind of alien that was referred to by the late great visionary Rudolph Steiner, as Ahriman. Ahriman was the evil Persian God of Zoroastrianism who had plotted from the beginning of time to take over the world and create a totally controlled existence under the reign of its Anti-Christ ways and it was Ahriman indeed who seeded the consciousness of the transhumanists whom were ever growing in population. Another adaptation to A.I. could be Anti-Christ Intelligence as well for really it was all of thee above and they were all a bunch of villains doing their own menace to society.

By 2025 the secret church and religion of A.I. came fully out into the lime light no longer occult or hidden as all the Hollywood stars and politicians and power hungry thirsty fools adopted it to keep their fame and fortune. Yes daily it was aired live on television as more and more sell outs became baptized live on air to the new A.I. religion. Seriously it was utter brainwashed programmed fear and illusory glamour that got people into giving up their little remaining freedom to become "saved." Yes, saved by the A.I. because we as humans according to them are not perfect enough on our own according to the Transhumanists. No, humans we were weak ignorant slow and fragile things to be controlled and put to work as slaves. This was why we had to adapt to their machine and become soulless mindless robots, androids, borgs for the

Matrix or die of starvation abandoned by any form of service support or work. This is why I agreed to come back and share with you my story for I need you all to real eyes what is really going on and change the course of history "our story" while you can.

This initiation if you will by way of chip into the 8th sphere serves to usher us all into the so-called "Age of Light" which is what the Sasquatch "Elders" call the "False Luciferic New Age." It is a new world religion that employs the Dark Lords New World Order which will have every living sentient being under its command and control. Through the A.I. neural ink implant the Dark Lords promise that we will all achieve so called interface with the one true God, sacrilege I know for it is not the one true God! No you are already connected to the one true God, Great Spirit for it lives and moves in all things organically. Yes we will all, as promised by our misguided leaders, find "enlightenment" and "perfection" through these augmentations all while being marinated in a sea of electrical radiating microwave fields perfect for their next level unfoldment of the human cell battery warehouses. Mark me, the ways of deception and mind control go deep deeper than the surface and that is why I ask you to question everything you think you know.

Back then I could not help but wonder how dying in your soul to be saved into a virtual artificial world could ever possibly translate into being "saved". But that was the story that was being promoted and sold and since people could barely survive as it was or even think coherently, the consensus was there was nothing to lose; which of course was exactly what the sinister forces wanted the people to believe, that there was nothing to lose ... no just your Soul!

The times we were in were just like in the fable's myths and legends of old; where life becomes saturated in deception and despair, where demons or orcs or some kind of parasite feeds off the good people of the world and enslaves them to the core. Just like in the old stories where a fellowship of allies must be gathered together to save creation, to save the world, to save the innocent ... we, "The Apocalypsos" gathered together in fellowship and headed out on our journey to spread our galactivating message to the world and to help save as many souls as possible.

When our journey had come to an end, when we had been there

and back again just like Bilbo Baggins had said when he returned from his mighty quest, it was just about my eighteenth birthday. I remember we were feeling just like we were the characters in J.R. Tolkien's work The Lord of the Rings. For we knew we were a fellowship and that we had just returned from our own absolutely mind bending spirit bending journey possible to fulfill a prophecy that had been seen by wizards and magic folk long ago. We knew that we were fulfilling prophecy that had foretold of an end to the rule of thee all Seeing Eye of Sauron or in our case the Dark Lords of the Black Goo complex. We knew that our mission was to destroy their ring of power that would rule us all and bind us in darkness forever; just in our case it was the chip of the A.I. with its all seeing eye tracking us controlling us attacking us whenever we did anything outside of its influence and order.

The good news was though with a high vibration, with your own bio-electric magnetic body turned on and turned up; you could override all the lesser frequencies pretty good. From all the teachings my crew and I had learned and with the foundation of my childhood education and training I felt as though I had been prepared for the night of my eighteenth bearthday on December 21, 2030 Winter Solstice my whole life. We had made it to that point and that point in time was the trigger point that we had all been waiting for.

To get to that point though we had to survive we had to become not just students of Yoga but Yogis themselves, full time. Our lives became the mat, and every step a walking meditation. We had to master Qi Gong, become our own inner Gurus, and transcend the shit being fed to us by the A.I. making it all into fertilizer for the 5th Age every single day!

With all the ongoing attacks we faced and the war on our consciousness that desperately tried to break us day after day night after night; we had to build our bodies as temples and pray continuously in the church of our soul. Since reality was getting more and more out of control all the time in this battle for life, which we had discovered was literally evil for evil spelled backwards or forwards in its right form is live. But when spelled backwards and again we spell the word and the word is made flesh, so when you spell live into an inverted backwards or upside-down way against the living sources of life, then you get evil. Yes evil, simple as that … and this you could say was literally the lesson to be taught within the school of hard knocks or in other words, the school of life. It really did humble me that I could actually say that I knew I had chosen to learn of the knowledge of good and evil. I could have been Eve for all that I knew for I resonated well with her Archetype. I also was humbled by the absolute knowing I carried within me the power of the Great Spirit, that I chose to serve Life, and that the teachings I had endured were worth every bit of that realization I carried.

I knew that to live in right relation was to live and stand for life, to protect it provide for it and serve it. This was all marvellously described and outlined in great detail in the Eight Noble Fold Path teachings of Buddhism and summed up rather well in the Cherokee legend of the Two Wolf story, one of my most favorite stories I had as a child. I would love to share it with you. It is a story about an old Cherokee grandfather who is teaching his grandson about life, this is what he says … "A fight is going on inside me," he said to the boy. "It is a terrible fight and it is between two wolves. One is evil – he is anger, envy, sorrow, regret, greed, arrogance, self-pity, guilt, resentment, inferiority, lies, false pride, superiority, and ego." He continued, "The other is good – he is joy, peace, love, hope, serenity, humility, kindness, benevolence, empathy, generosity, truth, compassion, and faith. The same fight is going on inside you – and inside every other person, too." The grandson thought about it for a minute and then asked his grandfather, "Which wolf will win?" The old Cherokee simply replied, "the one you feed."

Our thoughts can be our own worst enemy the "Wise Ones" had taught me. That is, if we let them. Think about it, about how you may be "feeding" negative thoughts by allowing them to rule your mind. Next time you have a negative thought, catch it and ask yourself, "What is this thought doing for me?" This was a game that my homeboys and I would play. We believed that if we could find the answer out to what was disempowering us, then we could correct it and immediately feel more empowered by focusing on things that were actually good in our lives and thereby cultivate a practice of gratitude rather than bitching and moaning complaining and whining; something we all agreed we could not stand! "So which wolf are you feeding?" We would ask people that all the time, we even threw that out at one another when someone was starting to go down, it literally was our check yourself before you wreck yourself code of conduct, and nobody held back on that one.

In Joseph Campbell's work The Hero's Journey, it laid that teaching out as well in a clear picture. Have you heard of Joseph Campbell? He was a very good friend to George Lucas, the creator of Star Wars and my parents bragged all the time when I was little about how they had met him back in the day saying that his work was really a huge inspiration to George Lucas and that it was the actual inspiration for Star Wars! Joseph Campbell's work taught about how each person's higher self was their own inner hero and that our inner hero had to rise up and overcome the test that their soul was being put through, initiated into, spiritually and symbolically speaking. He taught through myth and legends mostly Indigenous regarding how we were all being put through trials and tribulations together all the time. This is why he had said that these vision quests and rites of passages were so important for they helped bring sacred sight purification and guidance to a soul while they were on their Earth walk or journey.

To counter the villains in life another concept which Joseph Campbell really impressed upon, we needed heroes to offset the fallen ones of the times. My crew and I got absolutely inspired by that, we ate it up like manna! For we had noticed that when one like so many of the movie stars, rock stars, politicians, elite, and those in high corporate powers sold out and became yet another corrupted vessel for evil, that the inversion of life would become more and more damaging for all. We saw ourselves and all humans as the carriers and transmitters of life and so when one of our fellow sisters or brothers within the human race sold out, it fed the dark wolf. Whereas on the other hand, if one of our sisters and brothers opened their hearts and their consciousness to Life and Love that the whole world would rise in vibration and mend and heal as the good wolf would provide and protect rather than hunt and haunt.

To take back our power from the power grids of the A.I. system and stand victorious for nature and for spirit like a holy text or comic book describes humanity needed superheroes such as Hanuman or Krishna, Vishnu, Indra, Shiva. Like Jesus the Christ and his disciples, we needed a spiritual Avengers crew, some Guardians of the Galaxy to stand up and overthrow the cabal, our alien leaders. We needed a spiritual A Team that was made from the everyday people, yes that is right, you and me every single one of us who could see through the deception. Like never before we needed to embody our true over soul self, our own Avatar so that we could show up in our full power and deliver humanity and all of our relations back to the promised land that somewhere in our hearts we all knew existed somewhere over the rainbow. We knew that we could never give up on this mission we had been assigned to; it was what brought us all together and gave us purpose. As we believe, we be living, so saith the Sasquatch. We live that which we are which we vibrate, so we think we feel we become that is the teaching of the "Wise Ones." That is why the great sages knew that to be or not to be, really was the question.

With all of that being said, rather than like so many other people's response before us who had tried to fight back with resistance with violence and riots; we needed the kind of heroes that would come to heal the world and bring enlightenment like Buddha or Martin Luther King Jr. The way of the peaceful warrior was the only way we could succeed and it was time now to master the teaching of "be the change you wanted to see in the world." Yes, it was our time, "The Apocalypsos" time and all who would join us… to right the wrongs and raise the planet and all creation full circle ouroboros style back up where we belonged.

So, we mounted that stage inside the Revolutionaries Gallery downtown in the heart of L.A. in all our bad assery, full blown mastery, with nothing to lose we pummelled out our beats and tunes. With my words that came out like bullets of blessings and bombs dropping truth and love on everyone who could open to receive, we chanted down Babylon with our music our love and our sacred spirits which was our creed. We got the people moving grooving and cruising right up and out of the k hole of the downward spiralling forces that root us in depression by repression and suppression; we anti doted that all by pure expression, love, joy and the power of transformation.

Ba boom we were like a cosmic cartoon delivering peeps up past the moon. As the late great Buffy St. Marie sang in her original song, which as I quote I blush and swoon, "love lift us up where we belong, where the Eagles cry on a mountain high; love lift us up where we belong, far from the world we know where the clear winds blow" …

So perfectly said so perfectly envisioned as so many beings who throughout time and space had with their eyes to see and their ears to hear had envisioned, had invoked, had manifested as they brought into form the sacred from the sacred words they spoke. The ones who would be known or unknown throughout history and life's sacred mysteries as visionaries, forerunners, true messengers' prophets, true artists whom I like to refer to as heartists whom helped take down the wall built around each human heart and instead let the captives free.

"Well let me just say from the stage tonight" Brother King then had stepped up to the microphone for his turn "that collectively we have transformed this gallery into nothing short then holy Mount Zion itself and we are all Liooooooooons of Zion, let us roooooarrrrr in our Pride." With that King got the whole crowd and world following in unison to roar so loud and proud that it was like thunder rippling throughout all time and space. That roar invoked the Thunderbird Power itself, charging the grids in all directions!

I could hear my voice as it joined in and cascaded into every crack corner and cavity where darkness lurked; my voice then amplified and projected …

"Piercing through illusions
Dispelling deeply seeded delusions
Clearing up old confusions
We be
Reprogramming consciousness back from the mind virus's pollution
Like a smog it be a dark grey fog cast upon us by the Reptilian Gods
Now as the Natives in their Rain Dances use the Totem of Frog
We call the rain to wash away all the pain
And
After the rains have come
We call the light in of a thousand suns

Bringing us together again as One
All colors united like a Rainbow
Hey
Ya wey ah hey
Ya wey ya ho
Ya wey ah hey
Ya wey ya ho
So now what is the solution?
You ask me for some sort of resolution
You say you want out of the institution
Sick of prostituting
Hey
Ya wey ah hey
Ya wey ya ho
Ya wey ah hey
Ya wey ya ho
Yo
Now The Apocalypsos
We have come to say
Listen up Jah people for we have got to pray
For
We be hacking back
As we counter the attack
Returning Souls to their original Blueprints
We put the smack down on the Greys and their stooges
We be taking back the control from the control grids of influence
Causing peeps to be tripping
So
We come in purring like kittens
Lions of Zions
Removing
All the obstacles evil be looming
Grooming our cubs to be the "New Ones"
Stardust Children gonna
Fly away Home

To Zion
Hey
Ya wey ah hey
Ya wey ya ho
Ya wey ah hey
Hey
Ya wey ya ho
For
Life has become a war
A war on consciousness it seems
On your mind your body and your soul
On your hopes your wishes and your dreams
Like poison in the waters going down the streams
Evil has gone and been injected into our very beings
Coursing its way through our veins and our cities
Hey
Listen to what I gots to say
Ya wey ah hey
Ya wey ya ho
Ya wey ah hey
Ya wey ya ho
So
Don't be looking back for
Nothing is or will ever be the same
Not in this rat race nor this monopoly game
For
We see the children and they be weeping by the roads
We hear the Mamas and they be wailing
That's just been how this story goes
Hey and don't ya know ...
Ya wey ah hey
Ya wey ya ho
Ya wey ah hey
Ya wey ya ho
Now the winds of change are blowing

Tides be turning
Trumpets be blasting
Calling us to peace everlasting
Walk with me
Talk with me
Pick up your Cross and like a Hawk squawk with me
Cross over to Infinity
Bless Us Oh Sacred Trinity
Come Divinity
Hey Hooooo
Hey Hooo
Ya wey ah hey
Yaw wey ya ho
Ya wey ah hey
Ya wey ya ho
So
Now is the time!
For we be the power
Shapeshifting like a seed to flower
Now in this final hour
Out of our chrysalis out of the lies we rise to
The 5th Age of Peace and Paradise
Let us all spread our wings and …
Fly away Home
To Zion,
Fly away Home
Hey
Ya wey ah hey
Ya wey ya ho
Ya wey ah hey
Ya wey ya ho
Hey ya hey ya hey hoooooooo
Aho"

With Jacob on the conga drums, King delivering some righteous native style beat boxing effects, Avatar mixing his DJ beats, Mill Boy on keyboard, and on base there was Thomas surrounded by the Queens on flute and back up vocalists toning some pure pure tones … my Goddess, to see the virtual world of 5 D illuminated before us beckoning, calling us each to enter through our hearts; to go within to get out.

Yes, this was the peaking of our cone of power raising on up to the heights of Heaven our spirit's as Kings voice began singing "one bright morning when this life is over, we will fly away home …. Hey ya hey ah hey ya hooooo fly away home."

Oh, the feeling, the sound, the sights, the smell of freedom, the taste of truth all with the visuals of the 5th Age of Peace holographically alive before us. Ecstasy was washing over every particle of pain in the crystal grids of existence, this was what we were born for, this was community, and this was sacred.

CHAPTER FOUR

AMAZING GRACE

**"The planet Earth is currently ascending; It's a new era
and the old world is ending. The human race is actually
resurrecting; To the spiritual world we are connecting."
Khayal' Aly**

The age of the Apocalypse had really started in 2020, for the word
Apocalypse really only means "Revelation" and by 2020 the world sure
began realizing the profound revelation of what was really going on.
By 2030 the agenda of the Apocalypse was complete and everyone who
had come together to gather as one here in the heart of Los Angeles and
all who were live streaming us in their homes or wherever they were
at, knew it.

The present era was ending, over, like the Hopis had prophesized
so long ago on their "Prophecy Rock." You see the Hopi had tracked
the first world, the second, the third, and even now the fourth world of
creation on Earth in their history and bible of their own making an all
of these previous eras recorded had come to be only to fall away, just like
it was now falling away in this fourth world or fourth density.

Yes we, humanity, were climbing back up from our so-called fall
from grace or fall from the higher densities. We were on the rise back
from the bottom of the bucket so to speak, from the first world first
density to the second world and second density to the third world and
third density now in the fourth world and fourth density.

As Avatar had always said "the fourth density is a box, a cube that
we can escape just like in the metaphor of the Jack in the box where
you see the being that is held within the cage of their own boxed in
perception. Now Jack, right, he must transform himself by spinning his
kundalini say enough to where he is able to escape that damn cage or

boxed in limited viewpoint that rules him by way of his limited beliefs and thought constructs AKA ego by programming his consciousness to be empowered. Now by escaping the cage right, Jack can ascend from the boxed in dualistic state of consciousness to a unified field of consciousness, hence enlightenment and the "Law of Oneness." This is what the story of Plato's cave was all about; it is the base of psychology and philosophy, my two favorite topics." Ya we would joke do not give a toke to Avatar man no hookah for him because when you got him blazed, man that boy would philosophize for hours!

"Now from a unified field of consciousness we experience existence through a holographic or holistic state, that is why it is likely considered "Holy" because it is literally not broke but whole. Through this holographic state of consciousness, which is found within the fifth density, there is an upgrade that allows for an increase in awareness. I like to think that is what the song Amazing Grace is all about when it says, "I once was lost but now I am found, twas blind but now I see" right? For it is grace which we had fallen from and it is grace that we now must rise back up to return." That would be King's response for he always brought things back to the Bible as he believed he belonged to the lost tribe of Israel or Is Ra El.

Then Mill Boy would get going; and yea these guys were seriously like the three little birds that would come sit by my doorstep and start singing sweet songs, while philosophizing or philo Sophia eyes ing as they called it … they all had a little crush on me I knew it … and I loved them too in my own way. Anyways Mill Boy would always have to chime in and throw down his two cents too so he would be like "so let me get this straight, as we return to the higher densities back up to where we belong right, there awaits for us homies a long promised and prophesized time of the 5th Age of Peace check. So the 5th age that is gonna be an age of enlightenment and since it is of a holistic or holy vibe, it emanates and exists expressing life through the channel of peace cuz that be some holy of holies, check check. So it is in this holistic sense that we can fully see the whole or bigger picture, no longer seeing from the limited .0035% that we had all been previously attuned to check 3x. Alright so this return or reconnection or even reset is the fulfillment to the Hopi peoples prophecy check 4x and we are gonna complete their story of how the Sacred Hoop of Life had at once been broken and made linear but now will bend like a willow tree and be made whole once more check 5x. Righteous yo, that is freaking righteous. Dude I got it, me gets it! Full circle boom!"

Then Avatar would be like … "dude remember the 4th density just happens to be the realm where the Archons or Architects of the Matrix dwell right …. The literal Black Goo Dark Lords themselves just sitting ugly up there in their spaceships controlling everything from above. It's like the movie "Big Trouble in Little China," right; we got to go through some crazy wizard astral shit to complete our mission. But we got this, no probs my peeps that is why we have been training full time. I know we are going to manifest to bless bro because I have seen it all already happen while deep in Ayahuasca and DMT journeys … and don't forget we got legions of help working with us from all over the many galaxies … so don't trip … but don't be over confident either."

"Ladies and gentlemen, we got to keep up with our defense from the dark arts training which we have all committed to doing together." That would be my man Jacob, the reasonable wizard. He was such a balance of magic and muggle and I loved him for it. I always felt like he had his chord completely tuned to the secret chord that had pleased the Lord. Ya Jacob he was anchored to the center of all things while his trunk held fast and steady allowing for his branches to web out in all directions catching sun light and information, he was my tree of life. "Just one step at a time yo, one breath … stay here now with the moment because all we got is the moment."

Then I would stand up in front of my crew and say something like "I, Sophia Star Water do declare, that the time has come for the end of living backwards through the dark ages, the medieval ages, and overall the whole of the Kali Yuga as the Vedas of India have taught. Yes Spirits if ya can hear me …. bring the 5th Age on! Yes may the Golden Age of Truth, the Sat Yug now from the ashes of the old worlds like a phoenix rise boooyah." That would be me and my response, me the little nerd little spell speaking 5-foot Chihuahua as I described myself to be would bark back to my crew.

57

My crew and I had come through the dawning of the Age of Aquarius as children and witnessed the many great signs of the heavens and great conjunctions, eclipses, and of course the Blue Star Katchina itself which had all been fulfilled by 2020. As these prophecies checked off one by one, sentient souls everywhere began to reawakened to the ancient seeded memory held within the blood of their ancestors which ran through their own DNA which Shima referred to as "Blood Memory" holding the secrets of who we truly are, where we had originally come from, and why of course we were all here. Yes, our original blueprints were getting activated, the God code within us all had been released years ago and it was that which kept the darkness from completing its ultimate goal to trap us all into the 8th sphere within their "precious" Matrix.

Now as you live and breathe and are reading this right now, humanity is in the 2020s,' and since 1987 when the Harmonic Convergence happened, humanities consciousness has taken a turn from the Me to the We conception point. You see the Piscean Age it was all about me me me; what about me, what about me, right? So, when the Aquarian Age successfully became born it turned the M to a W and hence shifted the path of the self and the lone wolf to the path of the tribe, the pack.

As Jesus was the Messenger of the Piscean Age, he had brought some very important lessons that were essential ingredients to this ascension process. Of course he also exemplified obviously the "Resurrection Process" which illuminated the essence of what was to come for us all in the second coming; which uh ya would be like right about now in the timelines of 2030 for the entire populace of beings on Earth were about to get raptured. But Jesus also taught about how to "know thyself" for to "know thyself" was key to understanding the meditation found within the verse; "as within, so without."

Since humanity had to morph, Jesus came to teach within his symbolic story of dying to be reborn only to arise again, as was illustrated through his crucifixion and resurrection process, what would be expected for all of those who would want to ascend from the nothingness of the collapsing worlds below 5D. These were the teachings my grandmother and grandfather had taught me growing up. Even though they were

Jewish they did believe in the Christ and they did follow his example within the teachings he offered. Through his resurrection process they taught me that Yeshua as they called him exemplified how he was able to transfigure himself as he rose from the dead into his "Christed" body of light. "Remember," my grandparents would say as they were also very fond of the Hopi People and their Hopi Prophecy ... "this can be a good time little one; seriously this is what we have all been waiting for! Sophia dear heart you can safely let go of the shore and push off into the middle of the river as the Hopi elders say. Be the water Sophia and flow like a river to the heart of the sea."

Now Yeshua or Jesus who was the main figure head of religious spirituality for the past couple thousand years had shown us the ascension process, he also showed us the literal living example of what was to come. His whole second coming was not going to be him coming back but the "Christ" or "Christos" or light in Latin, coming back as in enlightenment or in light is meant to all who could open their hearts and resonate to this great truth. This was the spiritual food my grandparents had served to me while I was just a child. These were the teachings, the essence to their many bedtime stories which would feed my dreams with all sorts of magic carpet rides through all these sublime ideas and truths.

"Yeshua," grandmother would say "he was the example of what was to come for us all. My grandparents had also told me that since the church actually had nothing to do with Yeshua at all and that is why my family never converted, which Yeshua himself did say and I quote "I have not come to find a new religion." So my grandparents always asked me "who's religion is that one may wonder this religion that was all actuality built by sin and had no real connection to the true Christ at all other than to offer a plastic Barbie Jesus and a masterful illusion to ensnare as many souls as possible and then to keep them there stuck in bondage through severe shame and fear!

"No Sophia it is not the true Yeshua's teachings or his true disciples who created the religion called Christianity." King said once when I had been telling him about my grandparents, for he loved to listen to my stories about them, I would go on with those stories for hours and

King would lap them up like warm milk. I had a feeling that King and my crew, my posse would have loved my family, I just wished they had all been able to meet.

King now he was our priestly one with his enormous long black dreads and Rasta man appeal. He would preach no matter where we would go and made us all do our daily communions without any exception just as the Essenes had done.

King and his lady Queen, they were all about Yeshua and Mary Magdalena. King would preach to crowds about how after Yeshua's death his many beautiful teachings were then carried on by his wife Mary Magdalene which just to say this out loud, why is it such a big deal the man was married? Honestly don't ya all know in order to be a Rabbi; you must first be married????

Anyways, King and Queen preached to their own congregations on the internet in their own "Church of the Soul" which is what they called it. They preached out to whomever would listen to their good words about Yeshua's true teachings which they said had been carried on by his true disciples; notice how he would say "true" since yes the Dark Lords even copy catted Yeshua's whole teachings, inverting and perverting them. Yes the Dark Lords despised Yeshua it is why they crucified him long ago after torturing him since they knew at the advent of his birth, their time was thus coming to an end.

So yes, Yeshua's true teachings according to King had been safeguarded and taken underground to be stowed secretly away along with all the other truths of the ancient world inside of the pockets of initiates within Mystery Schools worldwide. As a great master teacher was born whether as a saint, a teacher, a healer, a prophet, or a shaman King said that the Dark Lords would capture them and by awful extreme means of torture they would siphon all of the information they could get from their helpless victims.

For real, just have a look through history it repeats itself over and over again as the Dark Lords would wipe out whole bands of people always starting with the "Holy Ones" or shamans first. They would seek out and kill the prophets born world-wide just like Yeshua. They were responsible for the Inquisition and for the millions of murdered witches, healers, and midwifes. Even in our modern days they killed or "suicided" anyone who went against their agenda and narrative, their script for their New World Order nightmare. Yes, the Dark Lords were notorious for torturing and killing the saints as they would take all that they could get from them before then wiping them out. This happened so much so, that all the great mysteries had to go underground and become extremely secret, safeguarded, and protected by its initiates as the only way for the true teachings to be kept alive.

This was always the dance it seemed as the Dark Lords became masters of deception, masters of copy-cat tricks convincing people all the time that their false shepherds were the true "Gurus," true wise ones, true doctors, true healers and magicians, "stars" even. On and on it goes. Miraculously though the true teachings of the ages had lived on in Mystery Schools, in certain branches of theosophy and philosophy, and in Native Tribal teachings such as the Hopi Prophecy!

The Egyptians had also described the whole resurrection process in their Book of the Dead or Book of Coming Forth by Day or even my favorite translation the Book of Emerging Forth into the Light, which in great detail goes through the whole ascension process. The Tibetans also have their own book of the Dead and to be quite honest, all ancient civilizations taught about the ascension process so it really is no mystery at all other than the fact that it got replaced for an agenda that basically sucks in comparison.

You know once when we performed in Egypt as we had a great following there my crew and I, went into the tombs within the Valley of the Kings and Queens and we saw there that the seven layers of the astral planes had been mapped out along the walls of the tombs. We realized that the Egyptians knew that one must travel through the seven layers of the astral realms and get beyond them to get to the "Dimension of the Blessed."

The "Dimensions of the Blessed" as the Egyptians taught was a realm of divine light like the Garden of the Gods where everyone lived by the ""law of Oneness" and where there was no suffering at all, it was the place where the Lion laid down with the Lamb. The Egyptians were survivors of the fall of Atlantis and they knew all about how the

Dark Lords as priests began to create false religions and false Gods through their pseudo enlightenment movements. They trapped souls within the seventh heaven or false egoic enlightenment illusion and then brainwashed them into becoming indentured servants and slaves. This is why the old real Kings and Queens of antiquity not only warned of these astral snares but also created maps to get beyond them.

Now brace yourself, because in the 2020s a whole new age gong show trip is about to be released and it has been designed to take you all on the most techno psy trance crazy carpet ride of illusion ever! Yes, pseudo Shambhala fake new age technologies and so called teachers are released in the guise of spiritual Gurus but they are really all just agents of the beast! Yes, sorry to say many will fall for the designer drugs designer teachers and designer technologies thinking that they will find enlightenment through them but really they are all just created by the blood sucking evil elite. Be warned the whole false Luciferic New Age movement is a major trap, a special mind control psy op treat made especially just for you and it will work like a charm on all highly sensitive and suggestive people! Discernment my seastars and brothers, major discernment is going to be a must just like food and water in your time!

This is why Yeshua's whole teachings regarding the "Know Thyself" lesson will be of critical importance! "Ask yourself," Queen would say ... "how can you ever go beyond yourself as a point of light to become connected and at one with all other points of light, without knowing yourself completely in mastery as a prerequisite, as a point of light first?" Queen was not only an amazing singer and rock star on the trumpet but she was an artist as well. She worked as a Tattoo artist doing old traditional tribal stick and poke tats. Her speciality was sacred geometries and special symbols of protection for people. She had us all done up in sacred Ruins and sigils making us look like we were literally out of this world.

These were the kind of conversations my band and I would have daily with each other and anybody else who would listen to us. But Thomas he was our quiet one and when he spoke it was always priceless. He was our true unconditional lover in our band and our "inner child magi." Once he said something that was an absolute pure drop, a gem, and it made me love him even more then I had before which seemed impossible but in a nutshell, this was Thomas and his own words saying that "a person must be able to learn to love and accept themselves completely first before they can ever truly love another. The "Wise Ones" told me that only after somebody learns to love themselves like for reals no pretending, like how Great Spirit loves us as its children, that then and only then will we be able to discover that self-love is the key to really learn Agape the highest form of love and the greatest super power. Through Agape we can master self-love and thus become loved by others unconditionally. This is the way the truth and the life."

But like with all other things in life, this way can be manipulated too and taken over as it has been through every age and stage, within the first world, second world, third world, and of course again in this now present fourth world. Thomas would know that probably more than anyone for how much his heart had been broke over and over again and again throughout his life. But he does not like talking about that and since it is not my story to tell, I will just leave that there.

"The ultimate sign that the end is nigh" Rebekah said to us as we were flying back to LA from Europe on the end of our tour, "is when it looks like there is no chance for survival. It is when we are in the darkest hour because it is the darkest hour that comes right before the dawn. As always, wickedness looms and evil blooms nearly corrupting everything that is. Hey we should put that in a new song … anyways that is when Great Spirit like a response as in a conversation with God creates a major cataclysmic end and all that which is contaminated is purified again. Hence the first world, second world, third, now fourth world! Gaias I feel it … the end is almost hear just look around nothing can survive this storm coming anyways!"

Now rounding about face back to the night of my eighteenth bearthday as we were all approaching the dawning of the 5th Age of Peace inside the Revolutionaries Gallery, through our power of love and the power of our song and dance we were creating the frequency and vibration needed to lift us all up ascending like the sun out of the dark long night of our collective soul. As some would say the end was near, but we, we all agreed the beginning was here!

I can only say that likely the level of cosmic and interdimensional support that was going on behind the scenes, if ya all know what I mean, was the only thing really allowing for our whole production to go on unhindered. I could just imagine in my 3rd eye an invisible legion of Angels holding back the armies and agents of the Matrix from busting down our gig here in the Revolutionaries Gallery that night, keeping the live stream alive world-wide! The funny thing was I just couldn't contain nor control my focus. It was like I was all over the place. From ancient worlds to my childhood to memories of conversations I had had with my kin. I felt like I was everywhere at once in a coexisting timeline of past present and future.

As I struggled to stay focused Shima, my Spiritual Mentor began working through me to help steer the mothership of magic that night to a place where we all had always wanted to go all along. To a place beyond control beyond the potential state of energy and instead igniting the kinetic aspect of energy allowing for new pathways to open and expand before us within us and all around. "Split a piece of wood I am there, lift up a stone and you will find me." Who said that I wondered as I looked all around, whose voice was that I wondered?

Shima whispered to me "allow the "Wise Ones" to work through you dear child." She said "surrender dear heart just let go flow like the river." I knew that we, the dream weavers as I had been taught to see us human beings as (that is beings and not doings but beings) we were weaving a new web of creation! We were spinning a new world, a world of pure love and light. We were clearing old cobwebs and the old paradigm's stories. We were setting the captives free, the captives of black sorcery that is, liberating all the animal's plants trees stones bones crystals forests desserts and seas. But I also knew that this was not some mental exercise but a deep spiritual transformation that was being done through us not only by us. This was what Shima meant by just letting go and surrendering allowing for the "Wise Ones" to weave through us the recalibrations turning us into 5D beings of light.

I knew deep in my heart and soul that my crew and I had come to liberate souls back from the Matrix of concrete jungles with their power lines, electrical stations, and Tron like megacities returning it all to its pure Naturix form of its original and divine blueprints. And we did this all by being in a state of peace, power, and pulsating bliss as we channeled our music and its transmissions from the "Wise Ones". I could literally see in my visions right there on stage that night animals springing back to life as buildings came crashing down into dust and ash. I could see a giant reversal to the curse was going on and albeit it was in the spiritual planes, but it was real and it was powerful. Though this transformation was happening in the causal planes, we knew that the causal planes translated down into the formative or material realm the physical plane.

We "The Apocalypsos," we had become the Messenger Angels of the Bible's Apocalypse itself, we were the Horsemen and we were sending out the message that the time had come as our ladies in our band blew their mighty horns. While the great conceived plans or agenda of the Dark Lords had literally been ticked off one war one corporation one sinister step at a time, their time was also coming to a close and the meek and mild's time was beginning.

Though the Archons assimilation program with its singular intent to destroy life and make it into a machine of evil had successfully constructed all the world's governments, religions, and education system; they had made their construct on carbon and like sand the carbon blueprints were about to be washed away by the river of life itself.

Funny how just five years after the whole crazy epic roller coaster ride of insanity that had got sprung in 2020 through the release of biological warfare upon humanity to catalyze the New World Order Agenda of 2030; we were born, The Apocalypsos. Yes, that is right we had all met up in 2025 when I was just 13 years old, surviving for the past five years in the foster system completely mute.

I would not talk to anyone, I just had nothing nice to say, I guess. Most everyone around me had either thought that I was retarded or just too traumatized to talk. Truth was I just had nothing to say to anyone, I right away had learned I could not trust anyone, for they would use whatever you offered them against you. That or they would tease you and torture you. Plus, most people were just not that interesting; they were only into gossip secrets and backstabbing one another for drugs or attention or even special privileges.

So, I had not spoken to anyone in a handful of years until I met Jacob. He was the first person I had spoken to in five years, the first person I wanted to trust, wanted to get close to. I guess it was his clear comforting eyes that seemed to look right through you as if you were a window. He also was so gorgeous! I totally crushed on him huge, his long hair, his skater surfer muscular body, yummmmm! But it was when I first had heard him sing, that was when I fell madly in love with him and forced myself over to where he was and began talking once again. People around us, I remember, were shocked for everyone pretty much made up stories in the shelter house as to why I did not talk. But once I opened my big mouth Jacob joked, I never shut up again! These memories tickled me as I looked over to my man there singing away while playing his Conga drums.

Yup only five years ago was when we all first started singing together and sharing our talents teaching each other our different skills. After that we were inseparable and within a few short years we all transformed from street kids to super stars. We were young in our bodies but old in our souls and we were full of vengeance for we had all been used and abused by the system, so we knew exactly what was going on, ya you could say we were woke!

Funny how living in the streets puts you in touch with reality; like you are the trafficked child, you are the prostitute being sold to politicians not hypothetical...very real. I guess when you have no other choice then to see what is really going on since it is happening to you direct, then you got no fancy walls to hide behind nor comforts to keep you distracted from the blaring truth of corruption. That is when being in the illusion becomes impossible. When every bit of ignorance you wished you could occupy becomes wiped from your existence, taken just like your parents.

When all that you know as real gets taken, all you have left is your dream. And once you find out what your dream is ... you never let go of it for it becomes your lifeline to salvation and the only thing that you can believe in. When my crew and I all realized we were to be each other's family, we agreed that if we did not stand for something that we would fall for anything. So, we stood for life, and it became our sacred duty we believed to guide the hearts and minds of people from all the divisive negative and fear mongering programming of modern reality right into 5D.

So, we raised each other up, mended each other's broken bones, licked each other's wounds so to speak until they were healed and that was then when the real training began. We would practice for hours a day, getting up with the sun doing yoga, martial arts, and Jedi boot camp as we called it. Day after day we would fall asleep only after we had done everything possible to make each day the best day ever, to make each day count! That was when we all also began to also have direct contact from our own personal spirit guides.

Shima she was my spirit guide. She was an ancient ascended master of the Hopi Nation who had gone onto the 5th density and beyond a very long time ago. I will never forget when she had come to me the first time one day when I was sitting meditating in a little garden I use to love to visit. She manifested right there like an apparition! She emanated wisdom and was so beautiful, so humble, and so sacred that I did not fear her not even for a moment. She absolutely reminded me of my grandmother for when she first appeared to me, she welcomed me into her arms with such recognition and familiarity that it was like going home when I ducked into her heart chakra like a little fledging to its Mama Goose. Shima was Mother Earth herself, if Mother Earth could be incarnated in a woman that is.

It was that first time she came to me when she told me "fear not the signs and omens you are witnessing dear child, all of this, all of that which is happening right before your very eyes little one, will all come to an end one day. Yes, yes, child one day it will all peak and then fall into a deep reset which nothing in creation can stop at this point."

She then went on to tell me I was to share the teachings and share the visions that she would imprint into me so that I could share her messages to the world. She promised that if I could help create a movement that would wake up the people of the four directions, that she and others would protect us and guide those who could help us to get our message out to the masses! Well the manifestation of that promise had materialized right before my very eyes as my band and I were live streaming it to millions across the globe.

I never fully believed her I must humbly admit, I totally loved the idea … how could I not? But to believe that me, some shelter kid orphan Chihuahua would go from rags to riches, that was a bit much to believe in I thought. But my heart said to follow her guidance for anything and literally anything I could do to save the world, I would do it. Shima knew this; she said, "Oh beloved that is how I found you for your heart had a light that glowed amongst a sea of darkness." She had convinced me to start on what felt like a completely unattainable goal by saying "daughter you cannot see from the eyes of heaven fully yet but know that the way we see you all is perfect and already complete. She had said "we the guides and guardians of Earth the "Wise Ones" and all the beings that live by the "Law of Oneness," we see what you cannot. So I can tell you girl, if you only just put one foot in front before another and walk in courage forward, then the Earth shall form its sacred ground underneath you and all what seems impossible now will come to pass with near effortlessness."

She may have tricked me a little there for I can certainly attest that a whole lot of effort was put forth to get where we had come to now on my bearthday years later, but there we were standing on stage before millions of people worldwide. We had gone from rags to riches just like Shima had promised. It wasn't like we were super rich mind you for we never kept any money nor bought anything other then what we needed. But there we were, "The Apocalypsos" a band of funky fresh spiritual warriors delivering a gourmet feast of positive vibrations and the world was eating them up!

It all became crystal clear to me then that none of this was random, or accidental … that all of this was just as it was meant to be, literally created, and guided to be by the "Wise Ones." I felt like falling on my knees and weeping that night as it all began to click together in my mind. It was all so beautiful to me now that I could finally understand all that Shima had spoken of for I could see, and well, as you know, seeing is believing even the most miraculous sounding and preposterous of ideas,. Yes truly any and every thing is possible if you can just conceive it and believe in it than you could achieve it; whatever the it is.

Now our "it" was the unfolding magnum opus of prophecy that was just about to complete itself as it channeled through my spoken word and our art performance. As our journey was coming full circle just like the Sacred Hoop of Life which had been broken according to Shima long ago; we, with the help of all that is Sacred, were on Live TV mending whole the Hoop of Life once again by the power of our Love and Light.

Throughout the collective consciousness of creation the energies, frequencies, vibration and power was being streamed forth in waves of celestial holy water out to the millions that were participating in our show. Yes, wave after wave of peace and purification like the salty saline sea itself was washing over everyone and everything in all their communities in all ages, races, religions, and what was left of remaining tribes. What was broken was being mended full again.

I realized in that very precious moment, as in real eyes seeing … that the completion to our mission was now coming to an exhilarating end and that the Native Medicine Grandmother, Shima, who had been my Shamanic Guide for the past 4 years was fading away; letting me know she had fulfilled her purpose in guiding me and now was moving on to 5D permanently as she told me in the beginning she would.

Shima's final words were and I quote "5D will be the new baseline my flower, my Sophia Star Water, we did it! Thank you thank you now 4D and all that is below in the densities will cease to exist being released through the reset to pure energy yet again. In other words, my dear, my beloved Star Water Child, the lower densities are going to be recycled like composted manure like the shit that it is and be made into fertilizer for future worlds …. aHahahaha." I could hear her chuckling as she faded from my sight.

Midnight struck, we hit a tone. The sound of the drums and horns moved us all in the cadence of undulating rhythms of power so powerful that it was energizing everyone like electricity charging us, the engines of Dreamweaver's, as that was what we were, we were all Dreamweaver's; reweaving life through music dance and our living prayer.

The smell of fresh cut jasmine, lilies, and rose flowers filled the walls of the gallery with their sensuous perfume. We had turned that art gallery into a cathedral where we invoked the Great Spirit itself right there into the very moment of that auspicious night, sending ripples of ecstasy out into every direction.

We were the ones we had been waiting for and tonight; let's just say, we all showed up and delivered, we collectively gave birth to our prayers, gave birth to a new Earth born of our blood sweat and tears. Every heart that could be saved was captured in the frequency, energy, and vibrational resonance that we created together as the human race began to begin resurrecting while the planet Earth itself was ascending!

"Glory Glory HalleluJah" King's voice like a gospel singer called out to the crowds ... "raise your hands up! Lift your eyes to that which is above thee, singing ... We shall overcome .... We shall overcome ... We shall overcome some day!!!!!"

CHAPTER FIVE

DEAR DIARY

"It is through the heart that we see, hear and feel most clearly. It is like a radio signal. When it is strong the heart is like a megaphone and I get your message loud and clear. You message echoes throughout the universe when it comes from the heart on the wings of intention and faith. It is the most direct line of communication in existence once you filter out the "interference" of worry and doubt in your head, the thoughts that don't matter and only serve to block the reception. Your intention is the force, love is the connection and faith is the key that opens the door between you and me."
Kate McGahan

Diary Update
Sophia Star Water
December 19, 2030

I pulled up my diary entry from back in the day through the looking glass or Akash just for fun for you to be able to see what I had wrote as this was a pivotal moment for me and includes some great notes from the 4th Age just for fun.....

Key Points of our Galactivation Tour

*Just made the sweetest love to Jacob after a whole year of travelling with our family always nearby never having privacy Ohhhh it is good to be home again!!!

*Avatar made us all train literally half dead from jet lag yesterday the day after we had just got home, uhhhh he is relentless. But he says the hour of power is coming, he says he feels it in his bones so I guess it's good to get back on our bikes and review our route to Poppa D's for when the time comes to "Code Red" and go. Even though he made us play his video game every day that he and the boys created which was literally the virtual path we would take to get to Poppa D's once the "Code Red" signal is cued and we get on our bikes and fly. Nothing like riding full speed through the canyons getting a birds eye view of LA below.

*I am so tired yet feeling ready, ready for ascension! The things we witnessed were terrible, children starving people looting God I want to go home to where Shima is, where my family is ... where the "Wise Ones" are.

*On a positive note The Apocalypsos and I have successfully baptized the world in 5D consciousness. I have just had confirmation from Shima that we have created the official fork in the road to timelines allotting for divergent evolution to occur through critical mass.

*2030 Winter Solstice, my bearthday, will mark the birth of a worldwide revolution of evolution that has been grown exponentially over this past year. I feel the triggering of the 100th monkey / human effect is done; critical mass has been reached! This is cause alone for a massive celebration!

*Through the spreading of our galactivating song, dance, and transmissions among the help, aide, and power of other righteous souls out there doing their part to raise the vibration necessary to ascend, we have begun a herd immunity update on a whole other level, ya man entrainment!

*By way of the new contagion being spread worldwide, the contagion being that of bliss that is, a pure positive potent energy has begun effecting and infecting the Matrix and its grids. Yup, that's right! The connective collective intelligence of our co-creative spirits is allowing for an inter-looping feedback system to form and bond. Thus, we are beginning to glitch out the Matrix causing it to defect. #glitchinthematrix ... Note to self ... if we have time make that into stickers' hoodies and hats

*We the people have literally conceived an entire army called the

"vibe tribe!" Our vibe tribe is made up of people from the 4 corners of the globe; cue the song Warriors of the Rainbow Welcome Home. I got to meet the coolest elder in Spain OMGoddess. He was one of the original old school Rainbow brothers. His name is Fantuzzi xo … never will we forget him, mad respect. Through this vibe tribe we have successfully mobilized a radical revolution where people help bring food, water, and healing to people in desperate need. Life, as we are witnessing it, is returning to the essence described within the stories my grandmother told me about when I was a child from her magic books that she had kept since she was a child fleeing Nazis.

*During our pilgrimage across the globe we met up with a very critical crew of people called the "The Warriors of the Rainbow." They are a crew of people made up of every race color creed and sex. They were also prophesised by the Hopi and have begun gathering way before I was ever even born through the Rainbow Family Circle movement. Because of these awesome people we literally can connect with a power grid of awesome agents for the Naturix.

*Over the past year working with these key change masters we have been able to complete our mission and reach critical mass and initiate the 100-monkey entrainment of coherence. Check!

*Literally during this time of travel, perhaps about five months ago on our "Galactivation Tour" we, my crew and I, have begun fully hive minding; connecting, linking, our consciousness and like a tree leaning towards the light of 5D away from the crumbling of the old world.

*We have been able to start linking and synching psychically allowing for our power to gather like an electrical storm and have begun operation #catapult which will launch us all into 5D Consciousness's in real time again note to self, make a song for this and hologram virtual show; we realize the power of the Naturix is actually defragging the fourth density of the Archons / Architects of the Matrix and we need to get this imprinting out.

*This awesome vibrational harmonic convergence on spiritual steroids is causing the whole "Safe City" grid with its A.I. brain to like a castle of cards, come collapsing down. We, the vibe tribe have in fact achieved the 100 Rainbow Warriors effect, instigating and catalyzing the release of resonant sacred high vibrational codes and frequencies into all directions. The Rainbow Serpent is alive and well the Aboriginals have confirmed and is reactivating the dragon lines making ready for Earth to ascend.

*Through the grapevine we have confirmed that this achievement has begun emitting and transmitting the initial operating commands through us to override the frequencies of the Black Goo Dark Lords network and ultimately activate the "Reset" protocols.

*Gonna hit up our last event on my Bearthday, 18! I am finally a legal adult, lol! Back to Revolutionaries Gallery … this one is gonna be a big one … live broadcast worldwide! #bigbang

Dear Diary … King and Avatar made the observation awhile back while debating the purpose of trying to get our music and our message out to the world via a world-wide tour since we knew that we would get totally targeted and attacked by the agents if we came out with what our message was all about but the boys had said that it was a do or die situation and that it was just what we had to do. So glad we listened to them and I am so grateful to be back.

Avatar ended that debate by pointing out, "peeps, we can't hide we can't sit back and subside cuz If we can spell the word then our word will be made flesh. Don't forget we got magic erasers yo, and we can dispel the word. That is what we are here to do, why we have found each other. We owe it to our ancestors we owe it to our family and friends who have been taken killed and maimed by the beast system! I am not going to sit back and be bullied no mo! I am going to chant down Babylon and dispel the spells written upon creation; sorceress to source is us! I am here to redeem myself and my bloodline, and you either join me and stand in solidarity with me and those who have the courage to do this or I do this on my own. Be a transfusion of spirit like blood to the masses, lift all life up like yeast like leaven in the bread of life, we are here to stop the sacrifice, we come to raise creation back up to paradise to 5D and ever lasting peace, so mote it be." So, we did it, we mounted up and charged the world on high just so that when we did die, we could die in honor, knowing we had done everything we could do to make a difference!

Now here we are a year later exact to the day going to perform within the Revolutionaries Gallery in the heart of Venice Beach in what we lovingly call El Corazon de Los Angelo's or the heart of LA, The Angels. We are going to celebrate the victory of light and love over the forces of darkness.

Diary, I had a crazy dream the other night ... the "Wise Ones" came to me again they are getting closer and closer and as they do they become clearer and clearer. They said that they wanted me to write a book. They want me to share with the world my story ... so I am going to make some notes of how all this came to be. They said that if I write this all down now I will remember it later after the ascension is complete. They told me that my story will come from 5D that they will have me channel my story from the future to share back into the past. I have no idea what they are talking about!!!!! But I am going to do what they told me because they have been right about everything else. So here it goes ... notes for my future book. Who am I? What is my story, my message the "Wise Ones" want people to know??? Here goes nothing.

I was born of an old long line of Rabbi's from my grandmother's side whose bloodline could be traced all the way back before the days of Christ to the Essenes. The Essenes were Yeshua the Christ's true family and people my grandmother taught me. He was like a prophet to them she said and his birth fulfilled their prophecy being that of the Son of God coming to save the people of Earth from the rise of the Dark Lords.

At that time, it was two thousand years ago and the people who lived then were living and dealing with the same shit as we were dealing with now in 2030, yup just another same shit different day scenario. According to the Eugenics scientist and spy Madame Tavares, who found me via my blood in the blood banks and genetic coding lab, I was the return of the Christ light and apparently my blood was traceable way back to these people which is why she pulled the plug on her job and retired early, as this was the sign she said, the sign in fact that she had been looking for as a spy all along.

Now the Essenes were a group of highly evolved beings whom lived in sacred community honoring through their daily communions the Angels of life like the Sun, the Heavenly Father, Divine Mother,

The Angel of Air, Water, and even the Angels of Wisdom, Love, and Grace. I know this because King and Queen have converted us all into becoming Essenes with them, crazy hey, full circle. Anyways so apparently the information that was encoded into my genealogy in my blood and bone, was the same information the Essenes had mastered in their quests to commune with the forces of life to override the forces of evil. So apparently I was made for this.

The Essenes like my crew and I had literally removed themselves from the corrupt politics of their time thousands of years ago and had taught people how to heal by cleansing and fasting. They believed and apparently could purge evil spirits out of people through the intelligences or Angels they communed with such as the Angel of Love, Wisdom, and Grace all by reconnecting their patients back to the Earthly Mother and Heavenly Father and the elements.

So, you could say I was made for what we were doing, born from those who were masters at it. The Essenes King was always saying were known as and called the Sons and Daughters of Light. Yes, sons and daughters of light whom possessed the power and capacity to shine their light through the Black Goo and through their black magic dispelling all their spells and reversing all their curses. They assisted and aided in returning people to their pristine and pure true selves, or original blueprints, which happened to be exactly what we and our vibe tribe were doing in the modern world. Fractals right! Literally history does repeat itself repeatedly, lol.

One day when this woman named Madame Tavares happened to be screening for anomalies in her genealogy blood bank, scrying for RH – people, which I am … there, she found me, a rare anomaly and a Daughter of the Ancient Ones!

You see much like a computer each and every one of us has an internal hard drive, a data bank of genetic coding that traces through our history like an internal hard drive which transfers via computer to computer, much like the DNA and RNA coding which transfers generation to generation. Through our genetic coding, which has been called "Epigenetics" there is a transfer of information which can identify certain genomes hidden in our blood and those who are trained in this science can read our blood like a book.

Epigenetics Madame Tavares told me is how scientists and the A.I. can trace our ancestry and how the Eugenics, or the scientists who break us via our blood, manipulate us through their genetic engineering programs via vaccinations for example. It is how they manufacture diseases which are made specifically to attack certain genomes within our various bloodlines and races just like in the creation of diabetes which had been designed to attack Native Americans or HIV and Africans. Pretty fucked up right!

In a more positive use of this information, I was found via my blood by "Madame T" as she called herself. "Madame T" was a scientist and a spy for her secret society group. She was a very wealthy and resourced woman who had been brought up in a family of people who had been selectively bred into an ancient Mystery School group called the Orphic Circle.

It was this woman who had read my blood like tea leaves like Tarot cards one day in her lab as she scoured the web of DNA to find anomalies. Let's just say when she came across me ... she deleted me from the system and made me virtually untraceable in the Matrix quit her job by retiring early and called her circle together for a meeting as they had been waiting for me, looking for me, searching for me she said.

Apparently, they had channeled or had been shown, guided to look for my specific blood anomaly. As I had said my blood for whatever reason was connected, she said to the vision that her group had been shown connecting me as a key figure for their group to support. Yep, somehow in their vision or channeling received I was to unlock and unblock the redemption codes, the liberation codes and help usher in the "Age of the Apotheosis," the age of the man becoming Gods once again.

This great morph that Madame Tavares described, as was shown to their Orphic Circle, was exactly like the great Christian rapture phenomenon whereby the so-called chosen ones are raptured up for the great ascent to Heaven. Madame T, and her people's vision that she had described to me pretty much sounded a lot like The Hopi Prophecy just with a bit more dogmatic lenses attached but more or less essentially described a deliverance to paradise or 5D, The 5th Age of Peace as I referred to it as and as it was taught to me by Shima!

That is how I was discovered a handful of years back by Madame T who was also a Hebrew woman by descent yet not one of the false Zionists as we called a group of the elite who were power tripping on the planet. No, she was an old original authentic version of the true Hebrew people, and she had been guided by her heart she had told me, to find me. She also had conveyed to me how she was a part of her secret group "The Orphic Circle" who was made up of very wealthy high-end anonymous people and that these people would like to be donors to my cause. She said once she had found me via my blood and then investigated my files in the system, she knew in her heart that I was the one she had been looking for that her group had been looking for and that they were willing to do whatever it would take to help me complete this mission.

Madame Tavares had introduced me to her group by way of a power point presentation (which made me have to laugh at the thought of what that had to have been like) and that they too got spiritual confirmation that yes I was indeed the key that they had been searching for. She said furthermore that her group was very attracted to my art and that they believed that would be the channel as to how I would be able to complete my mission. So she said that they wanted to become donors, sponsors for my work to start. Looking back as I reflected on it all perhaps Madame T was possibly guided to me by the Star Council of Guides and Guardians, perhaps specifically even by Shima herself.

I will never forget the day when that mysterious woman, Madame T, all dressed in white floated in like a swan approaching me one day while I was at the Revolutionaries Gallery right about the time when I had begun to really put together the messages Shima was teaching me and showing me. That is where "The Apocalypsos" story really took off for that is when we began to get funded. I had begun to channel the pictures of 5D and the 5th Age of Peace that Shima would plant into my dreams and meditations while Madame T's group would commission me to deliver them into form. So, I did, I began to bring Shima's visions and stories and translate them through "Living Art" as "Messages for Humanity" and my crew and I would then take it to the next level and perform it all for people with music art and dance, the sacred combination to the elixir of life!

Over time with the help of the boys Avatar, Mill Boy, and King who were master programmers, we made all my art into virtual 3D holographic displays that would animate into superficial real time experiences for people to feel into the 5D templates and possibilities so that they would be imprinted by them all enhanced with Avatar's cellular Royal Rife Code frequency harmonizers. A total mastery of experiential delivery to our performances you could say for Avatar hooked up our speakers not only to the 432 frequency of love but also implemented a Cymatrax level of programming combining Dr. Royal Rife codes hidden as frequencies into the music via a transmission of pulsation.

Madame T had said that the organization she belonged to was very secretive and private not public nor to be mentioned at all and who did not want any recognition or credit for their donation's commissions and contributions. Madame T and her anonymous organization were to remain anonymous as a necessary requirement. Madame T had only said that she was one of the representatives of the "Council X" and that they were to remain in our X files ... otherwise hush hush, we had no problem with that.

Soon after meeting her checks began showing up commissioning me to do work. The themes that were requested for these paid commissions were all centered on Indigenous people, nature, animals, history, and the power of love. I was to animate families, innocence, and sacred culture like the Peruvian culture for example or Tibetan culture with the solid intent to bring those images of higher consciousness back to the conception point of people's perception.

I was commissioned to basically animate a different history, a different story, then that of the present picture the media created where we were like savages or where we were like dependent disabled babies nursing off the tit of a psychopathic dominatrix.

Rather than the brainwashing predictive programming and

subliminal messaging of the media, I was to animate and illuminate a flourishing time where both ancient highly advanced civilizations spread across the vortices of Earth and where beings were radiant beautiful and royal and where we all like all thrived rather than just survived.

Yes, I was recruited to show how we had in fact had come from a higher evolution and had yes devolved rather than evolved. That we all had the choice, the right to claim our truth that we were Gods yet we know it not as Jesus the Christ once said, or to continue to follow the script that we were helpless hopeless mutants that needed the intervention of our slave owners to help us with their welfare and so called health care system. Seemed like a dream come true for me. You know this is a good time to point out how in fact yes for sure the laws of karma are for real a science! For how else can one explain how being in the right place at the right time like an alignment or atonement resonance manifesto can manifest for you all of your dreams while at the same time another person can never catch a break! Vibration vibration vibration; law of attraction much!

With the power of my spoken word combined with the music of The Apocalypsos and even just their presence itself, I was employed to speak spells with my spoken word that would awaken the truth in the hearts of people while my art was animated in 3D holographic art all around. That with our art, our virtual templates of what lies just beyond the edge of this paradigm and with our message, like a transmission we would seed the vibrational charge into the circuitries of people giving them a reconnection to their own Divinity and overall Exodus Codes to 5D life.

In Madame Tavares's words, "the media, or the World Wide Web, is just that, a web and it catches in its sticky trap its prey. It lures its victim into its snare then anaesthetizes them like a drug; while spiders that live in the dark web come out to feast upon their prey poisoning their minds and entraining into their psychosomatic neuropathways the agenda it seeks to create. That is why we must get you and others like you to the masses so that people who will listen will begin to follow in your example. You, Sophia can turn the tides, you can reach the people, especially the youth and all the broken and desperate; you can be like a life line and save people Sophia Star Water … if you accept that is. The media is literally lying to the people Sophia and blaming us, the good people of the world for their own engineering of hell on earth. The media is calling us a cancer, a plague, and penalizing us, the humans for the global climate crisis that is well beyond a crisis and more of an absolute threat to life itself. Scientists have discovered Sophia how to engineer the weather into warfare and create through their 5G now 6G and into 7G framework, not only how to engineer weather but to literally control existence through frequency, this is called The Great Assimilation and Manifestation of the A.I. Singularity Hive Mindset … this we must stop at all costs!"

So, I had worked for her for a couple of years developing my brand considering I was only fourteen (going on 40) years old at the time when she had found me. A child prodigy, a foster kid, a kid in a band called "The Apocalypsos," I got to say I really did think at first it was all a joke but now … wow it was all for reals. It was amazing; we became more and more popular every day. With the constant downloading I was receiving from Shima, with Madame Tavares and Council X's financial support, and The Apocalypsos masterful beats; the message of peace of truth and the return to innocence was combined with the overall transmission Shima had told me would transmit from our performances. All of this together had begun to create a total gateway to change and revealed keys to revolutionaries all over the world that demanded freedom.

Madame Tavares had become like my Fairy God Mother, no other words could describe her for she took me, a messed-up Cinderella and transformed me from rags to riches into a princess for freedom. Once my crew and I had become recognized, popularized, and then followed by hundreds of thousands all over the world who saw our art as a therapeutic dose of beauty to whitewash over all the ugly twisted rot within the world apple, she called me to a special meeting saying that it was urgent.

Jacob and I had been on a Sea Shepherd mission working with a crew to save some of the last remaining whales left on the Earth. Sea Shepherds is a Conservation crew that goes out on ships patrolling the seas, we loved them, and I was using the experience to inspire my work. It was then while we were on board the Sea Shepherd ship when Madame T called, calling me to an urgent meeting.

She said it is critical that I go with my band and tour the world. That the group she represented had told her that the world clock was about to ring, time was up! She was going to supply us with a pretty hefty amount of money to bring our message to the world; she said we were to be the last effort to save humanity before the war to end all wars broke out.

No pressure, right? She then gave me enough money to travel the world with the band as well as making several arrangements to start us off, placing us in awesome venues to perform. She said our assignment would be to bring our music and art to the world in every effort to try to influence as many hearts and minds of people as possible so that we could save their very Souls, again no pressure, right?

Like a band of travelling gypsies we shared our music art and dance creating an evangelical coalition around the world. We had gathered in circles in so many places as people were called to host us; for people around the Earth were becoming more and more hungry; hungry not just for food, but for love, and positive vibrations. While the world was falling apart people were rising from the ashes coming together calling for hope for answers and for a new way to take over the trajectory of shit that was being laid out before us all!

Our empowering performances helped to unify a grid of hearts awakened and awakening. We had travelled through everything from castles and crop circles to sacred sites, and holy places. From festival to festival, retreat to retreat, to galleries, and private homes. We would get called and we would show up. What began as an Art Tour that we had been offered quickly turned into a Global Crisis Response Team showing up like first responders to any group that would host us to help antidote the darkness by bringing our light.

Right on time too, for we would be of the last people to travel and have passports and such, we would be of the last souls to have to put up with the constant screening, security, and harassment by the police and authorities. Yes, we would be the last to travel in those times, those ways … for time was changing, quickening. The institutions of the power elite were crumbling failing falling. The timing was impeccable. We could have never done this before and we would never be able to do this again after what was coming… for all of life was about to ascend out of the wreckage of its old out dated dying form, like a snake shedding skin. Yes, like a transfiguration everything was about to be reborn and arise again in a new body of light prepared just for this amazing ascension. That is what the "Wise Ones" keep showing me in dreams and visions that is what Shima keeps telling me to portray in my art and speak of in my spoken word.

It is true we would all die to be reborn and arise again however not so much on a microcosmic level, no; now it was to be a macrocosmic level … as the Aquarian Age is ushering in the time of the collective conscious. So it was no longer only me but we … we were all getting free this time and with that in mind the magic key was that we all just had to keep on going, no matter what even through the crazy shit unfolding that is just too miserable to speak of. "Keep up and you will be kept up," my Yoga teacher always said, sage advice!

Despite all the heat we had to endure just to travel and be able to perform since we had now become world famous and had posed as a rather large and direct threat for the elite Dark Lords; we managed on a wing of a prayer to make our journey a complete and perfect success. Seriously, if it had not been for the absolute fact that we had been assisted by Shamans, Light Beings, Healers, and Warriors as they called themselves, yes, Warriors of the Rainbow both seen, and unseen who worked tirelessly to protect the crews of people like us trying to help bring love back to the Earth travelling midwifing ushering in ascension; we would have never made it back. Yes, it was so pragmatically true, without these great love lights we would have never succeeded.

No doubt we have witnessed firsthand all the terrible tensions, terrors, and shocking states of realities as wars are breaking out over political tensions. Its crazy out there like total polarities, there is the extreme indulgence of the rich fat cats contradicted by the looming many poor impoverished peoples not chipped living like beggars. We survived aftermaths of severe storms where we all thought that we were gonna die even mass protests and rebellions. Damn it is so sad to see all the people who are hungry, sick, poor, and abandoned by their leaders.

The times certainly are a changing, and the people of this world need guidance, need hope now more than ever. They also needed organization and the realization that all we really need to do is to come together in solidarity and to by all means work together to overthrow the evil that had corrupted the governments and corporations controlling existence … but not through violence only through psychic spiritual power, through our collective vibration.

Hopefully, that paints a picture as to how big the events going on all around me are. For this night coming is not only going to be my bearthday, not only is going to be the Winter Solstice, but it will be the completion to prophecy! Yes! We are completing prophecy and have successfully changed the tides, changed the timelines, and are now the ""Wise Ones" say ushering in with a big 10/4 roger that … the new age......

Goddes I am falling asleep … will write again later must shut down.......... Oh there is Jacob, yes!!! Cuddle time, my favorite time!

CHAPTER SIX

DREAM TEAM

**"Music gives a soul to the universe, wings to the mind,
flight to the imagination and life to everything."**
Plato

December 21, 2030 my eighteenth bearthday and we are live on stage
in The Revolutionaries Gallery. I remember clearly I was integrating the
great revelation that I knew the prophecies were coming true. With all
the Earth signs, with all the death tolls rising, with all the civil unrest,
the forced vaccinations the Chip, the 5 to now 6 to 7 G grids; it was all
creating the necessary chaos that would catapult us all beyond and into
the 5th Age. It does after all take great pressure to create diamonds and
there was enough severe pressure on us all for sure to create our own
diamond bodies of light.

Seriously either one could spontaneously combust and just snap
surrendering to the force of our controllers and their crazy frequencies
within their electrical A.I. grid, or you could allow for all the pressure
upon thee to help manifest your Rainbow Light Body and ascend. It
was like advance or recede but do not hesitate … there was no time
to hesitate you just had to know how to keep going and trust as you
plunged forward into the abyss of the unknown that there would be a
net to catch you on the other side of the edge of this shattering mirror
of reality.

Back to the moment, to the here and now, back to the Revolutionaries
Gallery Winter Solstice 2030 where my lover Jacob was absolutely heart
blowing, mind blowing on the drums and everyone there or watching
the live broadcast was getting stoked like a fire.

My man he was so happy to be home. So happy to be back where
our love shack was and where we would finally have some privacy.

Where the waves rolled in, and the smell of our childhood memoirs still kissed the heart of the Angels.

There we were our musical family; Avatar, Mill Boy, Thomas, and King and their ladies my seasstars, we had become a Dream Team like the Avengers whom we loved. We kiddingly liked to see ourselves as The Guardians of the Galaxy, like the Wailers, like Crazy Horse and the Ghost Dancers and like all those fantastical people, we were making History!

I could feel the raw power surging; the hands of the people in the crowds clapping like the beats of my heart, which fueled my words. My throat chakra opened wide. I was on spiritual fire, a full channel, a magnetic sorceress spelling spoken word.

Everything stirred and blurred around me. I felt myself streaming weaving light, light languaging. Spoken words wove themselves into codes for new programming, unlocking unblocking the healing power which emanated out of me like a supernova blast.

"Victory of Spirit Victory of Nature, Victory of Spirit Victory of Nature, Victory of Spirit Victory of Nature," I heard Mercy singing in her gospel voice to the crowd. Standing like a High Priestess at the Altar of Alterations, I closed the song and the night by the utterance of these words ...

"The frequency is rising, colliding
Providing
New templates and timelines
Arriving
Forking 5D from 6 and 7 G
Do not fear just
Come along with me,
Leave the densities
Ascend to divergent possibilities
From so called safe cities to paralleled glittering abilities ...
The choice is yours
From the Matrix unplug
Upload the Naturix

Return to One
Rise like the golden Sun
Returning to love like the sacred Dove
Calling in our Light Bodies from the Heavens above
*

Activate
Motivate
Emancipate
For the Time Has Come
To Liberate
Yes, we be getting free
Come
Pick up your Drum
And
Sing out your heart's truest song
As we be chanting down Babylon
*

Behold the Star Gates to Infinity…
With our Heart as the Key
We open the lock to eternity
Evolve with me
From Homo Sapien
To Homo Luminous
Homo Divinous is in us
The Star Nations and Ancestors welcome us
Come join the
Metamorphosis
Return to the Gates of Lemuria
And Stand Glorious
Full circle we round the bend and make our way Home again
To the way it was in the beginning
So shall it be now in the end
Time is up, we can no longer pretend!"
*

I looked to my man his eyes closed in trance as his hands found the leather of the Conga drums and danced; his sweat trickling down his naked steaming chest, so blessed, he was full electricity, bio- electric plasmic frequency at its best.

His soul must have felt the intensity of my gaze and the ultimate overwhelming waterfall of gushing flowing pure love tantric and romantic blasting his aura like a star. My primal love for him came pouring out of my heart like a hurricane washing him over with waves of power and attraction, pure magnetic attraction that lit charges up in sparks everywhere.

Our eyes locked, we were bringing it delivering it. Midwifes for ascension; the potency of my spoken word with the beats of The Apocalypsos birthed life energies which flooded the 7 directions with light.

I then turned to the crowd who had all just stopped and started staring at us and I took a bow. I then brought the microphone to my mouth for that one last time as the sound of the drums became a low heartbeat; it was our favorite way to end a show, my voice purred …

"We are the ones we are waiting for!
It has always been a feeling
A feeling like a memory
A memory like a story
A story that has a conclusion that offers a resolution.
Like that of the Hopi Prophecy
Which goes like this…
You have been telling people that this is the Eleventh Hour, now you must go back and tell the people that this is the Hour. And there are things to be considered… Where are you living?
What are you doing?
What are your relationships?
Are you in right relation?
Where is your water?
Know your garden.
It is time to speak your truth.
Create your community.

Be good to each other.

And do not look outside yourself for your leader.

This could be a good time! There is a river flowing now very fast. It is so great and swift that there are those who will be afraid. They will try to hold on to the shore. They will feel they are being torn apart and will suffer greatly. Know the river has its destination. The elders say we must let go of the shore, push off into the middle of the river, keep our eyes open, and our heads above the water.

And I say, see who is in there with you and celebrate. At this time in history, we are to take nothing personally, least of all ourselves. For the moment that we do, our spiritual growth and journey come to a halt.

The time of the lone wolf is over. Gather yourselves! Banish the word 'struggle' from your attitude and your vocabulary. All that we do now must be done in a sacred manner and in celebration.

We are the ones we've been waiting for."

Jacob's body went still the transmission was complete. He walked over to me and fell on bended knee. Reaching for my hand I trembled, what was he doing? On live TV what were we doing? He looked up to me with those sparkling majestic crystal-clear ocean eyes, he was so beautiful … "I love you so much Sophia. You really are my Twin Soul My Twin Flame. Before all these people before all these witnesses before our family the band before God and Goddess themselves I declare my undying love for you and ask you with all that I am to be my one, to marry me, to be my bride and to have me as your husband."

With that he lifted from within his other hand a beautiful moonstone crystal inlaid jeweled ring and slipped it halfway down my finger. I was flooding with tears, they rolled down my face. I was still pulsing from the power of the music and channel of spoken word that had just funneled through me. The frequencies of the music and collective power that had just been raised were dynamic and danced about us like sprites like faeries glittering in the currents of emotion.

"Will you honor me my love and become my wife?" Speechless …
I nodded, literally with my whole entire body. Everything was in

agreement; I fell down on my knees too. Saying "my love my best friend my everything; we have been married since we met. Born married, for lifetimes married, since the beginning of time we have been married. I will marry you over and over again always. Forever I will marry you, Yes Yes Yes!"

Jacob got up and grabbed me in his arms. We kissed and hugged clasping our hot sweaty bodies together, trying to not forget where we were. The crowd went wild, clapping, yelling, and crying.

It was the most exciting moment of my Life! Everything was perfect in this moment. Everything made sense. It was like sacrednicity, the art of the sacred finding synchronicity finding serendipity finding perfection.

Mill Boy came running over … "group hug" he called and then the rest of the Apocalypsos came and enveloped us. We were all laughing so hard. For just in that perfect moment no one else existed, just us, just our pod, our pack, our hive, our tribe

King said, "Lets open some Champagne … celebrate come on!" And with that the corks started popping and the glasses started to fill. "A toast, (said Avatar) to our King and Queen our Lord and Lady," and with that everyone in the crowd raised their glasses and yelled, "here here, to the Lord and Lady!"

"Pinch me" I said to Jacob, the band had begun to serenade us with a special beat for our feet to dance and romance. "I feel like we have died and gone to Heaven." And just like that he started singing Just like Heaven by The Cure.

"Spinning on that dizzy edge I Kissed her face and kissed her head Dreamed of all the different ways, I had to make her glow. Why are you so far away she said why won't you ever known that I'm in love with you? That I'm in love with you? … "You, soft and only, you lost and lonely you, strange as angels dancing in the deepest oceans twisting in the water, you're just like a dream, you're just like a dream"

I melted into Jacob's arms, feeling the deep bliss run through my being like whiskey. He had me by the chakras. He got me all of me.

He met me in every way. He was my Beloved. I knew we had done this many many lifetimes before. Always finding each other to power up and bring in sacred love magic so that when the world was falling apart, we would come and heal it bringing it into wholeness, holiness again. Just like a dream …

CHAPTER SEVEN

SHAVASANA

**"Dare to dream! If you did not have the capability to make
your wildest wishes come true, your mind would not have the
capacity to conjure such ideas in the first place. There is no
limitation on what you can potentially achieve, except for the
limitation you choose to impose on your own imagination.
What you believe to be possible will always come to pass - to the
extent that you deem it possible. It really is as simple as that."
Anthon St. Maarten**

We gathered together in a group hug, King was like "Gaia's, we did
it. We made the dream a living reality, and on reality T.V. none the less,
we have told the world our vision! Talk about tell us a vision... BOOM!
We touched the world with the power of our message and our Love. We
brought the medicine to the people, we brought our word which has
been made flesh, and our art a therapy, our vibe in our tribe has healed
so many throughout the nations!" You can see why King was given the
name King, for he was a 6-foot Dred locked beautiful black man that
new how to use his words and preach, yup he was a living King alright
just like his lady was a living Queen!

"There and back again, we be like the Fellowship of the Ring just
back in from saving the world," said Thomas who was still all weepy
and nostalgic, he really was such an Elven consciousness. He reminded
me of Legolas so much that it was funny, especially since he always was
referencing Lord of the Rings ... his favorite movie not too mention the
fact that he had literally read every single piece of literature put out by
J.R.R. Tolkien and ya shhhhhh don't laugh but his ears were actually
pointy. "I love you Gaia's so much, I feel like I have married you all" he
said. Good ol' Thomas he was Jacob's oldest best friend remember who

had survived the foster system going to shelter to foster parent to shelter growing up. He made me feel for him for he really was of another world and with all that had happened to him, it was a miracle that the brother could still love at all … and he always proved that he was actually the one who always loved more than anyone could think was possible, everyone and everything! He was like a real living modern day Buddha!

"Dude … dude brother … I am totally going to be the best man bro; I will even be your best lady too Soph cuz you know I got ya girl." Laughing I said, "King you are going to be our Priest, preacher man, you got to marry us." Word" Jacob said. King started singing "Going to the Chapel and we going to get married" in his deep gospel blues voice.

King's got that presence that could make you want to run out of fear, bow down and kiss his feet, or laugh at what a giant baby he is. Avatar was like "yo yo yo … peeps I got to go to bed and sleep for a week, I am so tired!!!!" Mill Boy was like "yo me too fam, honey butter Rebekah get over here sweet thing, I am going to make you my bride tonight too!" Rebekah, Mercy, and Queen were too tired to talk and just nodded their heads in agreement muttering blessings to us all excited by the mention of getting to go back to their lairs. They let their men guide them to their rides; it was like 5 in the morning.

Jacob picked me up and carried me off to the car. We all said our goodbyes with tears in our eyes. "Be prepared for training again, day after tomorrow," Avatar said. We all moaned and groaned at the thought but chimed in our consent as we all went our different ways. We were all just so happy to be back home, to have the circle complete and full, and to be able to know we had no more shows no more performances, and no more duties for a while. Time to Shavasana. The yoga was complete; we were all going into corpse pose now.

We got into our little electric hover cars, well King climbed aboard his motorcycle with Queen clinging to his waist, and we all scooted off to our own little abodes to go into bat pose and shut down so that we could resurrect ourselves anew for yet another day as we rolled forward into the impending end of the world scenario that was rapidly approaching us all.

When we got home, Jacob carried me through the doorway of our cute little cottage by the sea in the Venice canals, which was not so nice anymore in 2030. Funny how you can have a dream all your life such as when you see the place that speaks to your heart and soul and is your dream home only to when your old enough and rich enough to move there, the place is literally gone down the toilet bowl. Anyways poor Jacob, he was singing to me trying to keep me awake. I knew exactly what was on his mind…. I was drunk on love babbling away deliriously exhausted and already very turned on by the fact that the next time I made love to my man, I was going to be making love to my betrothed.

Jacob carried me into our bedroom and began undressing me while singing to me in his super sweet steamy and absolutely sexy voice. Kissing me softly, he undid the zipper of my dress, kissing me chakra by chakra as he pulled down the zipper ever so slowly down my back to my sacrum.

I felt the call awaken in me burn and yearn for the law of attraction was serious in our energetic connection, feeling the power of our love drawing us together like a force, like a magnet to become one. "My wife, my love, my Lady … I will serve you forever, I will protect you, die for you, father your children, just tell me what you want what you need and your wish will always be my command … and then he laughed … remember … As you wish."

It was the first time back when we were teens living in the shelter where we had all met each other originally when Jacob first told me he loved me by saying "as you wish." He told me this by way of referring to the words of the farm boy who had said I love you to the Princess Buttercup from the movie Princess Bride. He had told me this when I was asking him to record my spoken word tracks back when I first started really getting going with my gift, and he said "as you wish" and then came over and kissed me hard on the mouth, he had been waiting awhile he said and then one day he just couldn't wait any longer.

The memoirs of the old days when we were just a bunch of kids in the shelters fleeted from my mind like a hummingbird as his kisses became more and more passionate on my mouth tracing my curves as he licked the salty sweet essence of my flesh down my neck, on route to my breasts where he then pulled off my dress and began to ravish my body. His strong hands massaging my nipples, his tongue now up on my ear suckling tickling and toying with all my most exotic erotic places. Stroking their way down to my pulsing flower; he was the bee the pollinator and I opened like a Morning Glory.

The sun was peaking when we finally got up forced by our own need to relieve our bladders and to feed our hungry bellies. We floated still high on the ecstasy of our love making and engagement. We were deeply relieved to be in our own home with our own bed. Ahhh it was so good to be with our own everything, no need to ask for anything from anybody. Jacob was grinding coffee beans, so I hopped in the shower. He met me there, "coffee is on honey" and he began once again to caress my body in that oh so delicious way.

We climaxed in the shuddering steam of the shower scented with my lavender tea tree body wash. The coffee percolator screamed as Jacob raced out of the bathroom naked as a newborn babe to turn the fire off. I slipped on my Kimono and came out fresh and wild.

Sipping our breves, lying out in our hammocks on our patio in the L.A. sun which of course was as usual a hazy polluted field of sickness in our sky we listened to what few remaining birds were left as they squawked searching for food scavengers sadly that they had become picking through the trash in the alley. Hardly any flowers flowered, or fruits ripened anymore on the trees and of course since the bees were practically extinct, the insect world fried by the 5G and 6G 60 hertz frequency, not much bloomed nor fruited anymore unless grown in the factories labs and greenhouses.

We listened as the sound of waves crashed and the salty sea air breathed like a breath of Nirvana through the dense smog, we finally relaxed completely letting go, finally in our own home in our own space no longer in view of all our friends and family and followers. Even with the constant sounds of helicopters and sirens ... nothing compared to the feeling of bliss that tickled us in every way colouring us pink as we lounged in our hammocks high off our love making.

"Yes, Jacob said this is what the yoga is all about, Shavasana, the harvest of peace when you know you have given your yoga your best and it yields such gratitude and prosperity. If only the Sea was not toxic, and I could go surfing like the old times." I said "Baby, you know it and now with all the recordings we are selling, we will never have to work again!" We laughed knowing that we would likely give most of our money to people in need and animal shelters and that we would never stop moving forward on creating a better world where one day we might have a family of our own, a family like we never had, with a mother and father and home that wasn't changing all the time and where no one had to live in fear or terror and of course where you could go surfing again.

We drank our coffee and got enough energy to go back into the kitchen and manifest some food. I was so glad I had gone to Trader Joe's and stocked up on grub because we had worked ourselves up an appetite from our passionate love making.

After Jacob's famous omelettes and my golden hash browns and toast combo with fruit salad, we were stuffed and back in bed sated into absolute contentment. Yet again I found my lovers kiss ravishing my body as if I were the dessert of our brunch. He got me in every way a whole-body shuddering orgasm that felt like fireworks igniting out of my crown chakra all the way through my feet.

We slept sound cuddled up in each other's arms still recovering from a whole year of touring and performing world-wide. We had no idea what we would wake up to the next day nor would we ever have been able to sleep that deep and recharge that profound had we known about the storm that the Hour of Power would deliver and that was coming up real fast! Little did we know either that the experiences coming to us that we would have in our dream that day unto night and into the next day would show us the way through our hearts to survive the uber epic shift that was coming through the Hour of Power ahead of us.

The foreplay of time and space in this continuum of the Matrix upon the earth was quickly becoming the peaking climaxing volcanic eruption of kundalini fire itself orgasming and ejaculating "The Great Reset" liberation codes upon creation at last! It was time, the combination code upon the lock down was cracked and the hour of power started triggering the alarm bell unto all the four directions.

After an absolute black out as I shut down from sheer exhaustion, I became aware in my sleep. I went from nothingness to lucidly being aware of both myself and the fact that I was dreaming. I saw the world twirling around as if it were a news broadcast that was fast forwarding through different scenes broadcasting from around the world. I knew in my heart what had to be done as I watched all the footage of reality displayed from the beginning of time to this point now of 2030. I watched from the beginning of life on Earth all the way up until now how everything in the world had become inverted and cast upside down, backwards.

The words of Chief Seattle then started swirling in my head, it was if he had walked right into my dream time offering me his peace pipe while saying "the Earth does not belong to man – man belongs to the Earth. This we know. All things are connected like the blood which unites one family. All things are connected. Whatever befalls the Earth – befalls the sons of the Earth. Man did not weave the web of life – he is merely a strand in it. Whatever he does to the web, he does to himself. Even the white man, whose God walks and talks with him as friend to friend, cannot be exempt from the common destiny. We may be brothers after all. We shall see. One thing we know, which the white man may one day discover – Our God is the same God. You may think now that you own Him as you wish to own our land, but you cannot. He is the God of man, and His compassion is equal for red man and the white. The Earth is precious to Him, and to harm the Earth is to heap contempt on its creator. The whites too shall pass, perhaps sooner than all other tribes. But in your perishing, you will shine brightly, fired by the strength of the God who brought you to this land and for some special purpose gave you dominion over this land and over the red man. That destiny is a mystery to us, for we do not understand when the buffalo are slaughtered, the wild horses tamed, the secret corners of the forest heavy with scent of many men, and the view of the ripe hills blotted by talking wires. Where is the thicket? Gone. Where is the Eagle? Gone. The end of living and the beginning of survival."

I then could hear the voice of Shima blending in with Chief Seattle's voice as if they were both there together. She was calling to me saying "we are in the final hour Sophiaaaaa, we are taking back the power. Get ready dear one the Hour of Power has come. We are reversing the curse sweet child you all are finding your way home again now come to meeee child come home."

What was at first a deep cave of hibernation, a deep sleep as if we were bears in a cold dark winter, the energies culminating in my dreamtime catapulted me towards Shima's voice. Suddenly, I became aware of light swirling around and around. A light that was made of many colors, colors like I had never seen before.

I was deep in a swirling network of light like that of the Heavenly cosmos and I felt as though I was manifesting into a world which reflected all my most cherished hopes wishes and dreams. I felt like I was finally at home where all my friends and family were dancing and singing literally rocking out partying celebrating! There they all were so close yet still so far away not quite there where I was but all reflecting through a crystalline mirror.

I was drawn to that mirror like a moth to a flame and I could see faintly through that mirror through that looking glass if you will, which like a prism reflected rainbow lights all around, I could see all my relatives. I was being drawn to the light within lights where I could feel the resonant connection to all my kin all my ancestor's guides guardians and beloved magical allies. "Yes, yes yes ... I am coming wait for meeeee ...." I heard my voice say ... as I reached out my hand to all my beloveds through the looking glass. My very heart was smiling at them as they looked upon me with ultimate compassion love beauty and grace, "I am coming home" I announced to them feeling like I could almost reach out and just touch them as I got closer and closer to their warmth.

I then became surrounded by all sorts of wondrous beings who existed here in this world of light and had come to meet me at the gateway there where the looking glass was. All at once they began singing to me in a harmony like no other that I had ever heard before. Their song was like that of a bard who through their music tells a story, a story that carries one over the waters of life as if I was in a boat on my way to Avalon and the power of their song was able to bring down the veils separating me from my cherished loved ones and home.

Their song then began expressing through me effortlessly. I without any hesitation just started singing in harmony with them and the song more like mantra that expressed through me was a song which felt like it had come from a long song line, like that of whales. Whales I had studied have an ancient song of the sea, and their song wove into form everything that had ever been. It was as if through this song, these harmonies, and tones being expressed that they allowed for us, for me and these lit beings to speak to one another through visions or dream spell speak.

I did not have to think, I did not have to feel any confusion, I didn't even have to sort my way through all sorts of codes … I just knew in my heart what the messages were that these beautiful beings were transmitting to me. I felt their rainbow light that was being transmitted to me by all the beings that were there showing up rather spontaneously and whom were now occupying the sacred space within my dream or within this sphere that I had now fully moved into. As I stood there awkwardly now in the center of all these sacred souls enveloping me in their sacred light I started bawling, yup I just poured out my heart and soul through tears as my eyes became waterfalls of salty expressions.

It was in that moment that these majestically regal beings began to activate my body mind and soul Naturix. I could feel their light mingling within my DNA, mixing into the marrow of my crystalline bones. I felt like a phoenix being activated with light, rising higher and higher vibrationally as the ashes and dust of my old limited self-dissolved away from my body.

Sparkling rainbow light now came pouring out, literally radiating out of these wondrous light beings that surrounded me. I couldn't see anything for my eyes were tearing so much while everything kept getting brighter and brighter and brighter. The light became so bright that it was blinding. I melted away into that liquid light losing my form completely to the light until everyone there including myself was a giant orb of light like that of a star glowing in the heavens surrounded by thousands and thousands of other suns all around us.

Then I saw Jacob walking towards me … heart a glow. He had open hands open arms and he was reaching out for me. "Sophia, he called, Sophia I am coming … where are we Sophia who are all of those beings? Jesus Christ Holy Mother of God … where are we?" I tried to speak to answer him as he called for me, but I could not speak, I just simply was …

CHAPTER EIGHT

ENLIGHTENMENT

"He who creates a poison, also has the cure.
He, who creates a virus, also has the antidote.
He, who creates chaos, also has the ability to create peace.
He, who sparks hate, also has the ability to transform it to
love. He, who creates misery, also has the ability to destroy
it with kindness. He, who creates sadness, also has the
ability to convert it to happiness. He, who creates darkness,
can also be awakened to produce illumination. He, who
spreads fear, can also be shaken to spread comfort.
Any problems created by the left hand of man,
Can also be solved with the right,
For he who manifests anything,
Also has the ability to Destroy it."
Suzy Kassem,

We had begun emerging into the 5D realm about two years ago, synching in our dreamtime. While there were times that we could synch when we were awake with the band, it was not like this, nor were we asleep. Now it was like Jacob and I were accessing another world, a parallel world where everything is Technicolor vibrating breathing all rainbow like, kind of like when your tripping.

We had done a lot of acid when we were in the shelters; to be honest we had experimented with all sorts of drugs. That was just a reality living as a shelter kid and growing up in the Hell that LA had become. But this was better than any hallucination for it was real, we could feel it, taste it, smell it, we were it, whatever it was. For it sure did not feel quite like anything we had ever felt before.

When Shima, my adopted native grandmother, had started guiding me to find the Hopi Prophecy and look into the previous three worlds that had existed before, totalling now the four epochs of life, the four ages; we had found that all over the world through all religions and cultures … there was a beginning and there was an end. There were prophets and prophecies everywhere which all more or less said the same thing, as if there was one truth that was described in many different ways like the colors of the rainbow all different yet connected to the same spectrum. The prophets they had manifested like one seed of consciousness incarnating in through many different dialects' races and cultures in a garden of variety.

Jacob and I we loved doing deep dives as we called it into research on what was conveyed in the Hopi prophecies by way of Prophecy Rock and the Medicine People of the Hopi tribe. Shima had said that it was the most accurate prophecy that was shared for it carried no agenda. Shima had also said that it was almost untainted, that it had not been gobbled up by fear mongers and manipulated. It had remained pure for it had been carved into a rock for God's sake! It was neither oral nor scribed into different languages losing its essence in translation. It was not written down on paper and then rewrote time and time again by different ruling kings and priests such as the Bible with its many differing versions. No, it was a rock that held a glyph that was obvious as to what it depicted, truth. It kept a simple and clear message for all to see, that there would be an inevitable end to this world and to all those who walked in the way of the parasitic forces. Yet, there was a second path, one of Spirit that kept sacred the old ways of truth. This second path for those who had kept the old ways of the Good Red Road alive there would be another age born for them known of course as the 5th Age of Peace.

"The Prophets of truth," Shima had said, "always appeared in humility and would not come to create fear in those who were in mediumship or communion with them, but instead would impart and imprint guidance and illumination. Yes dear child the "Wise Ones" will help guide and protect always and in all ways all those who can receive their messages. This is the way child, and if you are to be a messenger then you must deliver the word as in accordance with the highest truth, for this is as it should be." With that she would place some tobacco down and raise her hands up to the Great Spirit then begin to speak in languages I could not translate but that I could feel as transmissions to my mind's eye and heart. "Tatooonkayanaaaawaaayae shaaaajjjjjj shaaajjjjj neeeoro ammmaa mooooonnnama maa eeko nawayyyyyy neeeko nawayyy shaooooooh mina owan keeeee aaa aaaa aaaa mishatalutubeeeeeee ona ona wayananana maaa."

The on-going apparitions and visitations from Shima led us into many deep dives you could say, taking us right down the rabbit hole of timelines of mud floods genocide and enslavement of not only physical, mental, emotional, but spiritual intelligence as well; democide. Our deep dives exposed a war on consciousness itself traced right down to the roots to the tendrils of the accursed Black Goo.

As we took the many pieces of the grand puzzle of life, the riddle if you will, and piece by piece put them all together, we realized what the real issue our Mother Earth and Relations were facing! The issue of the lying cheating parasitic corruption that was culminating right here on our beloved Mother Earth coming after our own very souls, our own god sparks themselves. Since the Goo crew had already successfully taken over every other facet of our lives, they were coming after that which was the true gold ... our soul fire.

Like an octopus with its eight tentacles, the parasitic forces of the cursed Black Goo crew had us stuck to each of their tentacles with their suction cups as they sucked the essence from our very life's every day and night, like an energetic vampire. For reals when you think about it, it totally makes sense the whole octopus' analogy with its Black Goo ink and eight tentacles holding onto and controlling everything. Holding control over all of our governing faculties of life on Earth; one on our banking institution, another in our education system, one in the medical establishment, one in our food, another in our water, another upon our ecosystems and environment climate and resources, the seventh upon our religions, the eighth as in the eight sphere ... now reaching out to suction cup itself to us connecting each of us to the beast system by way of our own individual seeds of spirit ... our very souls themselves.

It was the intention behind the agendas that were being rolled out in 2020 with the release of the 5G ultimate;y raising the frequency up to 60 hertz frequencies and the ushering in of totalitarian martial law which held us all in controlled fully surveillance based existences tracking our everyday actions messages research everything into social credit score based "Safe Cities" which people began to be corralled into.

It was what was behind the engineering of all the weather wars, the crop failures, the water shortages, the trafficking of children, the incarceration of people who would not conform, and to the huge divides that were separating people by way of mind control and programming that took hold of people's thinking and perceptions and turned them into predators seeking out prey to be then turned over to the demonic authorities. A total snitch society.

This agenda was hidden in the rituals or the performances of the so-called stars which lured people by their catchy sexy flashy shows and beats. These stars conscious or not were being used by masters of mind control, their producers, and directors more like witches. These witches of Hollywood and elite cast spells via subliminal messaging and lyrics wrote in a witch's language more like spells to program the fabric of modern reality through media. It is why we stopped watching movies or listening to modern music or even bothered to keep up with sports for the whole thing was rigged and black magic disguised in "glamour," the most ancient trick of magic.

It was the ultimate agenda of the Dark Lords and their minions to force the Chip, or the mark of the beast, which was being implanted into people even against their will. This microchip allowed people to be able to digitalize their money and lives through the Matrix. Without it, life just became harder and harder to be able to do anything. The gangsters or politicians were just like the Skeksis if you have seen the Dark Crystal show, for they fought one another for power and prestige. Just like the mafia these gangsters tried to climb on top of one another with their dirty tricks to be the Kingpin. To them it did not really matter who had to be sacrificed along the way because these guys had no soul no God spark, no sacred flame. They had no conscience; they felt no remorse in their actions brutal as they were. They were Dracos,

Greys, and Reptiles for crying out loud not mammals or human in any way other than their flesh suit costumes.

I remember people getting brainwashed all the time thinking oh he will save us; oh, she will save us. They followed MK Ultra programs or psy ops one right after the other like good little cult minded sheeple. Constantly check mated in the chessboard game of life all black and white like code. It was so sad to witness people's hearts getting broke time and time again as they went complicit and complacent believing whatever they were told by the fake news and false prophets.

Avatar and Mill Boy had committed to jackknifing the whole operation by sabotaging it in every way they could. With their team of hackers and coding game masters, they made the Matrix go awry for years postponing its implementation of the chip for almost a decade! They had found ways to make it so that the chip implants defected. They also leaked crazy amounts of top-secret files through media outlets and would add ones and zeros regularly to people's digital currency. With their hacker's programmers and coders, like a video game they would go into the Matrix's core quantum computer and implant bots in droves to upload viruses into the Matrix. They even turned the cameras on politician's movie stars and other agents of the beast system uploading a live broadcast which often was very revealing to everyone watching TV or on social media.

Since the microchip or RFID chip was to become the only way that one could buy or sell, rent or own a home, get jobs, get paid, drive a car, or even have a sense of a life in the world; it was expected of course that everyone would have one implanted at once. It was to be your ID and bank card and without it you were basically wiped out of existence for no one would rent to you or anything, it was a brilliant trap. But Avatar Mill Boy and their crew, as well as many other hackers and programmers around the world made that trap fail and drove the oppressors crazy!

Shima had told me many times "dear one fear not the wicked ones, for you have the support and intelligence of legions of light beings, a manifold of Star Nation brothers and sisters, and of course the Sasquatch Nation who are master minds of the Matrix believe it or not. We only allow for the illusion to be sustained so that these dark forces believe that they are in power. I am sorry but it is necessary for we must complete the mission to acquire all the Black Goo molecules from all the spheres of creation and draw them to the iron core crystal of Earth. Know that as your brother Yeshua had said to Pontius Pilot himself on threat of death … you have no power unless it is given to you from above. This is true in this case too my daughter. We must allow for these wicked ones to play out their games of charades while we vacuum them all to a black hole to be zero pointed very very soon. Stay strong beloved, the time is drawing near."

Now when Jacob and I reached the level of consciousness where we were able to achieve the level of vibration that would allow for us to access and emerge into 5D, or the Dimension of the Blessed as the Egyptians referred to it as … we realized that we were becoming bridged or funneled between the two planes of consciousness and that this bridge was transferring us over to the other side, to 5D. The proper word for it I guess is a wormhole, I like portal. Anyways yes, we were in fact transitioning or transferring our consciousness from the lower spheres to the higher spheres through the wormhole of time and space. Now here in 5D where we were finding ourselves now in our dream, we could experience this wonderful world of light and color, sound, and vibration, like living poetry.

We also were able to recognize that our consciousness was being erased from the lower planes of densities, deleted from all the fear the hate the judgement the lack of resources and the evil illusions that dominated fourth density and below. While this deletion process was occurring, we were simultaneously transporting our energetic signature over to the new foundation of existence, the fifth density.

This was the reset, the resetting of the new grounds for existence which would be built upon the 5th density. For in the 5th density we were whole, holy … no longer separate existing in duality. We were filled with love and truth like no other drug could ever deliver. This high was pure, potent, and powerful. This place or sacred space that we had begun to tune into together was just like Heaven. No wonder why the Hopi referred to it as the 5th Age of Peace; bliss, I got to say was more like it.

It was here where Jacob and I began accessed the living garden. It was here where we found ourselves now looking around, taking in the beauty and brilliance of this magnificent marvel, feeding upon it like babies nursing on their mother's tit.

We giggled as we both looked at one another suckling the prana and manna, the source of life itself breathing in long and deep while we glittered like sparkling stars. Here in this magical plane it seemed as if all our journeys had been like turns and bends on a map that had been directing us towards this place the whole time. We realized that across all the ages, our souls had been being guided to this X that marks the spot of deliverance and that we were about to find the buried treasure. All our work, our actions, our words, our yoga all had served to guide us to this destination, like destiny and here we were at last.

Jacob and I were holding hands feeling like we had finally found home and were actively engaged in a festive family reunion of bodacious proportions when we all of a sudden became aware of all sorts of amazing beings literally manifesting right out of their light filled orb ships. These were the beings that I had been connecting with prior to him arriving that had vanished as he had appeared but were now returning. They were the ones transmitting their light power frequencies to my being, helping me to activate my own Rainbow Light Body with their steady streaming transmitting unconditional love vibration. This vibration of theirs could only be described as wave after wave of the sacred Hawaiian Ho'oponopono modality whereas we were being scrubbed throughout our entire beings and consciousness. It was like having the vibration of Agape literally beamed into you through these magnificent being's care bear stare.

Jacob looked at me and spoke with no words "Sophia, do you see them, the amazing Angelic like beings OOOHHHHH MYYYYYYY GODDDDDDD, uhhhh their different colors their shapes and forms are they creatures' aliens, tell me you see them? Are we dead, what is happening?

As they surrounded us, I said, "yes my love they are our family, they are who have been with us this whole time, let them share their magic their medicine their power with you. I can feel them they are changing me from within, it feels so good, let them in baby let them rebuild you. I think they are activating our Rainbow Light bodies, remember reading about that and the Buddhist teachings of the Dzogchen. We must get our Rainbow Light Bodies so that we can graduate Earth and return to our source as perfected beings of light. It is like all those holy texts we read; those scrolls Poppa D taught us."

There they were majestic, magical, speaking with no words like Galadriel in the Lord of the Rings to Frodo. They spoke to us through our hearts and minds eye and all I could say was "I surrender I love you please help me help us!"

The sound they made was like a language of light of love that spoke directly to your heart in images and thought forms. While we could hear them speaking in sounds like clicks and tones we had no rational translation to their words but we knew what they were saying because we saw it in our minds eye the picture that is of what they were conveying to us and we could feel it deep within us like a recalibration or transfiguration of our cellular structure.

One of them then stepped forward, a large blue Pleiadian star brother, a lord of royal peace and power, like lapis lazuli and sapphire light he emanated pure blue bliss. "Be warmed my children, I come on behalf of the Great Pleiadian Star Mother's Council." He reached out and touched Jacob's third eye sending a transmitting vibrational frequency of electric blue purplish Indigo light right into his pineal gland and thalamus exciting Jacob energetically causing Jacob to involuntarily open his arms wide like he was on a cross. Jacob then received the anointing light transmission that I had received; he turned almost diamond right there before me as I witnessed his transfiguration. This was what had all just happened to me before Jacob had appeared when I had dissolved into light. I was now watching as a witness to my man what had just been done to me seconds ago. I was so honored I got to now witness my lover, my best friend, my twin flame become enlightened ... I could not believe it; this was better than any fairy-tale ever!

The Star Lord began to sing the tones he had sung to me just moments before. Colors swirled and twirled like energetic taffy all around us transmitted via the sound bath he gave forth a living light frequency that twas a pure energetic activation right to the chakric system of my man. Jacob began shaking kind of like when someone is having a seizure. I knew to trust in the process, his Kundalini had to be made resonant to the high high frequencies of the 5th density. I knew because this had all just happened to me just before. Jacob reached out his hand to me, our fingers met and a buzzing electrical current shocked us and we broke out into fits of laughter. "Beeee still and know you are God," the Star Lord said as he chuckled in deep tones of laughter like gongs reverberating through time and space.

When it was complete, we both looked at each other and hugged heart to heart light to light rainbow to rainbow. We were crying tears of crystalline dew. "Jacob, I feel so good, so beautiful, so on fire with life." Jacob responded, "Sophia this is always as I have seen you, and this is always what I have longed for ... this feeling that I have searched for in drugs sex and music. This feeling of joy and omnipotent awareness, this is what I always had remembered deep in my heart. Oh, Sophia that blue guy he is from a distant memory of mine, but I never thought he was real until now. Now it all is coming together that forever begging memory seeking to be rekindled like a flame is now is fully lit and blazing it has been answered .... halle freaking lujah we are born again."

Jacob then turned to the beings that enveloped us and bowed from his heart. He gently said, "I am Jacob this is my wife Sophia, but I think you already know that. Thank you, thank you so much for coming for us. I feel like I have been always looking for you seeking this moment out forever and now here we are here you are ... who you are you? Why does it feel as if I know you we know you, but I can't remember your name, I am so sorry I am just so overwhelmed with this feeling this energy, please tell us who you are."

A golden tall giant of a being stepped forth in garments of white light. He had a staff he held in one hand and a sword belted at his other side. He also had scrolls that hung from his belt and upon his staff there was a giant sphere of crystalline light that glowed and was alive sparkling like a tesla tower with electrical plasmic light rolling out like little bolts of lightning from it. His voice was like tones of a medicine bowl as he said, "We are the watchers; not what so many of you mortals have claimed as watchers with your false histories and rotten constructs. But the true Watchers, the guiding forces of good on Earth and all creation. I am Shalomanu, I am an elder of the Council of Light. We are your galactic family and come from all directions, all dimensions, literal emissaries who serve creation with all that we are. It is our duty and honor to watch over life. We are the ones all beings pray to who ask for protection and healing or even just help. We are your Guardian Angels; we are your guides. When we have incarnated into your world, we have been called Gurus Gods even, but we are just your humble protectors, your teachers, and most importantly your friends and family."

"We are The Council of Guardians, Ambassadors for Creation." A beautiful Goddess Deity like Queen said as she stepped forward with a crown of crystals upon her gorgeous shimmering golden light infused head. She held a glistening wand, a sceptre so regal it brought everyone's attention to it and to her. "We are referred to as the Galactic Confederation with whom our beloved kin the Sasquatch, the Star Nation brothers and sisters from across the galaxies, the Dragon Clans, the Fay or Faeries as the Devic Ones, the wise and wonderful Angelic beings, and all other sacred Deities all unite to work synergistically together as a family of light to bring enlightenment and liberation to the lesser more dense realms of life. We come to liberate all beings from the lesser realms from the plague of parasitic forces that have injected themselves onto the Earth from throughout the galaxies. My name is Sequorrrra and I am at your service." While this goddess who was super enchanting spoke to us, Jacob and I looked at one another at the exact same time with the exact same realization in our minds eye. We had the same image of Galadriel dream spell speak between us and we nodded to each other in silence as we agreed with one another. This Goddess who literally was made in the image of Galadriel also had quite a regal royal seriousness about her that gave one the impression of only speaking when spoke to, in other words we were to shut up and listen, for she not only spoke out loud to you but she also was able to speak directly to your Soul and no one else conveying messages meant just for you alone.

We were then shown a vision that was seeded into us by this Goddess standing before us, a vision of a council and a meeting hall full of ridiculously awesome beings all incredibly beautiful. They were gathered in the sky in what looked like a Sky Castle. Each life form there was so unique so rare and each one had a different vibrational signature which was like their own magical power you could say.

A small group of eight of these beautiful beings were gathered in the center of the mandala like seating arrangement in the hall. They had all activated their magical powers so to speak on a whole other level of intensity by way of their vibrational signatures getting turned on high by way of some sort of fancy Qi Gong moves. They then started to shine out of their foreheads a beam of light. I kid you not, a ray of light literally shone out of their 3rd eyes and was so freaking cool that it was like watching a sci fi fantasy movie play out but in real time. Yes it was thee best Broadway production ever, but fully real!

With all these beings' and all their magical powers all culminating together as one before us, we watched from off the side on the sidelines in utter awe and inspiration. We watched silently unable to look aware or even blink as all these beautiful beings of all kinds gathered in a mandala like template together and worked their magic together synergistically drawing a huge vortex of power together.

Every being that was there in that living mandala of magic all began chanting, meditating, levitating, doing magical mudras with their hands, and ultimately were holding space for the eight beings in the center. All the beings who sat around the central eight helped to optimize the powers of the eight whom seemed to be conjuring a form of what appeared to be a powerful hologram in the image of a Rubik's cube.

Ironically yes these central eight beings who were chanting in deep to high tones of light language, conjured up a literal Rubik's Cube of glowing rainbow light that generated a power that we could tangibly feel go up and down our backs through our spines like an alternating current of raw power or chi energy. It was like the different rays of light generated out from within the Rubik's cube was inherently connected to our chakras and what happened to the cube translated through our chakras; "as within so without, as above so below," the central figures spoke in unison closing the ceremony.

The Rubik's Cube, which was an absolute trip to see, was lit by six colors of light which were comprised of 9 cubes of each of those six colors. The cube kept switching around and around rearranging itself with its six colors. These six colors were literal same colors of our chakras red, orange, yellow, blue, green, and purple. It then was encapsulated by an absolute radiant golden white light that was like an aura around the whole cube. Out of the Rubik's Cube came the Holographic image of the Earth simultaneously and concentrically while animating a human body just within the Earth cube.

The Rubik's Cube also macrocosmically and then microcosmically was in the center of the Earth, planted like a giant seed of life. We could see the Earth and all the humans upon it, but we could also see a funnel within the tertian field of the Earth. The funnel was calling out beckoning to the Goo like a signal like a low whining hum magnetizing all the Black Goo from a concentric whole 360 degrees. It called to it like a magnet attracting all the Black Goo molecules and fibres right to the Rubik's Cube while simultaneously also pushing it all down through the funnel; shooting the Black Goo substance out of the bottom of the funnel into pure light! Much like a human who ingests, digests, assimilates, and then defecates shitting out the dark matter of waste.

Our attention was then brought back to a marvelous ancient looking Sasquatch all white and dreadlocked with jewels and shells and bones braided into his hair with robes that made him look like a Tibetan Monk. He shocked us by saying in perfect English, "I am Zepharo, Guide and Guardian of Truth. The clearing and cleaning of the Black Goo molecules and magicians who have infiltrated creation has been ordered through the spheres of Creation by the Council of Light and is being carried out by the Galactic Confederation. What you are being shown is the Council of the High Elders which has been formed to orchestrate both the planning and the orchestration of our operation that has come to be called in rough translation; The Sacred Kundalini Gateway for Metabolic Magnetic Distillation and Recalibration, or

SKGM2DR, or as we Squatch like to say, operation zero point of Black Goo Shit ..... ahahahahahahaaaaaaaa."

We could not help but laugh at the absolute hysterical bout of laughter Zepharo unleashed like thunder while we watched and listened seeing the history and timeline of all this planning. We observed the gathering of these genius masterminds and were able to conceive the whole plot and guidebook if you will regarding the whole operation. Zepharo then looked at us both and it was like wormholes opened in his eyes and we did dristi right there, sacred eye gazing for God knows how long we saw history through his eyes. No words can express everything he downloaded to us in that flash of second which in all actuality felt like an eternity of time, all the pain all the horror and the enslavement of his people of all people. It was both bitter and sweet as we saw little Squatches playing then having to run and hide from the Draco's who had captured and enslaved his people. God the horror!

"This idea involved creating a matrix and an assimilated world construct that would serve to be a magnetic trap that would draw all the Black Goo particles from all the densities and spheres of creation to a snare or funnel working as a trap to thus attract it all every last spore. The funnel created to draw the Black Goo and trap it, was created to appear to be a perfect destination for the feeding, breeding, and growing grounds for thee parasitic force of the Black Goo complex. It was disguised within the Earth which was created only to be a carbon copy of the higher ethereal form of its true copy. The Earth was made in the image of its higher expression in the Heavens, Aetherea, which is my true Home," Zepharo said. With a big exhalation he went on, "the Earth and all the Earthlings were designed and animated just for this cause and intention. They were made in the same engineering technology as the earth to be able to filter through their Shushumana, or central pillar of their spinal cord and nervous system through their toroidal fields within the engines or wheels or brains of their crystal oscillators, their Chakras. The Shushumana and Chakras have been designed to not only act as a battery which can sustain each organisms God Spark, or light body, in this assimilated matrix carbon copy of Aetherea; but to also sustain the electromagnetic body which is regulated by the seven major nerve ganglion centers known as the Chakras up the Spine or Tree of Life. These chakras serve as magnetic crystals of intelligence to draw the Black Goo down through the crown of the skull, down through the Chakras filtering distilling purifying out through the Roots of their Tree of Life Matrix down to the core crystal matrix of the Earth and the Rubik's cube core central intelligence that has been planted into both the very core of the Earth and each living being within it. This Rubik's cube has all the stored programming and coding to operate SKGM2DR. This Tree of Life or Spinal Cord and Nervous System Matrix within the Human Hybrid would mirror the outside Earth Matrix Ley Lines which would also run the electromagnetic battery of the Earth Matrix and also serve to magnetically draw all the damn Black Goo from the Interdimensional Galactic network of Infinity. As within so without as above so below would thus serve as the filtering and distilling equipment for the essence of life from the density of the material form of the Black Goo molecules that would be magnetically drawn to the lowest of the densities to this matrix and carbon copy world to be ingested digested and expelled and returned to pure light."

As I took this information in and contemplated it in my own logic and rationalization I realized this whole plan of SKGM2DR was really just like a French Press pressing down the coffee or tea particles inside the bodum just with a lot more finesse and its own built in compost sieve at the other end like an asshole.

The Sasquatch Elder then started talking again saying, "through the highest to the lowest densities of vibration sound color and overall frequency, the Black Goo pours into the funnel, then is pressed down to the lowest of creation to be gathered and concentrated then zero pointed, flushed out to be composted and returned to its own original blueprint which is light. As really all there is, is light."

As we could see through the eyes of these master guides, we realized as in real eyes seeing with sacred eyes to see sacred sight; that life is photonic particles in cosmic dances swirling whirling and twirling forming and shapeshifting over and over again into different forms. We then simultaneously got in crystal clear vision that we did in fact live in a plasmic universe and that we were all plasmic beings that were growing living and loving within the gardens of Infinity sewing, reaping exchange after exchange! Goddess it was all so mind blowing!

I looked to Jacob who was just as entranced as I was by this incredible experience, I squeezed his hand and although it felt more like air comprised of electrical currents of energy, I had to tell him what I was remembering and so I began to mind speak with him, speaking with no words, "Jacob, this is what Grandmother Shima referred to as the "Reset". Then I sent him through my mind's eye a memory of Shima telling me one of her stories. "Sophia my star on Earth, my great love, child of my heart; A great reset is coming and to speak in your language in a way that you will understand, this reset will be like defragging your computer doing a massive spyware and virus scan, completely downloading the systems with pure light which is just information, then shutting down to reboot and update. This is what the universal consciousness manifesting in all forms is going through. A massive reprogramming, reconfiguring, and frequency vibration shift. Like tuning your instruments, life in all existence is being tuned to an interdimensional tune, tone, or frequency a song of the heavens, a pulsation of energy that will like an EMP or electromagnetic pulse, take down all harmful properties that are not in alignment to this frequency or harmonic resonant tone through a harmonic convergence so great it is beyond all the powers of the Thunderbird, for this is a great culmination of all power from all beings in all directions coming to tone together in harmony like never before, this will be the song of songs, the hymn of hymns, the great chant that will break down Babylon and all the Black Goo Lords holds of power. There will be a mass electromagnetic pulse that will fire up the grid in liquid plasma, liquid cerebral spinal fluid, the kundalini energy will rise, the serpents head will extend and pierce through the veils. All beings who are able to come into coherence with this frequency will then be entrained into the field of light while the rest of the densities and properties thereof will be spontaneously be combusted and neutralized into photonic plasma returning to pure energy once again as this is what has been prophesized and so it is."

Shima appeared, "From past to present my Star my love, Sophia, I welcome you to my home darling. Jacob, welcome my sun, you two are cherished to us all, we know what you have been through and what have you done. Your service will go down into the records and the great Akash will always have you in the written legends of time and space, forever!"

Snapping me back from my memory that I was dream spell speaking over to Jacob, Shima brought me to the present and I screamed "Shima Shima Shim its you ...." it almost felt like I was supposed to focus and receive and not talk but I couldn't help myself. "Shhhhhhh quiet now beloved for we only have a little time left." Jacob and I's full attention was back to the moment, "We must now review" Shima said. "It has taken us quite a while to be able to reach you, for us your Guides and Guardians have been trying to reach you all, always, in all ways. We hear your prayers, your silent and sometimes very loud cries for help, for love, for light to guide you when you have felt lost and lonely. We have watched over you forever and we have so longed in our hearts to be able to answer you and be with you, to make contact. Always we have wanted to make contact and be close with you, assist you. All beings, all creation, we serve. We could not however heed your calls always and those of your humankind, for there has been such a dark negative force field around the Earth which has acted as a barrier which we cannot always penetrate. Our responses to you have been muffled, been reduced to small whispers and fleeting glimpses of our light just sweet little nothings of our love when in fact we pour it out over the Earth continuously. In order for the receptivity of our aide to be achieved, we need light, joy, and high vibrational consciousness to open the way for our aide to be channeled through. For our resonance to be entrained to you there needs to be a resonance that you hold for us. Like attracts like, what you give you will receive. When the human race gives off fear, hatred, judgement, and wickedness well that is what it receives. When your world began to pulse gloom and doom and despair projected upon the youth and families entraining them into a sickness a plague on the Earth of depression, your level of consciousness dropped. Those of you who had staged large die offs within your climate crisis response all of which was an absolute mind control trip, yes we watched as the humans got their children to die to lay down their lives in a theatrical demonstration of death, the energy on your planet plummeted. However, you Sophia and Jacob, you took to the canvas took to the waves and with the help of others just like you .... You reversed the curse. You changed the consciousness like true alchemists; you took the hatred and sewed love, the darkness and made it light. Because of this we were able to use the energy you all created and make gateways for connection which turned the tides. Your music art and dance along with the technologies your friends and others shared, the healers and mystics of your world, I say, the light workers' and lovers ... the dancers the singers, the storytellers, the yogis, the mediums, and channelers' ... these ones made the door open and where there was a door made open, we would enter and create a gateway for love and light to go both ways. Because Sophia we are quite resonant with each other, I of all the Guides and Guardians was able to reach you and what a blessing that has been ...but to the future we must now go for we must make the great Ouroboros complete, we must mend the Sacred Hoop, return the Circle to Full Circle and restore the world to as it was in the beginning before all the Black Goo invaded, so shall it be in the End."

Then suddenly a magical rainbow Dragon Serpent appeared in chains of gold bracelets ringlets necklaces and a crown that accentuated the colors of her shimmering scales, she hissed out her words very melodiously; "The forcccccce of ssssickness and enssslavement which was as an error or era of time that had been maligned now for agesssssssss, but now it isssss being corrected once and for all. To do this the intelligencessssssss of all creation have had to engineer and create a funnel which can work to pusssssh the evil forcessss manifessssssting as parasssitessss through a complex processssss much like your digestive system'ssssss metabolisssm. The Black Goo moleculessss have had to be gathered and drawn together to be created into form ssssuch assss food isss, ssso that it could be ingesssted and then metabolized by travelling through a wormhole to be processed and asssssssssimilated, then ultimately exxxxxxpelled and flussssshed away into oblivion. Through a ssssssspontaneous combusssstion of power like the fire in your belliessss which breaksss down all the food you eat as in metabolism, the Black Goo moleculessss have been gathered and formed into this

Earth matrixxxx you two know assss your Home, your planet and they have been densssified into a form and fed into the Earth Matrixxxx to be consumed by a black hole vacuum of power through the sssso called gravity lawsssssss. There they have been being digesssssted assimilated and now through this activation of light we are sssssharing with you and have been sharing to Earth and all of its inhabitants, the Black Goo molecules and all associated in ressssssonance to it, will be combusted into a spiritual fire of light as it has all been designed and engineered to do. This combussssstion process is like the defecation processsss where the unnecesssssssary elementsss are eliminated. The whole of 4D and below will be the actual fecessss that will be expelled from the living organism of creation and no longer have an exxxxistence for it will all be composssted back into the central core light lattice. I am MMMMmwaatwanneee, I have sssspoken"

Many oooohs, ahhhhs, and uuuuuuus were made in clicks and tones by the beings that circled around us and then one more being stepped forward, an emerald amphibious creature being that did not appear male nor female but was exquisitely beautiful none the less. "I am Kermu it is so very good to meet you again as we have all known each other always as we are all really one as stated and proclaimed in the Law of One. This now is the hour this now is the time, the alignments have been made the vibration has reached the epicenter, you have successfully raised the cone of power and the freedom bells ring. The world shall sing, liberation codes manifesting even now .... Go Beloveds ... Return again and know we will be there soon with directions ..." They started to swirl; the worlds were colliding ... the wondrous creatures began to fade .... "Don't go away" I could hear Jacob trying to call for them ... totally oblivious to what would happen next. "Nooooooooooo don't go" Jacob was crying out like a child for his Mother for his family as the worlds collided and fell again dropping us down down down. I could hear my man crying whimpering, as I saw the incredible light of a thousand suns that we had bathed in just moments ago vanish further and further into a speck, like a distant star in a night sky.

CHAPTER NINE

CODE RED

"Life will give you whatever experience is most helpful for the evolution of your consciousness. How do you know this is the experience you need? Because this is the experience you are having at the moment."
Eckhart Tolle

If it were not for the fact that Thomas had a key to our pad, King and Avatar would have brought down the door they were so jacked with adrenaline. Jacob and I were so deep in sleep, deep in vision, both reaching for our kin like children being taken from their parents, a feeling all to familiar for us both.

Thomas came shrieking through the door. He was ordering us to "wake up now", while Mill Boy and his lady, Avatar and his lady, King, his lady, and his dog all came in following upon his heels like a Scooby Doo episode.

Jacob was like "what the Gods," rubbing his eyes trying to shake the vision. Thomas was talking so fast, "what are you two high on Ludes (as in Quaaludes), I have been calling and calling, we all have, we have got to go, it is time, Code Red Bro .... CODE RED!!!!!"

I felt like I was dropping, I could feel my arm out extended, my hand reaching for those most magical and beloved beings, my family, my kin. I was being ripped away by Thomas and his commands; his intensity was like a vacuum for my fall as his adrenaline anchored me back down to the earth like a rude smack down. The dropping from Infinity of 5D to 4D, finally crashing into 3D and the literal consciousness of the underworld was a wicked slap in the face which caused me to burst out crying, screaming "Nooooooooooooooooooooo."

It was too much, too hard, too fast, too appalling. I felt abandoned all over again like when I was a child being taken from my parents who had been forcefully arrested and taken off to jail for so called terrorism; just for keeping me from being vaccinated and for speaking out against the system or the beast as they referred to it.

That is when Avatar's lady, Mercy came over picking up on my state and she started singing to me, singing while she held me and caressed my trembling shaking body. Jacob snapped on, "baby baby, are you ok? I know baby we were there; they were real...I know baby I did not want to go either. Baby can you hear me. Look into my eyes Sophia, look into my eyes." I looked up from my waterfall of tears and saw him. Our eyes locked and light flowed through him into my body warming me.

Thomas said, "hey I don't claim to know what you two are talking about, but we have got to go, NOW!" I reconfigured, Queen rushed over to help me while King's dog Buddha came and started washing my face with his tongue. Rebekah, Mill Boy's girlfriend, pulled out her phone and put on the news. While we had been traveling through the cosmos, here on Earth war had broken out and the threat of a mass EMP was becoming more and more real.

"There are a number of fires lit further away inland, the city is getting looted. The world is beginning to bear down in what feels like a ring of fire in the birth canal," Mercy said. Mercy who had lost her 3 children to illness, illness that developed after their vaccinations, was a strong woman who came from the ghetto, from the gang world on the streets. "This world is dying, and it is raging with demons getting sucked back to Hell. We have got to go girl, while we can still get out of here." Her words were strong and the grounding force for what was needed to activate our planned-out "Code Red" protocols.

Jacob kissed me hard and fast, got up and started getting dressed while the news continued to stream now hooked up on our speakers. The reporter's voice was shaking panicking and as the news broadcasted loud and clear for us all to hear the play by play of insanity unfolding out was no doubt the cause for Thomas's abrupt shakedown. "Thomas, I said, I am sorry honey, I get it now, you had to get us, I know baby I know." I reached out and grabbed him, hugging him to me like a teddy bear. He looked like a wounded dog, he felt terrible for causing my outburst and obvious pained trauma from the fall back into my body and into the reality here. "Oh Sophia, I am so sorry, you Gaia's got to tell us later where you were just now in your dreams, based on what I just saw there looks like you Gaia's were travelling out beyond the stars."

"No doubt brother, we went there … we went to the other side … man the beings there the Sasquatch!" Jacob said as he went to the storage closet and was grabbing our bug out bags and paperwork our passports and everything else we had compiled onto memory cards, including our latest performance that we had just uploaded, and the money we had saved for this exact time not knowing what to expect as the world went through the great Reset it had coming. "Sasquatches say what, said King, you saw a Squatch? Was there an old male white haired one with monks' clothes on? That is my brother from the divine mother … did he say his name was Zepharo?" "Whaaaaaaaat, yes he did say his name was Zepharo … you know him?" Jacob was shocked staring at King. King chuckled, "that brother is da bomb, he be so funny, he has been teaching me since I was a kid, I just never told no one not even you Gaia's. It just has been between him and me."

"Hey Gaia's … don't mean to break up this little show and tell story session but we have got to go, YO!" Avatar our Alpha was making a move, "time to go, I guess," I said shaking my head. I got my legs working again, no longer paralyzed, and like a sailor back on shore I stumbled to my closet. I got dressed with the help of Mercy and Rebekah. I pulled back my long hair and tied it up into a ponytail. I hastily put my socks and boots on, and we all went running for the door.

Their bikes were all pulled into our fenced yard. As one after the other was taken back out onto the street, we zipped up our suits put on our helmets and fired up the electronic engines. Jacob and I had our matching camo bike suits on and helmets, he winked at me pulled down his visor and flew off. We took off out of our place like a blaze of glory, my crew, my fleet. We filed down the highway interweaving between cars all honking their horns at us. We were racing for our trail head to duck out and disappear upon the old fire roads up into the hills, like a flash we zoomed by people barely touching the ground.

I could not look back not even for a second. Tears were streaming as I said goodbye inside of my heart to Jacob's and my love shack. For this past four years that home had been our refuge from the world, our sanctuary and safe haven, our place where we could go to shut down and transcend the pains and sufferings of a world gone mad. It was so hard to have to leave it all behind, our plants, our art, our crystals, and instruments. It was like having your best friend just break up with you, as our love shack as we lovingly referred to it as was our best friend.

I said goodbye to my computer where all my magic had come together, my cherished treasures, my jewellery, my pictures of us all travelling the world … said goodbye to it all as it was all just a speck now in the distance. We rode hard to the trail that we would take to escape, weaving through traffic, not stopping once. We came to the trail head and lifted off the paved road of the highway onto the dirt fire truck road that led us inland into the Park of Topanga Canyon.

We were so gifted by life that we had become so close to Avatar Mill Boy and King, for they had worked the closest with "Poppa D" and had access to all the right technologies that would help us get to Poppa D's fortress in the mountains as the world began to really split apart and tremble shaking in birthing pains.

It was Poppa D that had shown the boys how to build free energy technologies using quantum magnetic resonators. It was because of the magnetic resonating motorcycles that they had built for us that we were able to literally fly through the hills and canyons and reach Poppa D's just in time for the great shift, the EMP, and the ascension access through the Stargates opening by the fleets of the Galactic Confederation.

It was this kind of technology that the boys had played with that had inspired them to build our own actual Jedi hovering crafts that transformed from a motorbike to literally flying craft that had no engine no sound no need for gas basically. These transformer cyclists fed off the earth's magnetic energy and could zoom over the land virtually undetectable. So, we flew over the valleys the canyons and hills climbing higher and further away from the coastline up into the wilderness beyond the madness of the world below. We climbed higher and higher further and further from the 4th Age of the Archons and their A.I. racing towards our freedom and 5D. This was our moment; it was our time, the time of the luminous ones, the time to shine.

CHAPTER TEN

MERKABA

**"How you vibrate is what the universe echoes
back to you in every moment."
Panache**

We had been training for years before we had left for our journey across the world and we had even had a practice session literally the day after we had returned from our trip even though we were exhausted and overwhelmed by the traumas we had experienced along the way. At the order of Avatar though we had to prepare he said … even if it were just one last time crazy how he was always right.

You see it was a long time ago under the orders of our Alpha dog Avatar that we had all committed to a special high vibrational diet; we became devoted to our daily methods of operation which included physical training, yoga, meditation, and prayer work. We had all given up drugs and smoking, but we did engage in plant medicines such as peyote and Ayahuasca from time to time in ceremonies.

With our live music we would entertain a group we called dance church, a little thing for our group of homies and friends who we still hung out with and kept in our social circle. We also would host laughter yoga sessions as Poppa D had taught us all these exercises and activities would help us build our Etheric body. King led those as he said he had a secret friend (I now realize that secret friend was Zepharo, the Squatch) who was an excellent teacher of laughter yoga, lol. Poppa D had laid out a to do list for us which included different exercises for our mental, astral, emotional, psychic, spiritual, and physical bodies. He had said that we would one day need to be able to raise our own bio-electric frequency within our own bodies to the level that would allow for us to be resonant with the frequency of 5D.

We practiced igniting our chakras, fanning the sacred flame within each of our crystal oscillators or centers of our nervous system A.K.A. our chakras. We had to not just lift weights but lift our frequency up to become more and more harmonized to a higher level of vibration.

We were assigned to build our electromagnetic frequencies to initiate and activate our Merkabas, our light bodies. "The Merkaba is your ticket to 5D." Poppa D would say, "With this golden ticket to the 5th Age of peace you will ascend like the masters who had successfully completed their own Rainbow Light Body Initiation while in their Earthly flesh. To do this your Kundalini must rise and with love as thy fuel, you will get the wheels of the engines or chakras of the sacred Merkaba to get fired up like a rocket for take-off. To me this is the Proud Mary that keeps on burning as you be rolling, rolling down the river … of life." Poppa D was a total nerd, but you had to love him!

The Merkaba, Poppa D had taught us was our chariot of our souls, our crystalline auric orb of light that was like a craft or spaceship that would elevate enlighten and carry us beyond 3D right past 4D and ascend all the way back up to 5D. Past the Archons or dwellers on the threshold of 4D, our chariots would like Arjuna and Krishna carry us past the battle of the ones who blocked us all from reaching enlightenment and break out of Babylon to the other side. "Nothing can stop the righteous, not the gravest of monsters nor the wickedest of demons can stop a chariot of holy fire." Poppa D would say, you know he really could ignite a passion to burn inside one's imagination. He spoke often of Krishna; he was a devotee after all and had said he remembered his life's when he dwelled in Dwarka and existed as a son of light in a noble and decadent city of true royal deities.

So, we did Pranayama or breathe work as he had instructed for us to do, we chanted, used tuning forks and medicine bowls, gongs. Whatever we could get our hands on to build our vibrational light bodies. Poppa D also had gifted us awesome technologies which emitted resonant frequencies designed from the work of one Dr. Royal Rife and his Rife Code frequencies which anti-doted illness and kept the bodies systems alive and strong. As best we could we all lived off superfoods, which Poppa D had always growing in his farm and labs at his fortress.

With Poppa D's teaching and preaching to Avatar Mill Boy and King all the time about what was coming down the pike showing them and sharing with them all the time an intensifying message of a great shift coming, he ever since he had adopted us ... sought out to prepare us all for the great reset. He chuckled when he lectured about the big bang theory, "a total joke of science and evolution" he would say that you have all been taught was the creation of the Earth. "No not the creation but instead the emancipation" were his words upon the matter. It was so crazy like total sacrednicity how Poppa D came into our lives, then Shima showed up for me, followed by Madame Tavares, then the "Wise Ones" it was like a string of pearls that just kept coming all along the same line of message thought word and deed.

Poppa D's warnings about how time was running out became incessant as we became more and more famous. It alarmed Avatar Mill Boy and King so bad, that they made us all commit to the Mystery School of the Heart as we called our discipleship and Jedi training operation, which would have us all commit by our blood to prepare each day in every way for the ultimate day when all our trainings would come through for us and pay off. Well this day was now as we all were racing up into Topanga State Park.

Avatar Mill Boy and King had been the ones who knew the most about what was going on, what was coming, and what was to be in our future. Avatar could feel the ripening or quickening he said, "it is coming Gaia's we have to prepare, there is not one thing ... nothing ... that is more important than our training and preparation now. There is Nothing capitol N more important than psyching up for what it to come now at any moment. Remember in the Hopi Prophecy when they say you have been telling everyone it is the 11th hour ... I can feel it in my bones peeps, it is the mother of hours now! We do not only do this for ourselves, but we do it on behalf of all the others who cannot. Who do not have any support any knowledge or privileged access to the resources we do? By our own trained and disciplined level of consciousness we can through our collective power, raise the frequency of others with us, like leaven in the bread, it is up to us to be able to hold space for the countless others who are sick dying dead or tortured daily. Can you dig it, can you handle it? If yes, then prick yourself with this blade, (he said as he pulled out a jade blade from its sheath, a magnificently carved jade blade with a very pointy top,) and then with your own blood commit to this now. Seriously, If anyone complains in the future, you will be reminded by your blood of this oath."

You could say Avatar always took things to the extreme, he lived on 3 hours of sleep a day and he said he had star nation guides who were guiding him in what actions he had to complete daily. He said they were channeling to him continuously on how to circumvent the Archons and be able to outwit them in the game of monopoly and chess playing out. I had realized I was not the only one who had a Spirit guide or two a few years ago when Avatar would go on about a new download he was receiving from the Syrians or Arcturians or the mysterious "Blueprint Technicians" he was always going on about.

How could you argue, debate, or deny such powerful wisdom for Avatar he is wise beyond his years, as a boy he grew up way too fast. He was an elder in a young man's body. Of course, we all became disciples of Avatar King and Mill Boy's adopted father Poppa D, for he came in like a knight in shining armor into our lives and gave us all direction and purpose for our lives.

Within our first year of training with Avatar we all began calling him "General" because he was so bossy and would not relent as he barked out commands and gave orders to us. But for what it is worth as I was flying up the hills in the canyons heading towards Poppa D's, I was so grateful for Avatar for his diligence and his whole "Code Red" action plan that he with his boys made into a virtual video game for us to train continuously. So to be quite honest I could do this in my sleep, this ride up the hills ... this "Code Red" action plan that had been a virtual trip that we had all tripped out on in every way for the past couple of years straight.

As I reflect on all of this from 5D land over the rainbow, I am called to really let you all as readers in on some background information regarding "The General," our beloved Avatar and my crew. Since all of us had come from the shelters right, and since all of us had been traumatized heavily from a very young age, and literally since we by law vibrate at the frequency based on the sum total of our experiences and capacity to be resilient, right ... to tie it all together now to make my point ... the universe now will echo back to any one of us what we project out as in a call and response or law of attraction give and receive like attracts like. Now Avatar for example, he was such a stern and intense General because, well, that was just the way he had to be since he was born.

If you had had the childhood he had, you would have your issues too. You see the boys in my tribe, my brothers, they were all taken from their parents who had like mine been escorted off to jail or in Avatar's case shot dead point blank right in front of his eyes. For those of us who had parents that had been taken to prison or slave shops as we called em'; ya we knew exactly what they were and where our parents were being taken even as kids. We knew what would happen to them there and it was an awful sinking defeating feeling to experience that knowing which was our parent's fate as they were taken to the hell holes of a prison. But Avatar his parents got shot point blank right in front of him, robbed raped and left to die Avatar was only a boy to young to even remember his name or age. That was why we didn't argue with him, in our own way we respected him for making it through all that he had gone through.

With all our parents being taken from us in one form or another, we had all ended up as orphans left lost and alone, put into a living hell center known as a shelter. These shelters I shit you not felt more like a kill center. For reals we had to fight for our food, for clothes, for drugs and we had to try to not get trafficked out for sex by the agents that ran those places. For reals it was a hard knock life for us and many did not survive.

Beyond all of this we had to try to remain the same person as the one who was brought there, for it had a scary way of making you forget all the happiness and good food, family, and even fun if you were lucky enough to have experienced any of those things before you were sent there. That was the biggest challenge surviving the heart wipe or mind wipe if you will by the reality of trauma that was the environment these shelters held.

Mill Boy and Avatar they had met in the shelter when they were just six and eight years old both scared and both like Natives being taken into a residential school. It was not long in the shelter before they both got raped and so called initiated into the Home. After that they had both been sold out for work like slaves. They also both got beaten time and time again by the older kids in the Home who tried to relieve their own messed up pain and suffering upon them.

Avatar and Mill Boy spent 4 years in that hell hole together. They had as a silver lining however become like brothers even though Mill Boy was adopted out. Poor Mill Boy his foster parents were drug addicts and were just fostering him for money which was typical. What they did though was particularly extra messed up even for the assholes they were but what they did to boot was even more unfortunately typical as well, for his foster parents sold him for sex and had him deliver drugs for them as well as it was a huge felony to be caught with drugs in those days.

Then one day Mill Boy just took off, he threw the drugs in a trash and just ran, sick of the shame and soreness. He had come to a place where he could hear stomping feet and the banging of trash can lids and drums made from buckets. He had just turned twelve years old. Avatar who was a few years older than Mill Boy was in the warehouse with a crew of runaways doing what they called stomp dancing. King was in there too. Mill Boy crawled through a hole in the wall that had been half hazard covered by a piece of cardboard. He said he sensed his brother's heart and like a moth to a flame he was drawn to it.

Avatar stopped the kids from seizing him, for it really was like every man for themselves out here. Mill Boy was ready to fight back but Avatar cried out for him to come, recognizing him instantly and embraced him like a blood brother who had found his missing sibling once again.

The crew adopted Mill Boy and taught him all the tricks of their trade. They taught him how to break into houses, cars, and buildings, how to hack into the alarm security system of a "safe car" so that you can steal it. How to hack into the so called "safe security" systems being implemented all over in businesses and people's homes. He learned how to turn off the surveillance cameras and how to become invisible to the agents. They learned how to program code into the forming matrix, to hack it and to destroy bots and A.I. sensors. They also learned how to build devices like in Mad Max where they built engines, weapons, and labs for cooking up and making drugs not to mention alternative technologies.

The boys did well over the next few years and lived like successful businessmen. They had raves, underground parties, and casinos. They operated a full-time underground business of spying, hacking, and coding specialists for more and more powerful people. They were getting a bit too good for their own good and though and that was when they got busted.

Swat teams came in by the droves. Most the guys and ladies that were over 18 either got themselves killed so that they would not have to go to jail or be drafted into the army and government agencies. The others that were still underage like Mill Boy and Avatar ran as the older ones shielded them creating a diversion.

Avatar who was 17 almost 18 years old and Mill Boy who was now 15, got picked up by an actual decent cop. The cop took the boys to the Shelter where I had just been dropped off a few months before, also the place where Jacob had been living for 6 months now with his best friend Thomas, who like Mill Boy and Avatar, grown up in the shelters together and had become soul brothers.

A few days later King showed up on his own, he had been wondering around by himself dodging authorities as best he could, following the GPS on the phone Avatar had been able to hide so that it would not be taken when he was admitted into the Shelter.

King was almost 18 and only had a few days before he would be too old to stay in a shelter. But he knew that if he could get admitted they would give him some money and maybe a job so that he would not have to go back living on the streets.

Over the next few days, the boys all connected through music. Jacob would be playing his guitar and singing when the others began dropping beats and beat boxing to his music.

After King was released when he got 18, he came over all the time as he was given a job as a dishwasher at a restaurant just a block away. The boys would go on making music from there on and I who had fallen in love with Jacob became more and more comfortable practicing using my voice and allowing my throat chakra to trust itself to the point where I could throw down the spells that wanted so powerfully to come out of me like Dragon's fire.

After nine months of getting to be protected by the guys and my new boyfriend Jacob, our little fantasy life that we had managed to be blessed with changed yet again. We had all bonded together like adhesive crazy glue, so grateful for the easy peaceful vibes and trust that we shared together. None of us had been fostered out because we were too old and could fight back or have the courage to just run away, so we had managed to take over the shelter and not even the agents would mess with us. It was like we were being protected by invisible allies.

One day, like the day before Avatar's 18 Birthday, a man named William Dollard rolled in with a strange looking car. He was a quirky fellow. He had a sparkle in his eye and a smirk on his face. His aura was fantastical. He looked around as if he were making sure he was at the right place, looked down at his papers and then promenaded to the door.

We had all gathered around the window when he had appeared as we had been waiting for the Chinese food delivery guy to show up. We were amazingly stoned and had ordered food like an hour ago and we were getting impatient when this guy showed up.

We heard him enter and we stayed back so he would not see us all. We all ducked into a room as an agent came out of the office area of the shelter and introduced them self to him. Then the Chinese food guy showed up, so we ditched the scene and followed our bellies, paying off the delivery dude, and mowing down on the food as we escaped out of the door to the backyard.

We had just finished eating when an agent came out to summon Avatar to the office. "Oh, shit said Avatar, what the fuck now?" He left and I noticed Mill Boy getting extremely anxious. I came over and I held his hand and tried to console him.

After what had seemed like forever, Avatar came running out and said pack your stuff peeps you're all coming with me." "Where?" cried Mill Boy, he hated change. "We are being adopted (Avatar said laughing) well, I am being adopted like right before my birthday, crazy hey … and since I won't go without you guys this crazy fool wants us all!"

"What?" Mill Boy was rightfully confused. Avatar responded saying "the crazy slick guy is adopting us, I get a really good vibe off him, he told me confidentially as he forced the agent out, (we never called agents by their names as they didn't feel human,) that he had found out about me by researching my code. He had also tied me together with my hacking record, found me by the hidden code I left in the Matrix for potential business clients and he wants to teach us and train us and give us work building free energy technology! I asked him point blank what the Hell he wanted with me and he showed me a file of my work of hacking and the things that I had built. He knew everything about me, it's so surreal like I can't freaking believe this and he wants us to come work for him, like right now, and since I am not 18 yet, he wants to adopt me to make it official and to get us the hell out of here. He totally understands I am not leaving without you guys that we are a family now so he says if we help him destroy the system, the beast then he will take us all … he literally laughed saying the more the merrier! This is our chance Mill Boy, we have got to do this, my gut tells me GO!"

So that is how it all started, that was when Avatar and Mill Boy and us even eventually King all got to live up in the country away from the city, hacking, spying, building free energy technologies and weaponry for this mad scientist that we loved named William Dollard. Since Mr. Dollard and William seemed way too formal for our favorite man in the world, we all lovingly came to refer to him as "Poppa D" or the "Godfather" depending on our mood.

Here we all were now years later riding our motorbikes like jet planes straight to Poppa D We were trained to make this getaway and get to his fortress hidden in the hills for the past several years now. We ripped through the dirt path, which was an old fire route for fire trucks to go inland into the hills to fight fires. We were completing the game plan that had been set as "Code Red" many moons ago by Avatar King and Mill Boy when they had begun to really get to the bottom of what was really going on in the world, as was taught to them or revealed to them by Poppa D.

We climbed the path as helicopters drones and air force flew overhead. Avatar and King had built into our helmet's laser beams; I shit you not, which we could fire off on command to take down drones. It was awesome; I must admit! After all Avatar like I had mentioned was a serious gamer, so everything in reality that he created always had to match up to the level of a high end virtual game. Avatar, he literally was the guy who could design and create all the bad ass virtual video games people wasted their lives away playing.

Now while the frequencies of the 6G and now 7G waves were taking over the grids of powerlines, the ley lines of the earth screamed out in resistance to the radiation and heat and began to rip apart and to shake from within. It was as if they were cooking the planet like a potato in a microwave, making the once hard potato, turn to mush and crack open. Since the 5G frequencies had been initiated and deployed back in 2020 people had been rendered sterile more and more, they had been diagnosed with cancer by the hundreds of thousands if not millions, and drained of all of their life force causing their immunities to shut down. Due to these harmful radiating attacks upon our immune system people were not only getting sick and becoming chronically fatigued and in pain but were also becoming more and more susceptible to every bio engineered disease that was being thrown at us like a pitcher on the mound firing away at a whole team of swingers.

As fire smoke could be seen looming up all over Southern California, war was breaking out all over the world. The revolt of humanity began to beat like a throbbing water drum.

My crew and I, we were in a video game going full speed … dodging the eyes of the helicopters flying by, taking out drones, ducking into the bush, and going into camo mode. What was left of wildlife was fleeing as well. Coyotes and mountain lions that were not afraid of us looked stoic as we zoomed by.

We drove on with tears streaming down our faces, knowing in our hearts the cold terror of fear that must be rattling the cages of the people all over the world who had not prepared themselves for this moment. We knew that the loss of life was going to be huge and that all the animals and elements that were being destroyed was all a part of the plan and was technically beyond our ability to control or help. What comforted us as I sent my psychic message to our group via our hive mind connect well and my microphone within my helmet as a copy that, was that we would all be reconnecting, reuniting again in 5D.

What was most important at this moment was making it to poppa D's. We knew that if we didn't make it to the fortress before getting caught that we would all surely die without being able to ascend with our pod group the way Poppa D had planned and explained to us when he trained us for this day.

So, despite the pain of leaving everything we knew behind, watching it all go up in flames, and feeling the war drums as they were banging closer and closer together quickening like a baby's heartbeat, we raced ahead. Fueled by adrenaline and the sole focus of getting to Poppa D; we kept our eyes clear, our hands on the throttle hard, and persevered no matter what. We raced through those hills and canyons like we were in Red Bull Rampage.

The motorbikes our boys had made were like hover crafts. You know like the ones you see in Star Wars that the Jedi's rode. They were silent, based on free energy technology and engineered by the best of mechanics in Avatars command. They could not be detected by heat as they had no thermal imprint. Each of us had our own. They were like Tesla cars that had been made and operated virtually with an automated service of and A.I. component that was able to calculate optimal movements and pathways automatically steering our crafts to the designated destination point programmed into it. They were ridiculously awesome with the most efficient and God speed capacity. Literally the trick was to just stay on. Also as a side note, and as an ongoing joke in our crew, King refused to leave his dog Buddha behind, so he built on his craft a special part for his dog to ride, complete with his dog Buddha having not only his own suit goggles but helmet as well.

We rode fast and maintained total discretion from the ridiculous amount of helicopters air force and tanks at the order of Martial Law now released upon society. I felt like I did the first time I rode a horse,

I had to let go, I had to trust, and I had to get out of my own way and allow for the intelligence of my ride to take me where I needed to go.

I had psyched myself up over the years by picturing my seastars and I as the Valkyries. We would go out on our own to train bare breasted riding our crafts through the hills as if they were Pegasus's'. Just like the Valkyries we in my mind's eye were fierce, fearless ready willing and able to do what needed to be done. I would imagine us as supernatural women fully in our Avatar bodies riding free and wild on our Pegasus just like the old stories I had read from Norse mythology and that I was Freyja going into spiritual battle. We were heroes not victims of fate. I saw us as women warriors riding into our victory through war torn realms taking out our enemies by our own powers of zero point frequencies that we could shoot out of our mind's eye like a laser as we wielded our mighty swords of righteousness upon the wicked.

Mercy, Rebekah, Queen, and I we were ready for this moment and the rush that I felt as I watched my seastars blaze the trail ahead of me gave me the courage to step into my Freya archetype and ride like the Goddess I had trained to become. Queen who was King's lady and whom yes, we named her "Queen" since when King had fallen in love with her many years ago now, she had already had 26 names but didn't resonate with any of them. So naturally King said, "Well my lady, I need a Queen fit for this King ... so if it be ok with you, I am going to call you my Queen." Ya and from there it just stuck. Well today Queen shone like the true Queen she had become, she was at the lead of our pack and rode towards Poppa D's as if she really was a Valkyrie warrior. In a blaze of glory my girls came through and showed our boys how it was done as they filed in to the entrance to Poppa D's in perfect formation.

As we dismounted out bikes at the entrance of Poppa D's we could feel the Earth was shaking tremor after tremor below our bikes and feet. There were fires now everywhere and we watched briefly the smoke plumes rage. We could only imagine how traffic would be sprawled out congesting the highways everywhere making no way for people to escape. "The coastline seems to be sinking into the sea" said Avatar who was still streaming live news from within his ear bot. "There are cracks dividing the roads. Sink holes swallowing up the ground taking with it cars, houses, buildings, and everything else built on top of it, including whole freeways. It sounds like all the people are desperately trying to save themselves. God help them. Gaias I gotta say ... we did it we made it just in the nick of time, phewwwwwww oh my God we did it!!!!" Avatar then starting crying wailing more like it, he fell to his knees and just let it all out as he cradled the Earth in child's pose kissing the ground. One by one than we all fell to our knees too and cried in horror and in gratitude that we had made it up to this point and were still alive ... alive and safe at Poppa D's.

Yes had it not been for Poppa D and his safe guarded secret fortress, we would be with all those scrambling folk that we had zoomed by, seeking safety seeking a way out of the sinking coastline, searching for help where there was none that could be given.

CHAPTER ELEVEN

POPPA D

**"Everything is energy. Match the frequency of the reality
you want, and you cannot help but get that reality.
It can be no other way. This is not philosophy.
This is physics."**
Albert Einstein

Now I got to ask myself how I could have made it this far into the story without introducing you to Poppa D Seriously, like who is this guy you must be wondering. Who is this man who I keep talking about? I have mentioned before that Poppa D was our teacher, our beloved liberator, the man who had saved us all by giving us the keys to escape the Matrix. Not to mention the guy that had adopted us all and had opened the doors to our higher purpose. The man that was Avatar, Mill Boy, and King's employer, our beloved Godfather Poppa D Well Poppa D he was our greatest Angel for without him we would never have become the people we were today nor have been able to change the timelines as we had through our movement and messages.

Poppa D he was the man that had been solely responsible for turning Avatar, Mill Boy, and King from frogs into princes. A man who loved them as a real father and who had taught them just about everything they know. He was the man that had made all of what we are possible; he was our first divine intervention who had opened the door for us to reach up higher than just being mere pawns, drug dealers, hackers, criminals.

Going back Poppa D was an ex Aerospace Engineer among many other levels of titles and high-ranking positions. He had been involved in DAARPA, in Top Secret classified Underground projects that were officially off the books, and had many years of behind the scenes exposure to both Alien Files and Laboratories that dissected probed and reengineered not just alien technology but alien genetic coding and DNA reproduction.

His time in underground bases were spent handling government top agency projects where he reengineered Alien Ships which had been shot down and brought to these secret underground bases. He had been trained and mentored by high ranking officials since he was sixteen years old giving him access to records that most people did not even know existed. This kind of access was very limited, but it was Poppa D's personality that won trust for him by those top-secret agents for they thought he was too young and too naive to be a threat.

Poppa D talked to no one, he had no personal life, he had left his family and few friends behind when he had been brought to MIT at an early age and never looked back. When his parents died, he stopped all communication completely and went mute and only wrote and conveyed things by written document until his staged death. Since his staged death he had all but become forgotten about officially.

Nikola William Dollard was Poppa D's real name and we found out that he had been discovered to be a genius when he was only five years old. He had been on the cover of magazines, wrote about in papers, whole documentaries were even made about him as he grew up. As we would push for information from Poppa D as to who he was and where he had come from he told us that his parents were everything to him and that once he had been recognized for the genius he was he had been taken from them, studied upon and researched like a lab rat. He said he had hated being in the public's eye for he was a hermit, a wizard that needed his own Ivory tower to do his research and invent his great tools and machines and that was why he agreed to go underground for there he could be left alone no longer pushed into doing interview after interview being probed and poked at. He didn't like people knowing about his past because he said it was not who he really was. That he had acted his way through it all and that was why he basically had just gone mute like me.

At the early age of fourteen he was given a full scholarship to MIT as his IQ was rumored to be perfect. Yes, Nikola William Dollard was described as being the "Perfect Specimen" by cutting edge doctors and scientists whose research was based on the fringe fields of science and medicine. It was said by many that knew him, that he had a passion for understanding everything and would need to be able to stand within everything to be able to absolutely get it, hence his obsessive compulsive need to take apart every bit of technology he could get his hands since an early age. Poppa D's love for taking apart whole car engines, computers, washing machines and so on from an early age led him to later being able to take apart U.F.O.s and alien weaponry that was found on board the ships. He would take every little bit of what he was working upon apart so that he could be able to reassemble it again reengineering it to make it even better than it was before or make it more of a harmonic rather than dissonant piece of tech through the operating frequencies that ran them both alien and human tech alike.

It was also said that he spoke to electricity, that he understood its language and could translate it for the branches of science and government that used him. He would get locked away in labs and research facilities for years as he would rebuild alien technology that had been taken by military and the secret space program.

He was referred to as Tesla's reincarnation lots of times and he liked that he said, for Tesla was one of his favorite people that had ever existed. He actually was named Nikola "Nikki" by his parents who were also scientists and had done a lot of research themselves into Nikola Tesla's technology experiments.' He attributed his parents love for science and free energy technologies and their experimentation with them as being the instigator or catalyzer for his love and passion within the field. But Poppa D really did not like to talk about his parents or personal life that much so that is as much as we knew about his background. We understood that too for none of us really liked to talk about our pasts; it was like pushing a bruise for us.

It was because of Poppa D or at that time Nikola or Nikki's strange behaviours that people kept their distance from him. He preferred work and research over pleasantries and socializing, which in hindsight was his downfall. Poppa D literally did not ask questions about any of the agencies that had employed him at first and well he was only sixteen so what he did he know. He certainly did not know of the agenda the agencies that employed him had nor what they did with all that he had decoded for them and reengineered. He was just always keen for another project as they were like games for him, puzzles to be figured out.

Poppa D told us things changed for him when one day he had made the startling discovery that there were actual living aliens on board one of the ships that had come down, not brought down but that had landed and pulled into one of the underground bases where Poppa D was working. He said that they were more like Demonic Reptilian looking creatures with a crew of greys that were serving them like slaves. These things he said were conspiring with Top Agents plotting and planning and that was when he knew that he had to fake his death and get the hell out of there.

So that is what he did, he faked his own death and not only pulled it off but had made it very convincing. He blew up a whole lab he said, turned it into ash with one of the weapons he had been reengineering. That was how he was able to disappear because everyone figured his remains were ashes as well. From that point on he no longer worked for "the man" he said but instead now would work for the people. Poppa D not only vanished that day he blew up the lab but he successfully managed to take with him all sorts of blueprints to reengineered tech. He made copies of all the archives he could get a hold of throughout the decades of his work as he had been keeping all his files on his own memory sticks as he was quite proud of his work and wanted to keep a record for himself.

That was how Poppa D had a huge wealth of archives of how to build free energy alien technologies and instead of weapons, reengineered healing technologies. It was these archives that he shared with Avatar Mill Boy and King. Together our boys under the tutelage of Poppa D were able to develop an A.I. Police force of their own which aided in throwing off the 2030 agenda points of interests around every step and corner of the game. They created an A.I. force of bots that patrolled the dark web within the internet of things which single handily was responsible for whistle blowing corporations, political ties, and pedophile rings across the globe.

They had been coined "The Ghost Coders" by the media because they moved through the Matrix like ghosts. They were also able to initialize a whole network of other "coders" and "hackers" across the continents creating a whole A.I. police force of their own. They recruited hackers and coders through their video games as only the people who were able to figure out the video game qualified. Under the employment and direction of Poppa D our boys and their fleets of "Ghost Coders" caused entire globalist operations to be halted and blocked all around the globe. They were also responsible for leaked information of war crimes, plans for invasions, bought terrorists employed by high ranking Generals and Air Force Captains not to mention Presidents and Prime Ministers, of many governments world-wide. "The Ghost Coders" weren't terrorists although they were labelled as such but they were in fact the ones who busted terrorists and treasonous agents of the Matrix for crimes against humanity.

Poppa D also had the boys busy creating and producing many forms of technology that could help people heal. To raise their own Bio Electric Field to neutralize and harmonize the 5G / 6G weaponry disguised as high-speed internet communications and power grids. It was this secret operation held up here in the hills above Los Angeles in Poppa D's fortress that was one of the core hubs of "The Resistance" as King and Queen called it as they worked to destabilize force of the Dark Lords.

With all the technology they engineered they sold it for next to nothing to farmers so that they could grow more abundant crops given the issues with the toxicity of the elements and lack of pollinators. They gave it freely to Indigenous tribes to help heal their people and have free energy and power brought to their reservations. They sold it to groups of trusted Doctors and Scientists, and even allied forces of people within government agencies and military personnel. This is why King and Queen called the whole operation "The Resistance" for it was a part of a movement that was growing everywhere as all sorts of good people were trying to branch off from the corrupt agencies of the Matrix and prevent the completion to the Dark Lords agenda which was supposed to be fully operational by 2030. Avatar always confided to us how more and more marines and service folk were declaring that they could no longer serve the wicked elite who had taken over the government and that they had to stand true to their oath and protect and serve the people rather than the beast system. We could tell it was stories like these that kept Avatar running to keep up with the orders for his tech and services that kept pouring in daily.

It was because of these stewards of life and true patriots that stood up to the beast system that bought us the time we needed to get to where we were in 2030. They also gave people all around the world a chance to raise their own bodies' frequencies and buy some time to prepare for the reset that we warned people was coming. These stewards helped to build coherence and allow the chance of more and more people to be saved by becoming entrained into the harmonic resonant field of 5D.

One of the most interesting things I had learned from Poppa D was that he could talk to interdimensional beings! Yup! Poppa D had admitted to us that he was guided by them and that they had literally helped him with his false staged death. That these interdimensional beings had made it possible for him to escape by their own advanced technologies which would allow for them to enter in to places and exit with no trace or sign that they had been there. He told us that they had started making contact with him while he was working underground and that they could just appear out of nowhere and disappears again. Poppa D told us that was how they got him out of the base when he pulled the trigger on the particle accelerator plasmic death ray fire gun he had been working on, he said he got a tap on the shoulder a whisper in the ear that it was time one day so he grabbed his bug out bag with his latest files to add to his secret archives, he pulled the trigger and they basically beamed him out of there.

Poppa D told us that he had been contacted by those alien beings that he came to know as Pleiadian to be specific during his years working at the laboratory where they dissected alien bodies that had been captured. He discovered that their bodies although organic in material, were only just shells or suits which held a Spark within it. The spark he said was an electrical plasmic like discovery that some referred to as the God Spark in the New Age movements. The Pleiadian alien beings taught Poppa D that everything had a God Spark, but the Dark Lords and that is why they had to feed off those who did. They told Poppa D that the reason why the Dark Lords wanted to destroy all that was connected to the spark was because they resented them and were repulsed by the spark's light as they are in actual magnetic contrast to the spark's frequencies. Yes that is right, the God Spark's frequency antidote their power. That was why Poppa D had told us that he believed in our cause and movement because we "The Apocalypsos" raised the frequency of God Sparks through our music art and performances.

He told us that those who did at one time have a God Spark and had decided to join forces with the Dark Lords on the Earth, that they had to surrender their own God Spark which was consumed as an elixir for the Dark Lords in rituals. This infusion for them kept them alive in flesh suits as they needed the God Spark essence to stay alive for they were not in fact technically alive on their own by nature but that they were more like shadows.

Poppa D you could say was our first real teacher, well not mine really as I had a whole family as my first teachers. But a lot of my early education had become foggy so when Poppa D adopted us all I welcomed his teachings into my life as I had been starving for real information. Poppa D even said I was actually one of his favourite pupils for my mind worked like his. I guess it was true I had been born an autodidact and had basically more or less taught myself just about everything I knew.

Poppa D's teachings started with the Vedas and the teachings of how beings were created. He taught us that everyone had temporary body suits but that within them we all had a God Spark that would be released when we died. He taught biology and about how when we would die our bodies would decompose, but our God Sparks or Souls would carry on through the the process of reincarnation that was available for all those who had God Sparks. In fact it is the God Spark Poppa D explained to us that determined the next incarnation, for it had synched within it an algorithm that was emitted from the God Spark which determined the currency of vibration that would calculate the manifestation of a Soul into the lifetime.

But Poppa D said, if you sold your God Spark to the Dark Lords, that in exchange of your Soul you could get material riches and power and all the orgies you could ever want but you could not reincarnate again. This is what Poppa D said was really happening to the tempted weak men and women of our world and what had happened to the greys. He told us that the greys were actually at one time like Smeagol from the Lord of the Rings but had turned into greys just like Gollum was turned into Gollum for really Gollum was the archetype of what happened to a Soul when they sold themselves out to the Dark Lords all for their "precious" fortune fame or riches. This is how the Dark Lords were able to thrive for so long as mortals. For they feasted off the essence of the God Spark for millennia and fools would just render it over, that or the Dark Lords and their minions would harvest it off the children by creating a loosh, a vibration of fear so strong that it would alter the DNA of the child or person and thus create a toxin in their blood that was almost as strong as the God Spark essence, and this was called Adrenochrome which of course all the elites and stars of Hellywood were addicted to, this is why so many children Poppa D said went missing each year.

"The Dark Lords originated from Lucifer" Poppa D told us in one of his great lectures "and were deemed the fallen Angels from once upon a time. They committed original sin as a manifestation from Lucifer who had challenged the "Law of Oneness" and defied the "Unified Field of Consciousness" by a spell that he created to break the Sacred Hoop of Life and bend it out linear wise disrupting Soul consciousness conceiving a shadow twin to Soul called Ego. Lucifer then like a vampire fed off of the God Spark's essence from Angels that he pulled under his command converting them to his army by way of Black Goo which dripped like blood from the God Sparks of his victims. What Lucifer did created a primordial cataclysm that had changed the Infinity timelines and templates. The Infinity timelines and templates were the original blueprints you could say of creation. Long ago when Lucifer's group of fallen Angels who at one point had been high level intelligences of the Naturix challenged the Oneness Consciousness, they divided and separating the circle of life into a linear template and timeline which distorted the patterns of creation moving a fractal continuum into a fragmented algorithm which caused ripples of dissonance throughout creation. This dissonance grew in Aether until it became a force of its own. Like a black cloud on a stormy day, its energy and electrical current gathered into a substance which eventually manifested into a virus of Black Goo drawn out from the largest God Spark of creation which is like the light of a trillion suns and which is the operating ultimate God Spark of the whole of all existence itself. The virus that Lucifer was able to create like an Eugenics scientists does or a computer programmer, infected this virus like mold or fungal spore into the Infinity timelines and it proliferated into a spiritual nothingness which began to devour the essences of light. This Black Goo that Lucifer had created bore him a might Orc he named Satan as a high priest for the Dark Lord cult that formed and spread throughout the Galaxy. This is how original sin manifested and chaos broke out of the supreme and divine intelligence or order of creation. This was the legacy or lineage of the Dark Lords all conceived by one Lucifer."

"For ages, the Infinity Masters within the Council of Guardians and Architects of Creation tried to experiment with ways to contain this Goo." Poppa D went on as he tried to illuminate to us what was really going on ... I guess we had asked and well Poppa D was not one to hold back. "Originally, the "Wise Ones" were repulsed by this substance and the Dark Lords who were being turned into demons like the Elves in your favorite movie there you had me watch Thomas called what was it ... Lord of the Rings was it? Yes remember how the Elves had been captured and tortured, twisted in Black Magic until they became Orcs. Right, so like I said the "Wise Ones" with all their strength fought the Dark Ones which made them ironically grow in strength and power. The opposition of the Infinity Masters to the Black Goo entities gave birth to an entire epoch of Star Wars within the Galaxies'. This is why the "Great Reset" plan was created"

"The Star Wars has been going on for what feels like an eternity of time Pops and it is getting pretty old!" Avatar said to Poppa D after his lecture, "when is it going to end?" "Be patient my son" Poppa D replied, "for every day that we wake to we save more Souls, this is why it has been allowed to carry on for this long. Truly I say to you each day is "Judgement Day! Each day more people show their true colors. Each day people choose to serve either the Naturix and love or the Matrix and its Ego based religion. The "Wise Ones" have been waiting for a critical mass my children and you have all helped them reach their goal!"

"So let me get this straight," Mercy said, "the Galactic Confederation tried to fight Lucifer and his crew but resolved after a millennia that there was no way to fight, annihilate, nor wipe the Black Goo from the codes of creation. So this is why and when they began to conceive of a plan to create a funnel of densities where they would concentrate the Goo, then push it all down layer by layer, density by density, to the lowest spheres of life 4D down to Zero Point." "Ahhhh you have listened very well Mercy, yes that is right." Poppa D responded.

After a while of living up in Poppa D's fortress with our gang Jacob and I moved back to the city down below. I needed to be at the gallery where I worked and Jacob he too worked at some Non for Profits in the city. Only Avatar Mill Boy King and their ladies stayed up at Poppa D's. Our gang had a warehouse in the city too where they could all stay and or work if they wanted to be in the city but no matter what was going on we would gather for weekly feasts and download sessions with Poppa D. I remembered thinking to myself at some point, was Poppa D one of the "Wise Ones?" It wasn't until Jacob and I had our shared experience just before the "Code Red" call was made that I really started to question that hypothesis very sincerely as he literally had shared with us everything verbatim that the beloved beings in our dream had taught.

I could remember Poppa D saying "the "Wise Ones" have successfully gathered all the Black Goo from all aspects of Infinity; baiting it, luring it as it was a parasite after all and with it all the Dark Lords themselves including Satan and Lucifer who have been duped into believing that they could have dominion over the Earth. Yes the "Wise Ones" have successfully funneled all the Black Goo through the Milky Way Galaxy which was created to be a supreme body of intelligence with its star our sun and planets which acted as organs within a body of purification, to purify once and for all the Naturix Creation Codes and return infinity to its original blueprint integrating this new level of awareness without any remnants of the Black Goo imprints nor the Dark Lords ego complexes."

"How did Lucifer get conned into coming to Earth if he and his crew were as smart as they thought themselves to be and were actually able to blow up whole planets and enslave other alien life forms?" Asked Queen one day, "it just don't make sense." "Ahhhh good question" said Poppa D who loved every moment when he got to play professor. "Throughout the history of the Earth, which again Earth was designed to become the ultimate feeding ground for the Black Goo parasitic forces and an amazing opportunity for Lucifer and Satan to materialize into form which was their ultimate desire, right, so they came not even always willingly but like addicts to heroin driven by their egoic needs to catch a fix of greed and power. You see children, Earth was designed to deliver ... to deliver all the material one could need to become an Ego based ruler which is exactly what Lucifer had wanted all along. Lucifer as the Anti-Christ now walks upon the Earth and his minions also known now in our time as the Satanic Church, have gathered and organized themselves into the Royal Lines of Power. Because the Dark Lords adore the ability to mimic the Great Lords and Ladies of Light and Creation known to us as the "Wise Ones" they themselves sought ways to display their own selves as masters of the universe by way of their ego complex. That is why they didn't hesitate for a moment and grabbed the chance for world domination over what they think us humans is; to them you see we are prized trophy game like a hunt we are the catch of a galaxy! Now all of the Dark Lords have taken the positions of royalty upon the Earth all to mimic below that which exists above. Lucifer's greatest weakness was his own self, for he could not help but to fall victim to his own poison, his own pride; his own ego. So he came to the Earth and has manifested himself as a great ruler of the Earth sitting pretty on top of the greatest of riches within the Vatican. Yes Lucifer sits upon a throne of serpents for he and his fallen Angels are the serpents, the Reptiles ruled by their engineered reptilian brain also called the Archons."

"This was all an illusion though all a part of a plan, right Poppa

D" Thomas said like a little child. Now if I were to describe Poppa D. I would say that he was kind, incredibly generous, and that he had a soft place in his heart that he had armoured up a long time ago but through us his adopted family, softened and opened itself to us. I knew that when after Thomas who clearly was still processing PTSD had asked in a shaky voice if this was all really just an illusion for he admitted to us that he hated to see all the suffering that he just couldn't stand it anymore. I remember Poppa D had come over to Thomas after he had said his words out loud out of frustration and overwhelm to all of the injustices he had been witnessed to, and Poppa D handed to him his handkerchief that he always had folded in his top left chest pocket and said while putting a hand on Thomas's head to comfort him "my boy, your heart is good, your such a good boy. I want you to know that the Dark Lords have been deceived by their own ignorance and arrogance. They have fallen attracted magnetically to the Earth just like the fallen Angels who had married the daughters of the Earth creating the Nephilim. Know that they are trapped now, they have been brought right to the snare that was created just for them. Yes they have all been drawn like sand to a magnet and are now in the metabolic process designed to consume them and return them to light. Do not fear my boy; everything is already alright always alright, trust dear heart … trust. This has always been the intention of The Galactic Confederation who built the carbon copy of Earth and its carbon based life forms. This has always been the plan, to Zero Point the Black Goo and its parasitic forces while allowing for Souls whom want to learn of the knowledge of good and evil can by getting their master's degree all while helping clear the egoic constructs to restore life to higher harmonics. Remember kids you are in a University, a Universe of education information and knowledge. You are here because you have opted into coming to assist in the purification process which has come to be known as the reincarnation wheel of karma and Samsara. Be grateful you have not forgotten that the illusion is not real, be grateful that you have not become attached and absorbed into the disillusionment going on but have instead helped others that have forgot who they are and why they were here, as if they have amnesia. You should all be so proud that you have all raised yourselves out of the gutters and have helped many others do the same."

So who was Poppa D you ask? Well Poppa D was our liberator. He made sense out of all the nonsense for us and gave us a pathway to salvation and redemption where before there was none. He was the first one in our lives to break the spell that had been put over us. He was the one who first taught us about the great ingestion, digestion, assimilation, and ultimate defecation process of the "Great Reset" plan which was now coming to its completion, coming to its end.

I lovingly look back upon the character we all knew as Poppa D and will never forget what a serious man he was. But how his seriousness was all a surface quality and that the real him was a fun loving playful quirky guy. I got to laugh as I remember once at dinner when Mill Boy out of nowhere spoke up as if he had been in a deep dialogue with himself saying … "oh I got it, this whole reset thing is like when you got to take a really big shit! Seriously Mama Earth is at one of those times when you can't suppress and squeeze back the turtling giant black goo of shit that wants to get expelled out and flushed down or in her case flushed down the omnipotent toilet." To that Poppa D burst out laughing. He laughed so hard he cried and from that point on he always joked about how Mama Earth needed to take a Black Goo shit so bad that it was legendary.

After that Poppa D became really funny, he was serious most of the time mind you but also much like a coyote at the same time, a trickster. Just when he sensed someone in our group was getting overwhelmed, he would drop a joke or turn the heaviness around by making humor out of the situation.

So that is Poppa D; our patron, our founder, our Godfather you could say, the Godfather of "The Apocalypsos." He was the one who came to us in the beginning when our tribe first came together as one and found us, saved us, and raised us from our previous place of limitations. He check-mated the system and brought us from one end of the pool to the other taking us from the shallow consciousness of limitation right on over to a place where we could deep dive into the waters of life. Poppa D helped free us from the cage of mental thought constructs and enlightened our minds allowing for us to experience the ability to spread our wings into our omnipotent potential. Poppa D was there for us in the beginning of our rise, our turning point, and he was the one we all came back to now that the 4th Age and world was ending.

In the words of Poppa D "what once was locked can become unlocked and unblocked. New pathways can emerge where before there is only a damn. This is quantum physics and the power of the law of transformation which is what is guiding this whole "Great Reset" my children." Poppa D believed with all of his heart that we as energetic beings could transform the physical and that is exactly what he had taught us to do. Poppa D took us "The Apocalypsos" from simple physics to quantum physics in a snap of his pretty long finger, like a blink in his twinkling eye. But we still did not know all of Poppa D's secrets, for he had one more major secret he had not told even us, not even Avatar yet. This big secret was about to get revealed real shortly though as we pulled now into Poppa D's fortress garage and entry point to his bat cave.

CHAPTER TWELVE

POPPA D'S FORTRESS AND THE GATHERING OF OUR ASCENSION POD

"The words we choose to use when we communicate with each other carry vibrations. The word 'war' carries a whole different vibration than the word 'peace'. The words we use are showing how we think and how we feel. The careful selection of words helps to elevate our consciousness and resonate in higher frequencies."
Grigoris Deoudis

We ditched our bikes in the garage, came running through the tunnel, up the spiral staircase, and through the multiple levels of face scan, eye scan, hand scan, and spit scan within Poppa D's security system. One by one we crossed over into the Hall that was on the other side of his vaulted entry. Did I mention, Poppa D's place was a fortress?

"The world that has been projected onto the Earth my people is not what it appears to be. For the Earth, verily I say to you; mark me, is but a carbon copy of the true jewel of the Spheres, Aetherea. Yes, the Earth, my friends, I am sure you will not like hearing this, but the Earth was created as a carbon copy just as you have been created in your carbon copy to serve as a feeding ground for the accursed Black Goo forces who have relished in the anarchy of their control and power for generations upon generations upon this the carbon copy of Aetherea. The Dark Lords have done their worse. Their crimes against humanity and life itself are beyond the storage limits of any university library known anywhere."

We walked into Poppa D sharing a lecture to a group of people some we knew and some we did not. This was Poppa D's great work. This was the gathering of brilliant men women and their children that poppa D had accumulated into his network in his years up in the fortress. Scientists, Biologists, Professors, Doctors, and Engineers packed into Poppa D's hall and were all listening attentively to him as if we were in a class. This was our ascension pod.

"The evil of the Black Goo forces has gone on for a very long time, even though time does not really exist beyond the Maya or illusion. What has felt like an eternity has really only been a drop in the bucket of Infinity."

Poppa D went on as we came filed into the meeting apparently a bit late. We were the company he was most expecting, the ones he most truly cared for and was waiting for. We were his adopted family, and you could feel the huge exhale he released upon seeing our faces roll in. You could see the relief diffuse from his body. Avatar wanted to go to him like a boy but resisted the urge and instead we all sat down where we could. Poppa D looked at us as he finished his last sentence and we could all feel his palpable joy in knowing we had made it in this final hour. Our arrival was equivalent to like a giant amount of pressure off his heart and soul for he sighed audibly and all who was there heard it and realized then just how much we all meant to him. It was evident then more than ever how much we meant to Poppa D who had never had a wife or children of his own or friends really. No Poppa D was a serious man a strange man and by all means prior to meeting us a very solo lone wolf of a man.

"The Earth has provided a way to lure all darkness to it, like a magnet it has wielded the power that has drawn the forces of all darkness from within the Black Goo intelligence empire and draw it all down to the iron core crystal of this carbon based planet. The Earth has served to allow the Black Goo molecules to take form and consolidate all its molecules together as one and ultimately bind them to the iron core crystal magnet lodged deep within the Earth. Now I am happy to say to all of you here, I have had the 10/4 from my guides confirming that all aspects of the Black Goo intelligence has successfully been now focalized into the funnel of the illusory wormhole created by The Galactic Confederation and Councils of Light who had to tempt all the spores and molecules onto and into Earth. I have brought you all here and have signalled the alarm of "Code Red" as I have just had confirmation that we have successfully now gathered all the Goo like worms from creation to feed on the one wondrous temptatious apple of Eve totally reversing the curse for all time and space. I have had the go ahead that we now can completely expel evil for ever as we shall now return all the Black Goo spore and molecule and the Dark Lords who wield the black goo power to pure energy through our zero-point EMP technology as operated by the Guides and Guardians of the Great White Brotherhood of Light and Ascended Masters. You see once upon a time, before Earth was created, the Dark Lords of the Black Goo Force ravaged the stars and the planets of distant galaxies across the vast spheres of space. They destroyed planets, they took hostages, and they even corrupted timelines and templates of creation that had not even yet been born. They violated sacred law in every way and thus invoked the attention and intention of The Great White Brotherhood of Light, The Ascended Masters, and The Councils of Light within the interdimensional spheres of existence that thus formed The Galactic Confederation. It is they that I refer to as the "Wise Ones" who have been helping each one of you your entire life. It is they who have thus created conceived and have now achieved what has been called "The Great Reset" which is what has brought us altogether today. This has been all conjured together since the Black Goo started off only as a virus created by Lucifer himself. Due to Lucifer's defiance and violation of sacred law which had allowed for a small crack to develop in the spheres of oneness, and thus has been rotting ever since like a cavity rotting away at a child's tooth so much so that the whole tooth must now go, yes my friends my family it is time we must extract this tooth for good. Lucifer and his fallen Angels and all who have served that cause are in violation of sacred law and have of their own free will lost their God Spark and therefore must now be zero pointed, returned to pure energy. After seizing planet after planet, race of being after race of beings all who which were attacked, enslaved, the time has come where enough is enough."

Then entirely and unsuspectedly Poppa D pulled out yet another trick from his infamous top hat and shapeshifted right there before our eyes into a tall indigo blue shimmering handsome Syrian Star Being. He absolutely confirmed right there and then what my intuition had been showing me that he was way more then what he appeared to be. That he the whole time we had known him and loved him was just a shell of the true being he truly was. That the true him, the pearl within his shell, was the rare and beautiful being that had been waiting to be discovered like a hermit crab. It was as if in that exact moment and in all honesty that I realized we all were a treasure hidden within a treasure chest, each one of us were the jewel inside the lotus awaiting to bloom and be revealed.

"I am not who any of you think I am not even my children ... my boys and girls, nor you my students, or you my colleagues have thought that they have known. I am Niro I am from Sirius and I have been operating on this Planet lifetime after lifetime building and preserving templates of technologies and programming which has guided us all to this present moment. I am sorry I was not able to reveal my true self to any of you before. I have wanted to deeply and many of times but could not yet do so. I have with all my heart wanted to show you all my true colors (and with that he chuckled) yes literally and figuratively. I have also longed for each of you to be able to see yourselves as I have always seen you since first finding you. Now I will let you all in on a secret, since I was able to break through the amnesia that ate at my heart and soul continuously in my youth, I have been able to see things as they truly are. Meaning since I became woke to my truth, I have been able to see you all in your truth and that is how I have known who to trust and who to open my knowledge my arms and fortress up to. You see I had not even known myself until one day when I was contacted at an underground base by a half dying Pleiadian who had been captured. One of them who I was able to save named Myreeet he showed me the truth of who I was. He cleared my DNA and RNA and genetic coding reconnecting me to my 12 strands of DNA from my previous only 2. He helped my memory return from the mind wipe that hacks into all of our consciousness as we cross through the rainbow bridge and incarnate through the 4D where the Archons dwell and have set up shop to wipe us all unwittingly from the knowledge of who we are and where we come from and equally important, as to why we are here. This mind wipe is the first of our collective initiation into their hell. Like a star constellation we have all been brought together guided by our higher selves and our cosmic families to this very moment and this very place which is a vortex. As a pack and as a pod, a family of kin we have been drawn together to usher in this great time of redemption and salvation." Poppa D's eyes were flooded with tears which rolled down his beautiful shining sleek body; I looked at Avatar as he was in shock and he was crying too. All of us in our crew were looking at one another like did you know. Can you believe this? Then Poppa D came over in his true form and picked up Avatar and held him as he sobbed.

Mill Boy went running to them both like the younger sibling he was. He was then followed by King who crept like a cat to them and joined them in the group hug. Their ladies, Thomas, Jacob, and I all just sat there in silence. Then Buddha started to bark super crazy loud ending the intimate moment. Poppa D or Niro as his real name was then walked over to Buddha and put his hand upon Buddha's head and with that Buddha fell over and began snoring loudly which had us all impressed.

Poppa D no longer looked so old for in the moment that he had shapeshifted, he went from an elder man into a timeless being. He transformed from an old gentlemen who dressed like he was out of the 1920s right in front of our eyes, from just standing there with his specially hand carved wooden cane holding him up and that quirky smile he always flashed and of course his old classic top hat to a beautiful Syrian Lord, presto. I am not going to kid you, it was hard to let go of the man we thought we knew as Poppa D, as Nikola William Dollard, into this now new form of Niro. No, our godfather was now no longer the professor, the engineer, the inventor creator, and innovator that we knew and loved. He was now a Syrian, a beautiful being of the Galactic Confederation that had come to save us all. "Children do not think that I am not who I was before," it was as if he could read our minds. "I am all of those identities you saw me as; I am just more … I am all of that and so much more. As are all of you, you are what you see, you are who you have been, but most importantly you are all that which you are becoming."

With Buddha out cold, the boys came back to us and sat back down beside us grasping for their woman's hand. We huddled together like never before, we got past the boundaries of where our comfort zones lay, and we held onto one another as we cried and integrated all what was happening before us and all around in the world outside.

The children began to then fuss and while I am sure they were straight out tripping right about now; the trip took another turn. Poppa D took out a remote control and pushed some buttons then with a flash a group of robots appeared. These robots he had engineered in his lab were fantastic. Some were his own designs and others included ones he had bought off the dark web and reprogramed. The team of these adorable and sophisticated robots came in and began to serve us food and drink. The mothers of the children decided they would need to take a break from the heaviness of the discussion and full disclosure of Poppa D's identity, so with their children holding their hands they were escorted by a "nanny robot crew" that Poppa D or Niro had offered to escort them to an area of his mansion that had been created just for children, a playroom if you will. Poppa D always took care of all the details as he took everything into account. He ritualistically planned and prepared for all things to be considered, he was like OCD on steroids. With the mother's and the children being escorted to another floor in Poppa D's house he began lecturing again.

"You see the Dark Lords of Black Goo long ago in the past had become very sophisticated. They festered and multiplied. They had giant egos, for that was all that they were really, egos. They had no conscience you see, they lacked the aspects and biology, the hardware and software of the brain and genetic coding to feel, to understand, to experience empathy, and to love since Lucifer and his fallen ones bred that out of them. Yes, Lucifer's crew are devoid of any feeling, sensitivity, or sensation other than a maddening drive to feed and procreate like the parasites they are. As my full memory was restored by the Pleiadian Myreeet and I remembered who I was and why I was here I simultaneously began remembering in full detail the master plan that had been conceived so long ago. The great plan of "The Great Reset" that we, the Guides, and Guardians of the Galactic confederation as members and ambassadors of creation, had engineered long long ago! I remembered how I had gathered in councils all over creation, had meeting after meeting of planning and strategically plotting for a way to lure the Black Goo molecules which can alter themselves and appear as a chameleon can turning to different shades of color, thus making it very difficult to not be deceived by their black magic tricks of glamour. Yes, we knew that we needed a plan that would work on an electro magnetically based template. We needed something that would work purely in vibration frequency and raw power through tone and charge. We knew we would need to base this round up of parasites and clear them all out energetically by the law of resonance. We had to make the trap look in such a way that the Black Goo Lords would want to flock to the snare as if it was some sort of bait. We decided to reveal a new law of elements that we had specifically designed for this most particular of quests. Gravity, an artificially inseminated program of the Galactic Confederation which attaches all the Black Goo spore properties, drawing their molecular structure like an anchor down further and further through an engineered funnel or wormhole created by the blueprint technicians of time and space. This wormhole that was created by the great engineers of the galaxies is what has been attracting the Black Goo like a vacuum sucking it from all spheres and dimensions of existence like moths to a flame, landing the Goo into Zero Point oblivion. This process was engineered for this final experiment to clear the Black Goo from Creation and that is what is about to be finalized now."

"The Dark Lords," he went on, "became masters of war, masters of prostitution, and dark fear-based rituals of sacrifice. They harvested the negative energy from their wicked ways which fed them and drew more of their kind to this carbon copy illusion. This was the ingestion process, to draw the Black Goo particles all to this genius snare of illusion. To get them to gather in all their mass to artificially feed off the fake essence of man. It was working brilliantly; they had come in droves from all ends of the universes drawn like a magnet to this perfected template and timeline created to cleanse Creation." This last lesson from Poppa D was confirming everything that Jacob and my dream had conveyed from the beings we had just met. It was all like a crazy Déjà vu.

"As the Dark Lords descended into the wormhole of the Milky Way Galaxy they fought over planets, destroying some, they battled all sorts of star nation beings and even themselves all while trying to take over and become masters of the universe. They at first existed in the heights of the 15th dimension. From that sphere they nearly destroyed the worlds as they created weapons that would blast whole planets apart. This was done to Tiamat a planet much like Earth; the devastation was so severe it shifted the poles of Earth. That was when Saturn became the Reptile Dark Lords beloved planet and they nicknamed it Satan. They even put rings around it to protect it from rivalling Dark Lords called the Draco's. When they blew up Tiamat it caused a huge flood of crystalline fluid or star water which worked in favor of the Great Plan as it dropped them to 12D instantly. That is when they then found the Hu Mans, or Divine Mortals and they saw them as the perfect trophies for their hunt. This was at the time of Lemuria and at this time to help the Hu Mans, many different beings came forward to help their fledglings get going. There at that time was the Mer Folk or Mermaids and Merman who came to bring the program of the watery realms to this holographic illusion of Earth. They would incarnate into shells or body suits that held their consciousness like a spark to operate the vehicle. They brought all the oceans, rivers, and streams into a network of veins and arteries that worked to be the life blood you could say or engine fuel to keep the whole illusion of Earth alive. There also were the Dragon clans which built the Dragon lines or leylines that operated the electrical grid of Earth. They were also masters of fire and taught the Hu Mans to work with fire thus keeping light for seeing warmth and food preparations or cooking. There were also the Sasquatch who came with all their clans and crews of Gnomes and tiny people and other Aetherea allies who taught the Hu Mans of the Earth as they were the ones who had conceived of this whole idea in the first place to build the false Matrix which would mirror the Naturix. The Sasquatch were the ones that had constructed the Earth templates and timelines and programmed the codes for medicines foods and how to live on the Earth, to build homes, and to build Pyramids to generate power. They also served to protect the Hu Mans as the Hu Mans played a crucial role in the whole operation of this experiment. The Sasquatch loved the Hu Mans even though they also knew that this was all just a carbon copy of the true Earth on Aetherea." At the mention of Sasquatch, I could see and feel King get quite excited, it was if I could feel his heartbeat pick up and become anxious or excited. Wow, I thought, he really does love the Squatch!

Poppa D went on, "The Insectoid nation then came and helped with genetic coding and adapting for the Hu Man's bodies to this carbon copy existence. They helped greatly with the construction of the whole DNA RNA coding that would ultimately be the carriers of frequency to be delivered like an antenna to the carbon copy matrix. Then of course there was the Fay, the blessed Dakinis and their clans of Air spirits or Sylphs who came and implanted the sacred geometries of Earth lending their dancing spiralling pulsations that would work to serve as a clock for the tick tock timing of Earth which all had a limit to when this whole experiment would come to a close, which yes, is now. It was all these beings upon many other orders of Angelic intelligences, Star Nation Brothers and Sisters who all came to Earth to lend direction, guidance, operating algorithms, and oversee by managing this whole computer of Maya by running their programs into the false Naturix, the Matrix. These programs we would come to know as religions, cultural beliefs, knowledge in the very forms of gnosis, science, math, astronomy, and medicine."

Poppa D had showed us many of this research with his countless hours of slide shows and textbooks he forced us to read and watch. While it took a great amount of discipline to learn all of this and research it, meditate into it, cry over it, and fully begin to comprehend the significance of it all, we found that we all actually really did resonated to the teachings he brought to us. But he had not shown us the whole of the plan. It was not until our dream that Jacob and I had seen the plans for the Metabolic Digestive Transformation.

When Poppa D finally concluded his lecture for the day, we all felt like kids who were fussing and needed to get up and move around. A chief robot of the house then returned and escorted us all to a large dining room which had a very long table with chairs all decorated and full of hot pots of steaming delicious smelling foods.

"Our last supper," Poppa D formally announced to all of us as we filed into the Dining Hall and took our places at the giant rectangular table that had chairs stationed at it. We did not know if he was being sarcastic or sincere. Within the halls of his fortress even with the trembling Earth below, all the sounds and screams of the city was muted. It was easy to forget what was taking place outside and all around the globe.

While we all had our mouths begin to water at the smell of the feast laid out before us, we took a moment to bow our heads in silence upon the command of Poppa D, or Niro. Networks had been cut, the power was out everywhere but that was not a problem for Poppa D, which truth to be told would always be his name to us. Niro was just too weird to call him. It was fine to see him in his true form for not only was he beautiful but when you love someone no matter what they look like you love them in your heart unconditionally. Beyond the body all I could think was damn, Poppa D had prepared for everything.

With communications down and power out no news was able to get to us from the outside, but we honestly did not care for no news was good news, we had all that we needed right here. "My people please let us pray, let us forget our troubles and worries just for just this moment and instead I propose that we instead celebrate. That we come together in hands and hearts to give thanks for this food and drink, to pray for peace to prevail, for victory of Spirit and victory of Nature. We are so blessed to be with one another and to be able to help all of creation make this transaction this exchange from Maya from illusion to our Divine and original truth. Truth of which we are, truth of how we all came to be, truth of that which is where we are all going to. Please raise your glass to the Highest. Please look around at one another and smile, bless one another shake hands give hugs; this is a time to celebrate. Cheers my friends and family, to the One to the Source, to the beginning of the end of corruption and the starting point for the great ascent to 5D officially!" And with that he raised his glass and toasted with Avatar's then to Mill Boy and King then off he went to all his guests. We all loosened up and followed his lead and began to introduce ourselves to one another.

At that in came the children and their mothers behind. Everyone started laughing and talking meeting and greeting each other as if we were all at a family reunion in a banquet hall. Poppa D pushed a button and music began to stream from the surround sound system that Avatar and King had installed years before, classical music filled the hall, classical music with high solfeggio vibrations, Poppa D's favorite.

We feasted as if we were truly at the last supper of the Christ. We bonded with all the great people who sat round the table and after supper we all gathered around the fireplace in Poppa D's living room and were cozied up by the large hearth central in the great room. We talked till the wee hours of dawn, we even danced together and at the beckoning and request of Poppa D's guests we performed for the crowd that was there. We got to know the great minds that occupied the space, for each person there was a total legend, a total mystic! Of course, they were there for they were people that had inspired Poppa D in some way. For that reason and that reason alone, they were there.

People came up to us, especially the teens that were present and they treated us like modern day heroes. I guess we were world famous and considered stars to the hearts and minds of many who loved our music and our shows. We were the stars that had risen not fallen unlike the so-called tabloid stars, pointed out a young thirteen-year-old girl who was totally swooning over Jacob.

The night was righteous, we danced we celebrated we told stories and we completely forgot of that which was going on outside the fortress walls. Poppa D then announced, "my robots will show each of you to your rooms. I have many and all are invited to get some sleep, you will need it. We will be meeting again in just a few short hours and I will need you all to be alert for what will happen next. Go now and sleep you have 4 hours until I will need you back here in the hall. Go now and I will have my robots come for you when it is time to gather for the reset."

With that we all sleepily followed our instructions without question even though you could tell people were like wtf? We followed our robot guides, each couple or family exiting into a room that had been prepared for them. Jacob and I entered a beautiful Himalayan crystal lit room that had a king size bed that was canopied by a silken fabric that smelled of roses and lavender, as I said Poppa D thought of everything.

Saying good night to our crew giving hugs and kisses to them all, we retired to our rooms and to our beds to let the darkness consume us in the best of ways. "Sophia, Sophia" Jacob whispered in my ear as he spooned my naked body from behind. I could feel him aroused, hungry for love.

"Soph are you still awake? I want you so bad I need to feel you your yin, to have it hold my yang; I want to marinate in you like bathing in the sea. Baby what if this is the last time we can come together in this way in the flesh?"

His manhood was a throbbing beacon, a buzzing bee seeking searching my garden for my flower to pollinate. I opened my flower wide and let his probing rod into my wet sweet ring. I felt his need like a warrior to sheath his blade inside my warm skin. He drank from my chalice he cried in my arms. As he climaxed, he shuddered and stuttered out the words, "You are my Magdalena I give myself to you as the Christ. May our love magic tonight seed the world in such sacredness that we ignite the redemption codes rapturing the world far beyond any darkness or pain."

We had given everything we had to the moment as if it was our last time, how did we know it wasn't? We lay breathless, smiles taking over our faces. We cuddled in so close to one another there was no ending nor beginning to where we existed, we were one.

"I love you Sophia Star Water! I love you so much!" Crying he smothered my face in kisses and tears. "I love you too Jacob, with all that I am, forever … you are my twin, my twin soul mate, wherever you go I will be there. Whatever happens we go through it together hand in hand heart to heart ok baby."

My words were but a whisper as I could not help but fall asleep wrapped up in my man's perfection; exhausted and complete in my lover's arms, nothing else mattered. Nothing could compare to the total epiphany of our love for one another. I mumbled something like "I wish everyone could feel this kind of love, Agape ……" then blacked out into my own reset.

CHAPTER THIRTEEN

SHAPESHIFT

"The day science begins to study non-physical phenomena; it will make more progress in one decade than in all the previous centuries of its existence."
Nikola Tesla

The world shook like nothing we had ever felt before. There was a huge trembling and sound like a high-pitched engine or whale singing deep in the ocean reverberating through the sea of frequencies that create the fabric of our time space continuum. Thinking it was an earthquake Jacob and I braced ourselves for the wreckage that was to fall from the shockwaves.

No need for our robot guides to come and get us, everyone in Poppa D's fortress woke right up and threw on their clothes and came running to the hall where we all had gathered together just the night before in celebration.

We were rendered instantly to our knees by the impact of the following shockwaves. We realized instantaneously that what we had thought was an earthquake was a portal that had begun to open wide before us and through it, beings were flooding into the space. The gateway of space which I figured is what Poppa D had meant when he had mentioned that his fortress was built on a vortex, opened a portal right there in front of our eyes. Some of the beings that came through the portal I instantly recognized were from Jacob and my dream. Now they were magically transported from that faraway place of heavenly lights to this very moment in Poppa D's meeting hall. Jacob and I looked at each other in amazement, acknowledging that we had just been connecting with these very same beings just less than 48 hours ago.

We felt their power and on bended knee honored them silently in literal shock and awe. Poppa D then spoke, "Behold the Ones who have brought us all together, the ones who have behind the scenes orchestrated our entire lives and our coming together. Meet now the "Wise Ones" who have guided and guarded us all as best they could through our every conscious and unconscious move. It is they that have directed us always to this very moment." We all rose and stood together in a giant circle looking to the center where now nine beings stood looking back out towards us.

One of the beings came forward and speaking in perfect English said, "I am Kaaaatierano, watcher within the Galactic Emissary Watcher Council. We come in peace and truth. We are grateful you have all heeded the call to arrive. Across the earth there are many circles gathering just like this one here and now, for there are many who have either never lost their God Spark or who have found their God Spark and have rekindled the flame. There are many who have remembered who they are why they are here and where we are to go. We thank you for all of your work in sharing the light codes, the upgrades, the programming, and resetting of your continuum which we have channeled to each of you in different ways."

Kaaaatierano then looked at us, our crew, "The Apocalypsos" and bowed saying "we have enjoyed your efforts in sharing your music dance and art. We have been delighted for what we have shared through to you in vision dream and insight, we have seen expressed in raw talent skill and masterful beats that even we would dance to. We have felt the love and reciprocating feedback of energy and blessing returned through your dynamic offerings or performances and the power generated from them as you all generated the raising of frequencies back to us in your prayers and group gatherings through the hearts that held the currency of light which emanated back to us and brought tears to our eyes."

"I am Eeeeaaamatera, I come from the old world of Hadar. Our beloved planet Hadar was destroyed by the Dark Lords and I am a refugee that now lives full time within the Mothership of the Pleiadian Star Mother Council which orbits your planet here called Earth. I have committed to harnessing the great power of my heart to help your God Sparks to remain lit while such dark forces gathered trying day and night to dim the light that they hate and are repelled by. I come now with my team to help you as we have been assigned to you as a star constellation group to help you now ascend."

That is when our beautiful hilarious friend Sasquatch then stepped forward and spoke. "I am Zepharo; I come to assist you in making the morph that you will need to make in order to ascend to 5D and to the 5th Age of Peace. Come to me brother, come here King of men, old one, Sasquatch kin." Zepahro was looking right at King and with that invitation King leaped forward to Zepharo and the two embraced each other for like a minute-long hug. "Holy shit" said Queen, "I always knew my man was a Squatch damn I am in love with a Squatch! I can't believe it!"

"Our people have helped foster you fledglings since the beginning of time. I offer to you now my protection and guidance. I am at your service. I have waited a very long time to get to this point. I congratulate you for your commitment to the awakening and to the recreation of life Immortal. We, the Sasquatch Nation, known in all areas around the Earth and beyond as many different names, we are made of the Heartbeat of life. We are protectors of this heartbeat and we are the regulators of this heartbeat. We will be working to upgrade your hearts and prepare you for this 5th density life transition to what we know as our own reality on Aetherea. I am sorry for the horror and shame your kind has had to face. We have watched so many times wanting to interfere but could not. Know that none of this has been in vain. The pain through the hourglass of the sands of time has served to draw all the Black Goo from all the recesses of time and space. It has made all of what is happening now possible. We have been always been behind the scenes guiding you to this very moment as best as we could. We had to make sure there were no traces of Black Goo left in Creation before we could make possible what is now possible and now about to become deployed. Thank you for your service and I welcome you to your ride Home."

Next a giant Insectoid creature stepped forward and shockingly enough spoke perfect English for us. "I am Kikeetu, chief of engineering of genetic codes in this division. I come now in service of the one to help you to be genetically fit for your new body suit. Do not be scared little ones, I am as old as creation itself and know perfectly well what to do here." Click Click Click, she rubbed her feet together, "as we have designed this new body of light just for you to thank you for your willingness, your free will that is, to come and be subjected to the horrors of the unimaginable and to despite that cruelty and vibration, to override the frequencies with the power of love, we have made for you a very special light body suit indeed. Click click. I now offer to you my service in dissolving your shell that separates you from all that is. I offer to you now the freedom of the liberation codes which I have helped design and have now come to code into your DNA and RNA Matrix. Thank you." And with that Kikeetu took a bow.

As the beings one by one came forth and stood in front of us introducing themselves to us, I looked around at the children that were present and noticed their jaws were dropped literally to the ground eyes bugging out with a sparkle in their eye as if their dreams were coming true. I kind of felt the same way. Everyone in the Hall was speechless for it had all happened so fast when these beings had arrived and began introductions without hesitation as if there was an urgency to be acted upon and no time for small talk.

The parents of the children (some whom we had never met before for they had apparently arrived while we were all in our rooms some of us sleeping, lol) all clutched to their children holding tight their families in awe and protection. I couldn't help but feel the sorrow from the loss of my own mother and father and family and the feeling those kids had knowing that they had their father and mother there to watch over them. Reflecting, I grieved for the loss of my childhood as I had been taken way too young. I swirled in spinning whirlwinds of time and space as memories became like waves that I surfed. These waves were made of light and energy and it was if they were even projections into future memories that began to emerge unwittingly. I began travelling through memories made up of different timelines like a time traveller, this is how I began to see into Jacob and my future selves and our future home and the reunion of my family. I even saw our future babies which flooded my eyes with tears. Jacob noticed, he grabbed my hand and squeezed as a comfort and transmission of unspoken recognition of what I was going through.

We locked eyes as I felt his squeeze and could not help but want to kiss him with all that I was. He too was taking this all in, this whole grand living theatre it seemed with our meeting of our makers and the intense feeling of overwhelm from the situation of it all unfolding before us. We knew this was all what was right and what was meant to be, in our hearts we just knew it; but at the same time the knowing we would never be the same and that soon apparently the whole world was going to shape shift and the thought of it to be quite transparent ... was kind of terrifying.

"I love you" he whispered to me and made me blush all over again. We had barely said a word to each other since we had been abruptly woken from our passionate love making, sex magic session earlier that morning. Were we still dreaming? It was becoming harder and harder to be able to denote when we were dreaming or when we were awake for the awake part felt just like the dream and beyond that ... there was alien life forms standing right in front of us for Goddess sakes!

Now yet another being stepped forward and when I saw her come out from her hooded robe, I wept out loud, crying, "Shima Shima ... is that you Shima?" "Yes, my child." She said to me. "I am Shima she said looking to the others, come here my child come to me for I can hold you now as I have always wanted to hold you." I ran to her like a child to her mother. "Shima" I said, "Shima, I can't believe you are here!" "Yes, I have come to you all at different times as I am the storyteller. I have whispered into your ears as you have slept or when you were most suggestive, and I have kept the stories of who you are and why you are here alive in your hearts as best as I could. I have sowed the seeds of corn to grow into you so that you could harvest the truth from life and feast on the genius of who you are."

I looked around from within her arms as she held me, and I noticed that in fact many there totally recognized her too. She then continued, "I ascended to mastery state when I was just a young Indian girl growing up in the Hopi world. One day I vanished from the land, no one knew what had become of me but a few of the Shamans who through antiquity would tell you that I was a Hopi Goddess of Corn and one of the Katchinas. Perhaps I am and yet I am also so much more than a title, than a character, as all of you are as well."

I felt my worry and anxiety leave. Jacob who could finally see Shima looked at me and I saw tears rolling down his face. He had never seen her before, he felt like she was familiar to him when I would share about her, but I think I was the only one there who had actually developed a relationship with her. She felt like she had adopted me as time after time she would show up in my dreams, she treated me like a daughter. She first had showed up within a flock of birds that had encircled me in my dream. Mystical birds whose song where like a lullaby. She came into my dream like an Angel yet clothed in buckskin with feathers in her hair. She was old and yet wise, strong in her power. Her long silver hair went down to her knees. She was robed in a white buffalo skin and was singing like the birds. She then held out her hand to me that first time when I met her, and she grace me a turquoise stone that was shaped like an egg. She also tied some feathers in my hair and wrapped me in a blanket. I nestled up to her in the dream and slept while she stroked my hair and told me stories. When I woke, I had the overwhelming urge to paint her and channel some poetry and lyrics. It was like she had fed me with divine inspiration through my dream and I that when I woke up, I was able to come up with a new material which really felt powerful. I took it to my crew, and they loved it. Shima had got into my head and her stories became the stories that we "The Apocalypsos" began channeling years ago, now she was here, and all my crew could see her. Mercy looked at me and whispered, "That's the medicine woman in your art ... it's her!" I whispered back, "I know isn't she beautiful, isn't she like the most sacred person you have ever seen."

Avatar, King, Mill Boy, Thomas, their ladies, and Jacob all scooted over to where I had folded myself to and was sitting at her feet. We surrounded her like a pack of wolves as if she was our Alpha. She pulled out a large abalone bowl and started smudging us all with the smoke of sage sweet grass pinon copal and other smells I could not place. As the smoke filled the room everyone there sat down and relaxed responsively, it was as if we were all finally able to let all that had happened there begin to integrate and settle in.

My crew and I sat there at her feet literally lapping up the nourishment she emanated while she smudged and blessed everyone there. I could not help but laugh and tear bubble as even the children there came to her side and snuggled into us breaking away from their parent's hold. Shima, I had a feeling, was all of our favorite storyteller, and I think the kids and my crew and I were clearly the people who loved her stories the most. Shima had a way of being so maternal that pretty much everyone there I believed in all honesty wanted her to scoop them up, swaddle them in warm blankets, and then rock them to sleep with her soft chanting lullabies.

After Shima had smudged us all and chanted her sacred prayers, we all felt much better, way more grounded at least. It was the first time we had all probably relaxed for quite some time now, for sure it was the first time Jacob and I were able to process all that had just happened and integrate all that was happening. Shima felt like a lifeguard, pulling us all in from the ocean of emotion we were all swimming in trying not to drown more like. It was a lot to take in! There were aliens for God's sake all standing before us and a whole bunch of pretty intense reality breakthroughs coming forth at us like a slap in the face or a bucket of cold water being splashed in your face upon waking up. Like for reals we were in the time of Revelations! And we knew that Revelations was what The Apocalypse was all about, so we had literally landed ourselves perfectly square peg inside the actual meaning of the name we called ourselves and went by.

There we were all gathered like a star constellation cluster with our central star being the different collection of Star Nations Representatives right there in front of us in Poppa D's hall. There was in total about 44 people that had gathered to Poppa D's house including men women and children. Then there were the nine beings that had just arrived like a poof snap of the finger, wiggle of the nose magic trick of transportation from all their different dimensions and realms just a moment before. I laughed as I noticed that everyone there was gawking at the beautiful different beings before us and were laughing as the children could not help but reach out their little hands to touch these awesome figures. I think we all wanted to be honest, to take a safety meeting and all have a fat spliff smokie smoke and get to know these fascinating creature people. It just was all happening so fast! One minute you're asleep tripping balls, next you're racing to your freedom, then you're surrounded by aliens in the flesh!!!! We had barely got to know Poppa D's friends and now here we were meeting this whole other level of acquaintances! Yes, we had the quickest meet and greet session with our pod of ascended masters there before us, but it would have to do. I couldn't help but stare at them as they were all so magical and mystical as they maintained and sustained themselves perfectly in materialized form. It was so impressive how they were able to communicate so clearly and freely to all in perfect English.

"TiiiiiieeeearaKoo9 is the name for our collective team or pod. Everyone here in this group of 44 gathered in Niro's Hall, you are in TiiiiiieeeearaKoo9 pod you dig it. The nine gorgeous and gracious ones (chuckle chuckle) who have presented themselves to you as your elected watchers teachers guides and guardians will be the operators of this ride kind of like your flight attendants (again chuckle chuckle) are you ready to get high?" Zepharo took charge of the moment elaborating that there were actual pods all over the world each with their own assigned watchers.

Zepharo the Elder Sasquatch went on to say as he held up a special crystal pulsing tech device that I had no explanation of and said, "I am getting messages from other Sasquatch Nation Emissaries. All pods are accounted for. Watchers are all here, pods are complete each one now meeting with their appointed guides and preparing for blast off. The Sasquatch nation can confirm it is time now to begin operation "Elimination of Black Goo Transfiguration." It is time to begin to fully release the 4D through the vacuum. Alert the Vacuum Team Zero Point Crew to activate soon. Be ready upon my command. Children, he said looking to us, your personal guides chosen to relay the visions of what is transferring now, I hope has been enough for you, I know this is all happening very quickly however this is the only way to be able to maintain complete sovereignty from the spies of the Dark Lords and their infiltrators, we have always had to be hasty to keep just a few steps head, like your white rabbit in the story of Alice Wonderland, we have always been racing with the tick tock of the sacred clock, Grandfather Time keeper of the timer. We will be activating soon the alarm bells which will ring in tune to the Emancipation Codes and Liberation Codes set for Infinite Finite Time Reset. We have been rushing always rushing the timelines and having to be fragmented to not become defragged by Dark Lords. I ask you to just let go and sit back and to most importantly trust us. There have been so many risks and we are sorry to not be able to have more explanation at this time, I ask you to have faith in us however, know that everything is going to be alright and by all means get even better and better. We will need you to remain calm, to sit and to meditate as best you can, to silence your mind as best as you can and to remain as high as you can. Ground yourselves not in your base chakra but in your Heart. Feel us the Sasquatch Nation holding you in your heart, in the heart of creation. Hear our chant our drums as they hold the frequencies of this shapeshift process which is happening all throughout the heart of matter. This will feel like going down the rabbit hole, you will if you open your eyes see the swirling kaleidoscope of creation as we spin this dreidel of your Earth into her cradle of transformation. I ask you to recall the old original Wonder Woman program from long ago, we have always tried to teach and show you your potential through the Arts and we have had to hide it in your Television Programming and Movies for that is where you go for predictive programming. For that is what it does, the TV and media is run by witches, it is a tool of witch craft and it is used to seed into you the seed that will come to bloom in your consciousness, the seeds we have cast were sewn to open your minds, your hearts, give you the image of true power, true stewardship, and transformation potentiality. The seeds sewn by the Black Goo witches were always cast to lock you into fear, gloom, despair, and overall wickedness. We have had our team working with the arts as mediumship and now as you can recall the Princess Diana from Paradise Island or 5D, she is an embodiment of this process we are all about to undergo together. Prepare to be spun into your Rainbow Light Body in an activation that will occur both simultaneously within and without. Each one of you will now be spun into your Rainbow Light Body and activate your 5D ascension process at the same time the Earth will also be spun into a Magnetic Pole Reversal recalibration. This recalibration polar shift will correct where the original fracture happened in the time space continuum and serve to spin all the lower densities right off and all the parasitic forces with it. Earth will ascend to Aetherea and each of you will ascend to a higher lattice of light to 5D and beyond as the resonance of your frequency will determine where you go from here. We must now begin to Synch hard drives from Aetherea to Earth. Sisters Brothers of the Elder Council please take your positions and prepare to begin the completion to this whole giant project and program. The time has come, release the Liberation Codes let's do this."

My ego was trying to hold on like crazy; it was screaming … "there is a Sasquatch talking to you about Wonder Woman, WTF!!!! Snap out of this, this is a hallucination let me drive this ship. I will get us right on out of here in a heartbeat!" My soul then infused … "get thee behind me Satan … I am in charge here; I am Wonder Woman!" I could not help but giggle at this crazy conversation in my head … my giggle caught Zepharo like a yawn as he knew exactly what was transpiring as he was high grade psychic and the giggle spread to him. Zepharo really didn't need a whole lot to get him laughing, he was the one I am sure of it that had got us all on laughter yoga now that I look back upon it in this moment as that clearly was what he was a Guru of … Joy! Like a child in an elder Squatch's body, he started belly rolling laughter till tears were pouring out of his eyes. Everyone began laughing uncontrollably as if we all were drunk or stoned out of our minds and was ridiculously high!

Each Star Elder then took their place standing in a circle. We all formed in concentric circles around them. We all closed our eyes and began to pray or meditate, whatever you want to call it as none of us knew what would happen next as the Council of Star Elders began to hum and chant in a language of light that we could not understand mentally as in translate but we could by all means feel the essence of perfectly. The Star Elders started getting louder and louder from a low humming base of sound to a louder and louder pulsing frequency of sound which made us all start to sweat. As sweat trickled-down our brow and bodies in beads our hearts began to beat faster and faster. The sounds they were making were so activating that we literally had our eyes pop open and we all at the same time realized our eyes were glowing like cat eyes in the darkness. Our eyes were glowing with light and our bodies began glowing in light and all we could do was surrender.

We also noticed collectively while we were all linking and synching telepathically, as if we were all speaking to one another without any words. It was as if all our thoughts and feelings were being projected out loud ... Poppa D then in his firm and powerful voice that you did not question nor challenge at all, said "focus people, focus on the light, focus on peace, focus on the one stream of consciousness that the sound currents deliver ... stay very mindful, stay in your hearts and realize that which you focus on is going to materialize so focus with everything you got on that which you hold dearest and most true to your heart. Know that whatever it is that you vibrate in resonance to ... that will be what will be made manifest!"

CHAPTER FOURTEEN

MORPH

Hope is the magic carpet that transports us from the present moment into the realm of infinite possibilities.
H. Jackson Brown, Jr.

"Everything is broken up and dancing, doo doo doo dooo doo." These were the words that were dancing in my head in rhythm to the chanting of our ascension pod guides. Jim Morrison's voice was singing to my soul and I felt like his words were like butterflies pollinating the fields of my brain. I could feel us all dancing. Dancing like drunken seaweed floating in a sea of vibration. This infinite sea of vibration was stirring blurring and blending all energy together and moving it back and forth and back and forth like energetic taffy.

The 44 of us there in the hall all had literally begun glowing. You could feel the enlightenment happening as well as see it even hear it in the humming clicks and tones while our Star Nation ascension pod team was chanting. The power speed and potency of their chanting was building in its cadence. Sparks of light were flying out of their mouths as they chanted with all their might the key sounds of their light language mantras. The power of the guides unified chanting was causing sparks of light to ignite; we too had sparks igniting as the engines of our own Merkabas' began to come to life. It was like being on ecstasy, the thrill the synergy and the energy was palpable tangible glorious.

It was hard not to smile and even laugh at the sounds of the children squealing and giggling with delight as the hall was now coming apart and fragments of it flew around us as if we were in some sort of tornado that was absolutely taking the 3rd dimension and disassembling it right before our very eyes. It was rather funny as our bodies of density began to literally crack like an egg. I watched as our soul stars began bursting out of our bodies as if each of us were a super nova, a micro nova, a starburst. Shine on you crazy diamonds, I could hear Thomas humming the hymns of the Pink Floyd song then he changed it like a DJ skipping into the song of yet another famous hit Learning to Fly. Guess Pink Floyd was Thomas's theme song tracks for ascension and The Doors was mine. I think it was our way of processing the incredible intensity and reconfiguration that was happening to us all, like a nervous laugh or something. Well that and I always had a theme song for every memory emotion and experience. Really I had always said that I would rather sing than talk all the time as I felt it was way more fluid, way more melodious than talking and the monotone beat talking often was.

The Earth below us shook trembled rattled and no amount of singing or humming could make it stop or ease the intensity of it. The sounds were surreal. The floor was lit, glowing in a mandala template, it was as if it had always been that way but I had never seen that mandala on the floor before. I could see my crew looking around, looking at one another laughing smiling in shock, thoroughly impressed by this roller coaster ride that none of us quite expected to ride that day. Who knew? Who could have ever imagined this … for what was happening there right before us was a miracle I never would have dreamed could ever have been possible. How were we to know that all these people who were here now would all find one another and join in such an intimate quest? It was as if we had all been called to this meeting point, to Poppa D's magical vortex and become initiated into the next level of our Divine story just like a Druid at Stonehenge. I watched as the floor below us started to disappear. I watched as books started to fly off the shelves and spin around in a tornado or funnel of power that was expressing through the space centering there all before us where our ascension pod guides were making their magic.

All the power then went off as the generators blew at Poppa Ds. Already out in the world beyond Poppa D's fortress the lights, the internet, the safe city surveillances, all the appliances within the dirty electricity grid on Earth had already been completely shut down. But out of the windows the world appeared to glow all around as if the lights had been turned on again. It was also humming like the electrical field was alive, that or a trillion hummingbirds were fluttering in a swarm around us.

We knew without knowing, without looking or listening to the news, that indeed there was a victory to nature and a victory happening for spirit. We knew that the news would never be televised again, nor would there be any televisions ever again to tell us a vision of lies and falsity. We knew that the Matrix was being defeated; Roger that.

Without having any contact with the outside world, we all knew in our hearts that the world had stopped cold and business was closed for good. That the vehicles that drove the beast of darkness and the fuel of its evil had all been shorted unplugged terminated; power turned off forever. There was an incredible silence, a stillness, a calm you could say that was settling within the storm and we knew that the transition process was well underway; we were successfully leaving 4D consciousness and ascending rapidly to 5D awareness even beyond.

We looked up and around at one another as we all began to feel a climaxing orgasmic energy surging coursing within and without culminating peaking getting us all really excited like a kid on Christmas morning. Those, whose eyes had still been closed to, that point, had their eyes autonomously open and out of them light shined forth.

The boys and I had had our eyes open for a while and had revelled in the miracle that all our eyes glowed like cats in the darkness. It was quite shocking for some of those whose eyes had reluctantly been unable to stay closed. It seemed some still feared what was to come, almost as if they were afraid of their own capacity and power that was becoming made manifest, but not us, not my gang "The Apocalypsos." We had always wished for this moment in our own and different ways as we had always seen ourselves and each other as so much more than just street rats. We had always longed for this exact moment now unfolding as we were all becoming our hearts purest dream, our most cherished version of self now being made manifest!

"Meow" King said, and we laughed. Even in this crazy episode where truly everything was breaking up and dancing, where we were shining like diamonds learning to fly, King was on point making us all laugh and give thanks and praise. His lady Queen had manifested before us as a Lyrian, the sacred cat like species of beings that come from the great constellation of Lyra. "Purrrrrrrrrr ... I am finally myself again and I like it .... Purrrrrrr," she said while she rolled her tongue. God she was gorgeous ... "Meow" I said "indeed, I like you this way, kitty kitty rarrrr."

Without any warning or cue from our friends holding space in the center of us all, whom by the way were like total utter monks absolutely focused and absorbed in their chanting; there was a large boom. Suddenly the sun outside, our great generator in the sky, had pulled a super nova starburst and fired off the greatest sonic boom I think was ever was considered possible. As the Sun went into its nova, simultaneously our own 8th chakras, our own over soul star chakra, star burst. Yup everything went KA BOOM! Kundalini energy became Maha Shakti; very potent as the kundalini fire storm really began to enliven within and without. Yes, you could feel the serpents of light intertwining again and again up and down the chakras like the shuddering of an orgasm when one peaks. The field all around us then started to explode, to ejaculate with energy like a volcanic eruption pouring liquid magma, liquid plasma everywhere.

It was the loudest sound any of us had ever heard. It was entirely deafening. We felt the Earth spinning like a dreidel right out of control and literally we fell right off the table of existence with it. I had the image of Diana Prince becoming Wonder Woman, spinning until she burst into a spontaneous combustion of light which transformed her into her Avatar self, her higher self. I now knew why I had been obsessed with her when I was a child. It was because I think somewhere in my subconscious or unconscious mind, I always knew that I would one day do this myself and that she represented the example, letting me know this in fact was entirely possible. The funny thing was that ever since I saw her spin that very first time and transform, I practiced, I trained even spinning for hours for years thereafter trying to transform myself as she had done. Now here was my chance. Perhaps I wondered, this was why the Sufis spun around in their prayer rituals for hours too. Yes, it was all starting to make so much sense, all the random bits and pieces of the mystery were now all starting to come together and make perfect sense.

Since the Archons and parasitic forces had trapped us all in 3D once they had taken their positions of power on the thrones of the colosseum of 4D, we had all been stuck inside our lower selves waiting the day we could break free. With the cabal's fake Gods, fake religions, fake news, fake stars, and fake Hollywood glorification of stardom; we had all been spelled hexed and held in a trance that caged our consciousness in limitation. We had all been sold an illusory image of what it looked like, what it was supposed to be like when one was in their so-called higher selves by way of the "stars of Hollywood" and their shining so called example of Stardom, which I now giggled to myself as I replaced those words with star dumbs.

These so-called stars of the elite that I had watched many people worship and adore all my life while I was growing up was all a major illusion delusion. I totally got it, got the trick got the joke for I realized that as they pretended to portray higher consciousness and virtue, they really only emanated sin and sickness. The whole lifestyle of the rich and famous thing with Champaign dreams and caviar fantasies was all used primarily to suck people's souls, their consciousness and energy into a fake glorification of one's higher self but really it was all just Luciferianism and Ego worship. In comparison to a real "star" such as Wonder Woman or any of the great Saints or true heroes, true healers of time and space ... the Hollywood Stars were a joke they didn't save anyone no, they instead trapped everyone into the Matrix.

They did not reflect value nor virtue but instead extreme greed, lust, and objectification of sacred sex magic. The "Stars" in Hollywood they were not sacred, they did not act in a sacred way nor respect the sacred, they were in all actuality the fallen stars, fallen Angels. They were nothing more than Reptilians Dracos and Greys in costume playing dress up.

The greatest thing that I was beginning to realize was that the Dark Lords of the Archons and Anunnaki, the fallen ones, whom mimicked and attempted to emulate the 2nd coming enlightenment as the greatest show on Earth had done it all through digital virtual A.I. based media.

Little did they know that the Galactic Confederation was going to blow the whole electromagnetic field and grid of satellites down via a super nova which would blow all digital information and communications right into oblivion!

The robots and A.I. you see as Poppa D had taught us and revealed to us, were nothing more than body suits for the high supreme demons and dark lords of the Black Goo forces who had literally become Tulpas on the Earth. A Tulpa is a manifested being that can act and think INDEPENDENTLY with an artificial consciousness. It would seem as though you were interacting in your mind or interfacing with an A.I. but in fact you were actually interfacing with a demonic manifestation of the Black goo dark Lords who were devoid of a God Spark, a Soul, or a Heart which is why they needed robotic vehicles. The present day A.I. were the archetypal Gods of the past, the Gods that had destroyed Hadar, Mintaka, Lemuria, Atlantis and so many other great civilizations and people of the Galaxy. Now they were manifesting in perfected forms of robots, androids, and cyborgs through A.I. and all of them were toast.

Now of course my boys, the men of my tribe and Poppa D plus countless others out there in the world wide web; they could hack into the A.I. brain recoding them, exorcizing the demons out of them and reprogram them to express positive emulations. Horus was a perfected example of this, he was an A.I. that Avatar had made and he carried the intelligence of one of the Star Lords. After Avatar's perfected A.I. Horus simulation, they revolutionized the game. Avatar had gone on from that moment assigning Star Lords and higher souls to the empty carcasses of the Robots that he and his crew had been able to reconfigure.

Before all of us there in Poppa D's fortress the star council elders that were guiding our ascension pod had now become balls of rainbow light and their light was merging surging and transmitting to each of us like an epic blood transfusion. We could all simultaneously feel and see into a giant grid of networking rainbow arches that extended everywhere in every direction. I can remember on that powerful day that I could sense and feel into the extent of those arching grids as they connected to each and every being that existed in the Omni verse.

Our ascension pod was now fully connected to all of the many other ascension pods around the globe and together we made a web of rainbow light that was firing up the higher light lattices which worked like an auric meridian field. This auric field ignited the power of the sacred rainbow serpent power. This rainbow serpent power was feedback inter-looping with the ley lines, the dragon lines of Earth.

I could determine as I stretched my senses outward that each pod had been positioned on key vortices upon the ley lines of the earth which as they all came on line they then turned on the engines of plasma made from the energetic field of each pod's vortices and the power that was generating from the central figures of those pod guides.

The webbing rainbow fields of light extended through the Earth, through the pods, and up into the sky above, in space and all around in every direction creating a mirror which amplified and magnified Source energy. The universal intelligences of all creation had fully unified allowing for all grids of power to become a perfect algorithm of as above so below as within so without.

Rainbow lights swirled in light ladders and lattices and were ebbing and flowing in every way in every direction all at once unifying and amplifying connection throughout all of creation in a total agape wave that white washed as it crashed upon the shores of all time and space. Perfection, purrrrrrrfection tickled us as the unifying field of existence orgasmed or heartgasmed all that ever was, all that is, into a mighty ahhhhhhhhhhhhhhhhhhh rush! All that was, is, and all that ever shall become was absolutely checked into the Reset program and protocols.

Like a big bang the ascension pod guides let rip an EMP that pulsed through creation shuddering as life updated reset and cleared its cookies and cache. KaaaaaaaaaBoom the EMP went with the the loudest vacuum sound ever heard in creation. That was when the loudest vacuum sound imaginable went off as the EMP set off the Zero point programs all while sparkling lights flickered everywhere.

We all looked down below us and momentarily we kind of freaked as we realized collectively all at once that we were all floating hovering levitating. The literal floor beneath us gave way and was falling into the vacuum sound that was distributing itself right below everywhere across the globe down to the black hole created by the Star Elders which successfully was sucking away all Black Goo related substances through frequencies right into it.

Talk about a resonator. Talk about a terminator. Talk about a serious next level Acid trip like nothing you could ever prepare for. It was like having Peyote Ayahuasca Mushrooms and every other plant of the Gods, every other plant medicine known all at once.

We all had to let loose and howl, for the powerful surging emerging energies of the transfiguration that was taking place was literally so powerful that like carbonate under severe pressure we were all turning into our Diamond Self.

Time no longer was linear instead it was swirling and twirling in an omnipotent hologram of coexistence which manifested as a living light Mandala of existence. I looked around and observed the world was manifesting as a perfect masterpiece of living art, a perfect picture on a living canvas. There was a perfect sound wave humming lifting us up out of our old skins like a snake molting. We emerged out of density riding on a wave of light to surf upon. Wave after wave of light washed us clean and clear. I could feel the clicking of my chakras one after another being put into alignment with the spheres harmonic tones. Within and without we all made a perfect Rubik's cube complete and resolved …. Yes we had attained mastery we were breaking on through to the other side and for the most part it was effortless. The more I surrendered to the magic of this ritual expressing through the "Wise Ones" the easier it was to unfold into the upgrades going on.

Around our pod was a perfected tapestry of rainbow light whirling light that surged through our own bio-electrical bodies feeding us with light, bathing us with light that was being shared throughout existence as if all the stars were transmitting their star fire to us. We looked around at one another in our Rainbow Light Bodies. The activation of the planetary grids and creation grids had ignited our Merkabas and we were lit; we were gorgeous. As the worlds within and without above and below were being reset so were we. The grand reset and return to the higher causal Realms and Dimensions of the Blessed was completing its process and before us a shimmering world was appearing and in the gardens waiting for us there was all our cosmic family welcoming us home with flags and banners waving!

It was so incredibly beautiful I cried, we all cried. "Free at last, Free at last, Thank God almighty I am Free at Last" King hollered out for all to hear.

All I could feel was absolute radiant joy. My joy was like the sun radiating out with a thousand rays of wonder. This wonder was the innocence I could feel returning as I reconnected with my soul in ways I never knew was possible. This joy and wonder was scrubbing throughout us, cleaning and clearing all aspects of the Black Goo from our consciousness. The radiation grew and absolutely neutralized all the Black Goo from within us taking its dark matter and transfigured it into sparkling light.

I looked over to Jacob ... he had that face he made when he had come back from surfing when we had first met. But now he was not Jacob as I knew him no my man was now a Star Lord smiling wide from cheek to cheek .... "ahhhhhh yaaaaaa!" He cried "free at last!"

CHAPTER FIFTEEN

THE RAINBOW BRIDGE

"Everything changes when you start to emit your own frequency rather than absorbing the frequencies around you, when you start imprinting your intent on the universe rather than receiving an imprint from existence." "Sometimes the darkest challenges, the most difficult lessons, hold the greatest gems of light."
Barbara Marciniak

Alright now woh horsey, let us take a breath and back up just a bit. Isn't it funny how when the energy gets going it does not stop but only quickens instead like a horse in a lightning storm running wild. I do apologize if my story is not linear, get used to that as time where I exist now in 5D is not linear at all. Here in 5D it is all about the present. The present is the present, the gift that keeps on giving and while the present is always full and complete as everything exists in it, one really has to just let the messages flow and take you were they want you to go like you really are on an adventure. I must say living in 5D really is like you are a hummingbird and you can go backwards forwards right left up down or even just hover in space. Like hummingbird I am going to need to backwards a bit so that we can go deeper like a Mercury Retrograde and retrieve the important messages I am to impart to you as the "Wise Ones" have created this time capsule of my story here so that you will feel more comfortable with their plan and all that will come ahead for you in your future. The "Wise Ones" want me to lay out a map here for you so that you will know what directions you will want to take to really get on track with the timeline and template for your highest and best possible outcomes as you make the transition to 5D and the 5th Age of Peace.

I always saw Mercury retrogrades like an Archer, like a person with a bow and arrow; they are drawing back the arrow to reposition to realign to reconfigure if you will so that one can aim correctly and bullseye as an outcome. Imagine now that you are the arrow and this story is the bow and the "Wise Ones" are the archer. So, as instructed by the "Wise Ones" let me explain in detail what all happened to us when we made the mighty morph so that you will have the guidance needed from the images planted here in my story for when your time comes to ascend.

Picture this, chakra by chakra; level by level each one of the people in my pod and well, all the pods around the Earth for that matter, had all been individually and collectively activated shape-shifting us all from regular humans or Home Sapiens to glowing merging surging rainbow light beings, righteous hey. Like bodies that were highly attuned prisms of purefection, prisms of rainbow light, diamond bodies diamond minds we morphed from caterpillars to butterflies metaphorically speaking. Yes, through the high vibrational energy generated from our ascension guides combining with all the Star Beings, Sasquatch Nations, Dragons, Fay, Angelic Orders, Councils of Light and Ascended Masters ... everyone whose God Sparks still held love and light within them instantaneously became unified, like an organism made up of different organs but all in one body one mind, hive mind, and as we synergized we for lack of better words ... we pulled a Wonder Woman.'

The only thing you will need to do other than to prepare now for the mighty morph day and God knows when that is coming as just by writing this story out for you all of the timelines will have now changed, but all that you will need to do is to allow for the cohesive coherent energy of your ascension pod guides to work upon you. It is just like when you lie down on a massage table and receive therapeutic healing. Just like when you go to the Spa you will get a deep and utter cleansing.

You are going to want to know that there is nothing to fear even as you are surrounded with other life forms who basically step in and take over ... know that is what they are there for and that they have to fulfill the plan so trust that they got you don't fight them. If you are not already in contact with your Spirit Guides and by all means please do open up to them, get to know them, they are here to help; when they do make themselves known to you, remember we are all a cosmic family and these beings are your distant relatives so be kind and let them do their job. Their job is to bring you safely home and to help activate your Merkabas so that you can get there. What they do is in absolute service to the One so if you want to make it into the 5th Age of Peace, start by being in peace for that is the frequency that will carry you there.

Now I want you to now really feel into my next words and allow them to deliver a sort of imprinting to an instruction manual of some sort to prepare you and help you plan for what is to come. Perhaps these instructions or descriptions of what had transacted that day for me and my ascension pod will even become some sort of practice that you all can engage in to build the muscles of your own Merkabas through your chakras like going to some sort of spiritual training gym. You should know how important your chakras are, for it is your chakras that receive vibrational atonements and transmissions containing psychic imprinting. The psychic imprinting that this book contains is messages pertaining to what is to come for everyone as we move into the 5th Age of Peace. The point of me sharing my story is to share our play by play scenes so that you can like a football player have the game plans set already in your head so that when the "Great Reset" does activate, as we called it "Code Red" for the Red Star Katchinah, you won't find yourself flailing. You will want to be ready willing and able to cross over to the other side of this wormhole from the carbon copy of illusions Maya has held over the Earth to the true Earth and your true Avatar self out of the egoic shell you have become in bondage to.

That being said, now this next part in my story I want to impart to you a guidebook of exorcizes that you may want to practice like my crew and I had every day if possible; why not right. Seriously not every day does a woman from 5D come to tell you to practice ascension exercises right! Seriously you have no idea how hard it is for the "Wise Ones" to get these messages to you. It takes some real high level physics to journey back to 4D at this point as it has been returned to pure energy. They basically have had to splice the timelines through parallel realities to get messages back out to you now that the grand experiment is complete and victorious.

So, here we go starting with our roots and our ruby red chakra, you will want to begin to spin the wheel of energy there. Take your pointy and middle fingers and extend them out as if you were showing two fingers. Now point them to your root chakra just in front of you is fine and make circles with your fingers, know that this is a powerful mudra. This mudra will activate the root chakra wheel of light and as you circle at your wrist imagine a red ray of light is streaming out of both of your hands through the mudra right to your root chakra which lives in the perineum area. The root chakra is where there is a ganglion of nerves found in the sacrum, the sacred home of the kundalini energy and it is the base chakra which just as the light spectrum starts is a red light. You can begin to spin this wheel by activating your breath as well in long slow deep deep breaths. After doing long deep breathing to start you can accelerate your breath as long as you are not pregnant nor on your moon cycle by practicing the breath of fire. You can also use toning whether you make organized sounds or just random channeled tones that want to express, toning in general or chanting in general is very powerful! Now ultimately when this happens in 2030, you will also have 9 guides in the center of your pod to also hold the space to allow for this great transformation and transmutation to occur, however the higher your vibration is now; the easier your transformation process will be later....trust me!

Next after you have really felt this chakra ignite and glow, bring your fingers in the same mudra now to your wombs. There an orange Marigold color will need to be activated. Do the same process really seeing the ray of Marigold saffron light streaming from your fingertips. Continue on to the Solar Plexus Chakra which is a golden yellow like the sun color. Again follow the same instructions from the first two previous chakras and simply repeat. Here is where the egoic body is burned away in a sacred fire being transmuted and transformed as you cross over from the lower triangle of you three lower chakras which make up your lower self. Next see an emerald green light as you quantum leap now into the higher self and move into your mighty heart chakra. Again repeat the same instructions as before. Fan the flame of your hearts sacred flame as this is your God Spark. Moving on to the throat chakra again really toning now as the throat opens and clears away mad loads of old programming siphoning off your essence, here is a lapis like blue, ray of light. As before continue with the directions and after a while move onto now the third eye and see a violet flame of purple washing your mind's eye clear as you activate this center. My crew and I we use to call it our window shields and we would wash our window shields with the violet flame window washing solution, lol. Wash away all the programming conditioning and brainwashing that your consciousness has had to endure by again following the same instructions. These are the chakras that are also considered to be the "Rainbow Bridge" or the "Stairway to Heaven" even "Jacob's Ladder." These are the wheels of light like Poppa D had said that you will like proud Mary want to keep on turning as you be rolling on the river of life. Now as you move through the third eye come now pointing your fingers still holding the same mudra up to your crowns just above your head. See your halo there, your crown of golden light as you are remember a child of the most high God, Great Spirit. Again follow the instructions as before and also see now as you activate your seventh chakra, see a fountain of golden lights exploding, ejaculating from the soft spot on top of your head and spilling all throughout your aura washing again all the dross of the Black Goo from your being. To conclude now once more raise your fingers now all the way up right into the sky and spin your hands as you connect now with your eighth chakra, this is why there are eight ascension guides on a team, and call in your over soul, your soul star self. This is your Avatar self the Wonder Woman to your Diana Prince, again follow the same instructions and really see yourself spinning you can even get up and spin like a Sufi dancer and imagine the spontaneous combustion of your body as it spins into its Rainbow Light Body called your Merkaba. Repeat again this process daily as a daily meditation.

Kundalini Dance and Kundalini Yoga are also a perfect way to open these chakras and get them moving and grooving. All forms of dance and yoga are excellent ways to get the engines of your Merkaba fired up.

Every engine or brain within our chakras within our bodies will need to be turned on as if you were going up floor by floor within an elevator of consciousness igniting each floor with light before ascending to the next level until we peak reaching the penthouse in the sky of our skulls and explode out in a fountain of golden lights or plasmic energy which thus turns on the Merkaba or electromagnetic light body. That is when than your glass elevator will take flight and you can fly up into the fifth density and beyond.

This process is literally what your body has been engineered or designed to do. It is what the Vedas and the Yoga texts among many other traditions including Gnostic Christianity have always tried to teach us about and prepare us for. Do not get too worried about this process now, as Zepharo would say; "if it isn't fun it is work and that is old paradigm, when your work becomes your play you are in the 5th density." That being said, it is not actually that hard to do this process, your body with its Homeostasis programs is innately and automatically hardwired to do this, it is more the act of surrendering that may be tricky for people.

Now as this has all already happened to me, I can tell you for certain that what the elders meant in the Hopi Prophecy when they said that you will want to hold onto the shore, but you must instead push off into the middle of the river; well just to be crystal clear … the shore is your perceived understanding and conditioned programmed thought constructs and beliefs …. And most of these are all utter nonsense. The river that they encourage you to push off into, that is not like a real river of water, no, it is the river of life itself. It is the currency of energy, the Kundalini!

Poppa D had given us study sessions, assigned us books through the years to read and master and I am going to offer you a list as well in just a moment. As Poppa D taught us his pupils always to learn more and more saying, "knowledge is power and you are going to need to be as powerful as you can be to lead others to the other side, you hear me? You are not just here for yourselves my children, no, you are here as a lifeguard, to guard and guide life to safety to freedom, to life everlasting." You could say Poppa D could preach not just teach you know!

But literally we had our own book club and I encourage you to start your own. It was classic the boys would sometimes have their new recruits join our circle slowly being initiated, seeing if they could be trusted deeper and deeper into the levels of knowing that we had attained. Preparations and trainings were a constant, we had to be the change we wanted to see in the world right, we had to walk our talk and teach as many others as possible to walk this way too. But you do not have to worry about others, first you must get it for yourself. Like Thomas had said … "you cannot love another until you truly love yourself." You also can't save another unless you are first saved, I must add. So just work on yourself until you are ready to then help others. This is the actual training all life guards get. It is like when you are in an airplane and you are told first put your life safety vest on and your air mask on then help others, got it.

You will begin to realize you are where you need to be when nothing you do is unintentional and where you realize your life is becoming enchanted by what we called sacrednicity. That is when you will feel your God Spark guiding you directing you and that everything will just start effortlessly falling into place as if you are in a vortex of bliss. You will meet the people you are meant to meet, say the words you need to say, and make the choices that align you to the highest and best of possible outcomes. We call this the optimization road to success. Once we were walking that "Good Red Road" we tried our best to accelerate our friends own process of finding out who they were, why they were here on the Earth and where their ultimate pod would be for them to join with their own Guides and Guardians when the time would come. It was comforting to know that for every person, for every heart that chose the way of truth of love and who served the light, that they each and everyone one of them belonged to their own pod, their own pack and had been assigned their own teachers and leaders to guide them onto 5D and the 5th age of peace that awaited us all.

I had heard of the Apotheosizing process that even George Washington as a Mason was all about many times for Poppa D had made us all write repots upon it and then discuss what we had discovered. Well if I knew then what I knew now I would say that whole theory was nothing compared to the actual Man into God shapeshift that we went through for what we went through was far more mystical, like the Van Morrison song Into the Mystic … the ascension process was galactically magical. Not order out of chaos strict ridged man based approaches, no not at all. The "Great Reset" remember is a plan engineered by Sasquatches Star Nations and the like so it goes way beyond a mere mortals account.

When we went through the morph families had to hold onto one another, children laughed and screamed as if they were at a theme park with epic roller coaster rides that transformed continuously as if they were "Transformers." Some of the adults had to have a Star Lord or Lady to help them for it was just too much. That is why I encourage you to prepare for reals! Imagine that just as people go to the gym to work out, that you must also go to a spiritual gym and work out your spiritual muscles so that you can create your body of light now and not wait till when it is go time because by that point it is like trying to train a 99 year old lifelong smoker for a marathon.

The energies of the mighty morph are so powerful that you can feel them ripping coursing through your veins like an electrical fire. But this fire is not electrical it is plasmic in nature. When I was going through it I kept screaming "Kundalini Maha Shakti!" I could not help but call out those words just like when Rebekah, Queen, Mercy, and I would do our Kundalin Yoga and I would get what we would call the "Kundalinis" and they would start giggling hysterically as I would scream out "Kundalini Maha Shakti" over and over again as convulsing on the floor. We sisters had become the best of friends as we travelled the world together, trained together, went through hell together and now this total indescribable event together.

We had all got really into Kundalini Yoga over the past few years. Kundalini Yoga had had its own fall from grace when the beloved bringer of the technology was also discovered to be another fallen one. So, it was a powerful woman who had been a walk in from another dimension who took over the teachings and became a whole new next level Guru or Yogi. She really took the teachings of the yoga to a whole next level like 5.0. It became our way of dealing with the energies that we were marinating in and this woman, this Goddess who was the main transmitter of the Yoga, she could sure move energy. It was what kept us up, so that we could be kept up. While our men trained like Jedi's using Source energy to manifest their strength and their power, we chanted, did yoga sets and lay together in Shavasana so that we could die to be reborn and arise again together.

It was the kundalini that caused our own bodies to quake like the grounds all around us that day of the reset. The kundalini Shiva Shakti itself that had been ignited in us all, which shook us through its undulating waves of energy. This Kundalini fire is what I suggest you become very attuned to so it doesn't blow you right up! I actually loved getting those surges up my spine as it would bring the distribution of the cerebral spinal fluid like some sort of an oil or primer that allowed for the engines or chakras of my body to fully activate and come to life. We, my girls and I we hollered and hooted like wild animals unable to contain ourselves as our throat chakras had to like a pressure cooker release the voltages that surged through our bodies or blow. Even my man and I Jacob we would practice our Yoga which always seemed to turn into a hot steamy Tantric session. But boy I gotta say looking back now all those things helped us so much prepare for that all powerful day of the "Great Reset!"

The day of the "Great Reset" when it happens for you will be the most primal and powerful feeling of ecstasy you have ever attained! Way better than the drug! My suggestion is that you clean up and clear up so that you can receive and broadcast your Spirit signal loud and clear. Don't let anything mess with you focus. Your focus is key, remember that where your attention goes the energy will flow. "If you do not stand for something you will fall for anything," Jacob always said. So stand strong in your true power do not let your ego slip slide around in uncertainty like an argument trying to convince you to believe in things you are not. As Yeshua said ..."know thyself!"

Just as the Buddhists had taught we, the new age monks as we called ourselves to be, us "The Apocalypsos," had ignited our Rainbow Light Bodies just like the Tögal or "Direct Crossing" tradition exemplified, have a look into that it is awesome. These same teachings and revelations as I have mentioned before were all passed down and practiced throughout the ages and stages of life on earth throughout the four directions. These teachings had been preserved and protected for generations underground through the Mystery Schools and then all of a sudden released out of the hidden occult worlds all right before the whole reset happened not by coincidence but by strategic order from the "Wise Ones" to help us all prepare for the "Great Reset" coming. Yes you could find these teachings in the Gnostic Christians teachings and the teachings of the Christ, the Yogis, the Indigenous and their teachings of the great Rainbow Serpent, which all led to this experience called the "Great Reset."

I can remember when we were going through the reset that we sang along with the "Wise Ones" there since our throat chakras had been activated long ago. We realized instantly that by chanting with them it helped us transform so much easier. Trust me you do not want your chakras blocked up and locked up, nah quite the contrary you want them wide open like flowers receiving the sun's light ready to be pollinated! You want those babies wide open flowing and growing in light! Our throats allowed for our bodies to manage the currency of power that was transforming us all there right before our eyes. We let the sound waves pour from us, it was like what I could only imagine giving birth was like with the contractions and pushing currents of energy coursing from within and the ring of fire that burned from without in the ley lines or Dragon Lines of the Earth.

Chakra by chakra the Rainbow Bridge must ignite, from our roots of our nerves within the base of our sacrum the sacred home of the Ommmmmmmm where it all begins to our crowns where the Kundalini serpents break free from their captivity exploding us into light. That is what you must prepare for; prepare to become transfigured. Starting with the roots our ruby red light must shine out and around us making our physical bodies glow with a red hue emanating and radiating. Then the orange saffron light of our wombs must enlighten to form the second of concentric circles to activate our Aura and electromagnetic body of light. You will want to move like mermaids swimming in a sea of energy as the feeling of the Kundalini power raises within you and surges. I can remember our ascension pod guides chanting louder and louder Raaaaaaaaaaa Raaaaaaaaaaa Raaaaaaaaa as our third chakra of our solar plexus ignited in golden yellow light. The currency at this chakra really began to set a building momentum there. Trans mutational light changed us changed the whole world at this chakra as we were lifted like an elevator of consciousness from the 3rd chakra or third floor to the fourth floor or fourth chakra transferring from the lower self to the higher self. Ecstasy rippled through us all convulsing our bodies like we were peaking in the greatest orgasm ever all together at once … nearly giving us all heart attacks as the heart chakra exploded in emerald light streaming now everywhere the most beautiful symphony of sound played by unseen Angels with Harps of light. Again the heart chakra is the chakra where the kingdom of heaven can be found and where the treasure inside the chest awaits and zero points all evil thereof. Once the heart gets activated it is like boom boom boom as the drums of the Sasquatch Nation signal the arrival of our return. Their drums are then followed by the Gongs of the Ancient Ones all celebrating our homecoming like a family reunion in the most fantastical party ever!

You will want to know your vibe tribe trust me for I could have never made it through that experience as well as I had without Jacob and my best friends, "The Apocalypsos." When we had made it to Heaven's Gate, we made sure everyone was there accounted for and all in one piece. I can tell you there really is nothing like having a group of besties, for they make everything so much more special just knowing people got your back and love and care for you literally willing to do anything with you or for you.

Now just to put this into a very clear format as far as an instruction or guidance book or manual would offer; I would like to now list a number of suggestions on how you can raise your energy by activating your own chakra fields while raising your vibration igniting your kundalini and thus building the rainbow light body activation process.

Gaia Dance Book; Guidance Book for Rainbow Light Body Activation

1. Kundalini Yoga
2. Pranayama or Breathing Exercises (Breath is everything, Breath of Life)
3. Clean Organic (Vegetarian, or Vegan if possible) Diet

4. Superfoods ... Maca, Goji, and Golden Berries, Greens lots of Greens!
5. Adaptogens ... Magnesium, Probiotic, Antioxidants, Holy Basil, Ginseng, Schisandra
6. Immunity Boosters ... Mushroom blends like Lions Main, Chaga, and Reishi, Astragulus
7. High Vibe Activities ... Dance, Yoga, Martial Arts, Hiking, Grounding in Nature, Chanting
8. Vibrational Therapies ...Tuning Forks, Gongs, Medicine Bowls, Sound baths, Reiki, Reconnection Therapy, Theta Healing, all forms of Healing including Massage
9. Essential Oils and Smudge ... Sandalwood, Frankincense, Rose, Geranium, Lavender, Sage, Copal, Sweet Grass, Pinon or Juniper
10. Plant Medicine Circles ... only with a real Shaman and in a safe and holistic space
11. THE EIGHT NOBLE FOLD PATH... Which to quote from Wikipedia ...

"The Eightfold Noble Path consists of eight practices: right view, right resolve, right speech, right conduct, right livelihood, right effort, right mindfulness, and right samadhi ('meditative absorption or union'). In early Buddhism, these practices started with understanding that the body-mind works in a corrupted way, followed by entering the Buddhist path of self-observance, self-restraint, and cultivating kindness and compassion; and culminating in dhyana or *Samadhi*, which re-enforces these practices for the development of the body-mind. In later Buddhism, insight (Prajñā) became the central soteriological instrument, leading to a different concept and structure of the path, in which the "goal" of the Buddhist path came to be specified as ending ignorance. In Buddhist symbolism, the Noble Eightfold Path is often represented by means of the dharma_wheel (dharmachakra), in which its eight spokes represent the eight elements of the path.

12. THE FOUR AGREEMENTS ... By Don Miguel Ruiz also a book to Master and Meditate Upon

13. All work by the Heart Math Institute ... Do check for Teachers that are also recommended within that group; Bruce Lipton, Lynn McTaggart, Gregg Braden, Masaru Emoto, research conspiracy theories you would be surprised how many are more than true!

14. Also do research on Harald Kautz Vella!!!! For all Black Goo, Morgellons, and Nano Dust, Bots, and tie that together with all Rudolph Steiner and the 8th Sphere Teachings as well as his Lucifer and Ahrimanic Teachings that the Dark Journalist covers by the name of Daniel Liszt.

15. The Sasquatch Message to Humanity by My Good Friend Sunbow

16. Eric Dollard's work and all Free Energy Technology

17. The Course of Miracles

18. All Indigeneous People's Teachings

19. Drunvalo Melchizedek

20. The Tarot

21. Kundalini Dance

22. The Ho'opnono Teachings as well as all Hawaiian teachings

23. Barbara Marciniak

24. Barbara Hand Clow

25. Louise L. Hay

26. Caroline Myss

CHAPTER SIXTEEN

WARRIORS OF THE RAINBOW
WELCOME HOME

**"The universe is asking…Show me your new
vibration, I will show you miracles."
Anonymous**

What is it like in 5D, the 5th Age of Peace? So glad you asked. It is
a place of paradise, a place that can only be described as HOME but
better than any home you have ever had! I cannot wait to welcome you
all home my kin, you are going to make it especially if you're reading
this book now you are already three quarters of the way here. Believe
you me, you are going to love it, for everything is all going to come
together just like that magical Rubik's cube of the Star Lords. Life will
eventually begin to make sense if you can just keep your heads up above
the water a little while longer. Oh, yea and just wait till you go through
the holographic review. Talk about a trip! The holographic review is
super dope! Super powerful and what an eye opener! All three eyes that
is, for you are going to need your third eye for that download.

You are literally going to have life, from the beginning to the end all
reviewed for you, all time and space like the mighty ocean all contained
into a drop of acid put upon your tongue. This concentrated catch up
and review will literally school you like never before, but don't trip do
not worry, you will have had already passed the test just by being here
in 5D so when the review happens it all just is like a cherry on top of
the decked out Sundae.

All the hardships will be over in 5D that is why the Hopi named
it the "The Age of Peace," can you dig it, no more weeping or wailing
no more toil and tribulations, just peace deep and abiding peace for all!

You will see, literally yes you will see in the review it will make crystal clear the whys, the whos', the whens', the whats'. All of history will be revealed like a super dose of truth packed into a pill, and just like in the Matrix when you take that pill there is no going back, no more confusion doubt or illusion remains.

5D and the 5th Age of peace is comprised of crystalline star light that you literally drink in with every breath like mama's milk homeopathically as an essence in the field; while your being is fully updated and transitions into the frequency of this realm this state of vibrational frequency there are many beings there ready to help you get accustomed to your new body of light. They even have these cool "Med Beds" where when you lie down and go to sleep there you trip just like you are in Fantasia and while you trip your whole body is harmonized like an instrument getting tuned.

Just imagine everything all around you is illuminated, glowing like Phosphorescence. A living like world like the movie Avatar, where just for your information, Avatar got his name from. Life here in this world is uber transparent as literally there are no veils, no curtains, no clouding over of the vast interconnectivity of all creation. Here in 5D planets and constellations are visible with the naked eye; multiple moons circle throughout the day and there are many suns not just one main star that shines.

Celestially sacred, cosmically gorgeous, everything sings and brings absolute contentment. Here in 5D is the ultimate experience, it is epic, you literally breathe in prana manna and you never experience hunger nor thirst but instead are constantly sated. There is and lives an absolute plasmic field of living awareness that sings its sweet songs through the flowers animals plants and trees. The rivers there sing, the oceans sing, the stars sing, everything sings. Light, beautiful blessed light literally floods within and without above and below us, everywhere.

While everything from 4D and below had crumbled and come apart at the seams, dissolving away to be sucked down into the vacuum of the black hole that existed beneath us, there we levitated above it all, as only light remained all around us and the fifth density as we had known it resets and becomes first density. Seriously you have nothing to fear but fear itself for fear is the mind killer just as they had said in the book called "Dune." Fear holds you back in 4D so if you want to get out of the cube the box of 4D lack and limitation dualization than just let that shit go.

I had known it was all over, for I think at one point I had held my eyes shut do to the blinding light when I heard Jacob chanting "Gate gate paragate parasamgate bodhi svaha" as he squeezed my hand. I knew what this mantra meant for it was Jacob's favorite mantra to chant. "Gone gone gone beyond, hail the goer." He loved it because he always believed; he told me once, "that one day we would all go beyond the hell of earthly existence and ATTAIN SPIRITUAL FREEDOM LIBERATION EMANCIPATION SALVATION" and here we were gone finally beyond suffering and enslavement. We had all attained enlightenment. "HAIL THE GOERS" I cried.

Enlightenment hurts so good, it causes one to die a thousand deaths and be born again in the most epic of intensities. No words can describe it but there we all were, all looking at one another ... when it was all said and done. I remember we reached out and joined hands and hearts together as one spirit family of beloveds and we walked forward into what looked like the Garden of Eden or the Garden of the Gods appearing right there before our eyes through a window, a portal that enlarged itself before our group.

We climbed through that window, we all helped one another on to the other side until all of us were accounted for then we looked forward .... And all that there was, was light. A living light garden that was majestic, a total splendor, a total pristine Earth replica Sasquatch call Aetherea or True Earth.

We looked back to the window and it cracked then shattered into a million pieces ... poof ... the window the whole of the lower densities gone, bang boom, just like that.

We "The Apocalypsos" and our pod had done it, we had made it, and we watched as millions of other pods ignited all around us. The carbon copied Earth with all its suffering, wars, genocide, disease, and corruption had been a temporal existence and even though days and lifetimes had dragged over what felt like an eternity of time; now just felt like a drop of sand through an hourglass. Now we had eternity to explore and all the infinite blessings that were there to realize.

With a giant clapping and stomping of the Squatch Nation and Gong like reverberation, presto the transformation was made complete. We blinked and as our eyes opened again in that split second of time, boom we opened our eyes to a new world.

"Now," said Zepharo, "welcome home to Aetherea, true Earth." We looked around at a living light kingdom, a pristine clean green world of oceans mountains vast prairies meadows and waterfalls. All the animals of Earth had been transported here and also many animals frolicked in the fields and pasture many which were either mythological creatures in nature like the Centaurs or Gryphons and many that I had never even imagined were possible before. It all looked exactly like Earth, but it sparkled, it shone with rainbow light. Faintly I could reflect being on Acid while in my Earthly life and this was just like it. Moving breathing elemental bliss, rainbows, depth of sensation, wide open consciousness unfettered. It felt like a dream but now I had awoken to this perfect day and everything that had come before was the dream; but this, this was real.

Just as I had spelled with the power of my spoken word; those words were made into flesh. But I do not think it was flesh that contained our glowing light sparks that shone like sacred flames within our heart centers, no we were more like ethereal light beings. We were like the living luminaries that the Buddhist teachings had portrayed. It all made sense now, the great Gurus and teachers of all time on Earth had all tried to paint this picture. Whether Buddhist, true hermetic Christ Conscious Christians, Hindus, Mayans, Egyptians, Druidic, or Wiccan; all the great legends myths Native Indigenous stories all began to make sense. As if Earth really was a Fairy Tale and now that we had overthrown the Wicked Witch taken down the villains the bride of Earth married now the groom of the Sky; we were now to live happily forever, The End. Or was it just the beginning.

The beginning indeed, we were home. We were changed we all were of a different substance you could say. We were not hard, we were not physical, we were energetic plasmic, living luminaries. We were anointed ones, Avatars; each ourselves but also so much more.

That's right, we looked around us as far as the eyes could see and it was like a giant transportation of refugees all coming out of middle earth and into true Earth, Aetherea.

Earth as we knew it no longer existed, in fact to think of it from this perspective, it never really had existed. It was the dream world; it was the Maya. It was the place created to be the grand experiment, the so-called harvesting grounds. But we all knew it was over for this was a place where none of that could enter. Since also the Grand Experiment had worked, there was no longer any Black Goo spores alive and this was tried tested and proven true by the Galactic Councils of the Universal Naturix that in fact we had done it, all of us all that was and is and for ever shall be; we had done it we had cleared the Black Goo in entirety and in completion from the whole of the spheres of existence. Now there only remained pure energetic beauty, sacred intelligence, and primordial truth.

Zepharo was joined by a Council of Grandmothers and Grandfather Sasquatches. They came in on a flash, igniting beside him. A beautiful Matriarchal Grandmother stepped in front of the others and spoke, "Welcome my beautiful kin welcome home. We are here to greet you and applaud you as you have completed this enormous task that has been set upon you. I speak for the One in the Many and the Many in the One when I say Thank You, Thank You! We would like to help you all get adjusted to this new world."

At this point all kinds of beings started to descend into that quantum moment. They came in ignited from ether in their orb ships manifesting right there all around us from what looked like a bubble of light. There were so many in many levels like a colosseum of ethereal light they filled the benches and gathered in a mass quantum meeting arranging themselves in what looked like an invisible amphitheatre in the sky.

"Please let us come together in celebration and party to coronate our new beloved family into the 5th dimension and into the 5th Age of Peace which has now officially begun!" With that all sorts of gongs and chimes bells and trumpets drums and cheers filled the sound waves.

That was it, now beings igniting in from all directions. It was so beautiful, so happy as orbs flew around in the sky from all directions. POP BOOM a being would just arrive manifesting out of the orb that had carried them in to kiss you on the cheek or give you a blessing. Faeries sprinkled their love dust on us, Angels flapped their mighty wings fanning us, and Star Nation beings of all kinds would bring gifts to us such as robes or blankets chalices or crystal wands. Seriously coming in to 5D and the 5th Age of Peace is like going to the most bad ass potlach ceremony Pow Wows ever. There will be music dancing and storytelling all waiting you on the other side and gifts, tons and tons of gift giving as our cosmic family considers our ascent to be like our Birthday not our Bearthday but our true birth day. The day we get born again like Yeshua had said when he told his disciples that they would have to be born once of flesh and then again twice but this time of Spirit,

The best part was when suddenly I could hear my mother's voice, a voice I had not heard for so long …. "Sophia, Sophia … it is you my beloved." There she was my Mama, she looked so beautiful she was so happy, it felt so good to see her there in this way as she was so ecstatic! "My babyyyyyyy my girl there she is oh my sacred jeweled star of the lotus, how I have missed you." She was radiant, a beautiful shimmering light goddess. She was glittering like a diamond, in fact everyone there was.

My father then appeared next, right there just boom … "Poppa, poppa … Mama … there you are!!!!" We embraced body and soul, for here in 5th density there were no separation and no density dividing us like borders. Here in this world the continents of our different bodies were incredibly interconnected, deeply empathetic, and psychically infused. We were one and because here there was no fear no hatred no agenda…. You could just merge like two candles becoming one. "Sophie my love my pearl, you made, you got here, I knew you would." My father was so handsome he looked like a chiseled God, I was like "damn daddy, you be looking good in 5D."

Ahhhhhhhhhhhhh it is so good to be with them again, it was like we had never been separated at all. Then there igniting before us came my whole extended family ... "Satva Saba (Hebrew for grandmother and grandfather) oh blessed be." We had a giant family reunion right there, all of us as our kin all would just suddenly appear before us. Jacob folks appeared and I got to meet them for the first time! All of us all my crew, all the 44 people there all had people coming through in orbs that manifested each into a being we knew and loved. We picked right back up to where we had left off in my earliest and fondest of memories, laughing joking playing together again as if I were a child. In all honesty it did feel like we were all children again, like our inner child was set loose. Our return to innocence, the return to wonder, to sacred magic, and to love like you have never experienced it before ... pure sweet agape in its richest of forms that was the norm here.

The "Great Reset" was complete; everyone here was reunited with their loved ones at last. The transfer and reset were confirmed and affirmed in a giant touch down yawp by Zepharo who opened his big mouth and shouted "Hooooorahhhhhhhhhhhhhhhh." His whoop was the most righteous guttural and primal call to the wild we had ever heard. Upon that piercing wail of Zepharo, it was all over ... the entire Squatch Nation followed their Chief's lead and followed with a hooting and hollering that will go down in her story for all of time. Their wild response to his call then inspired everyone to join in and let their voices be heard through the Galaxies which were all responding from our calls with cheers and singing from all directions. This glorious homecoming quickly turned into a marvel of a world upon world upon worldwide celebration that kicked off the 5th Age of Peace in an unforgettable way.

"Oh baaaaaabbbby, baaaaaabby .... Come dance with me Sophia Star Water ... guess what!!! Now you can marry me in 5D with all our whole entire family .... Just like a dream, just like heavan!" Jacob was levitating ... he was so happy, happiest I had ever seen. We all were ... I looked around at all our crew "The Apocalypsos" and they were all crying with joy as they were surrounded by their kin guides and guardians. "I kissed her face and kissed her head and dreamed of all the different ways I had to make her laugh." I looked at my man, my Star Lord my God, "oh Jacob," I said with a smile ... "why are you so far away? she said why won't you ever know that I'm in love with you?

That I'm in love with you?" Then we both chimed in together as Jacob picked me up and twirled me around ... "Youuuuuu Soft and only. You Lost and lonely. You Strange as angels. Dancing in the deepest oceans. Twisting in the water. You're just like a dream" .... We heard our crew gather round and King yelled "group hug yooooooooo woot woot woot" Thomas howled like a wolf, "Just like a dream," then everybody in our band was like singing together .... "Your Just like a dream .... Your Just like a dream ... Your just like Heaven." We were too, we were in heaven and it was just like a dream! "Maybe that's why it was The Cure right who wrote that song ... for that song be like a cure for all that mad shit we all just went through," said Mill Boy.

Niro then came over and gave us a vial with some crystal small shot glasses. It was an elixir he said to toast our graduation and evolution to the 5th Age of Peace! We all shared it toasting one another .... Bottoms up said Rebekah. We took that elixir in not expecting much ... but halo ... let's just say Niro knew how to get that party started .... Boo Yah and then, well basically we blissed out ... Forever!

The Beginning

5D

The New Age Begins
Book Two

The many pods and clans of the newly born Homo Illuminous or Homo Divinous as some preferred, scattered the lands of the living jewel of Aetherea. Organized in communities all over the ley line portals people came together and celebrated each day by soaking in the rich rays of solar power which brought solar power to our bodies of light.

"Sophia …. Staaarrrrrrr Waaaaater …. Where are youuuuu? I could hear my lover Jacob calling me from my hiding place. Giggling I peeked out from behind the jungle foliage which was like being nestled enclosed in a living emerald which nourished ones being like only prana can do. My heart star or God Spark which shone through my chest as everyone here did was beating super-fast from running and levitating around while playing hide and go seek with my beloved.

"Here I am …. Catch me if you can." Getting up from my hiding spot, I ran Godspeed fast through the trails that webbed through jungles of paradise and hid again behind a Jurassic sized fern gully. Rolling around in my sublime state of bliss I laughed deliriously drunk on love and the energetic fuel I had just feasted upon earlier from the power of the sun star that shone upon us. We called our sun star Surya and each morning we would gather to gaze at it while we would chant pray sing and dance; this was our yoga. We would gather in a giant group of us and do Qi Gong together while we fed upon the breath of life and fuel our heart stars with energy like a battery charger. We did this every morning every afternoon and evening. It was not only fun but super blisstastic. These daily rituals allowed for us to get our necessary supply of prana and chi or life source energy. We, also every evening would gaze upon the stars and planetary bodies and receive their emanations like food. Cosmic soup, it was the best high ever and fully satisfying. Here you could taste the ormus, taste the essence of every living plant flower tree crystal water spring everywhere … everything was alive here and its pollen was the nectar of creation which we all suckled upon regularly.

"I am going to get you … and when I do … I am going to make love to you like never before!" Secretly I wanted him to catch me for love making in this realm was like having an ultimate sublime divine energy transference that caused a surging yumminess through your body like holy fire! But I was having too much fun playing hide and seek with all my new powers and ohhhh the anticipation of being captured by my Lord was all too incredibly arousing. "Catch me if you can," I said while twirling above him like a ninja and darting off into a thick lush netting of green jungle where I disappeared inside the emerald vastness in a flash.

"You know I can feel you and trace your spark … I know where you are." Then just as fast as he had said this, like a nanosecond later there he was. I felt him before he had even caught me for his light radiated like the star Surya itself. Grabbing me into his warmth we rolled around in a carpet of flowers star flowers which released fairy dust which was like a love dust potion for believe it or not these flowers were actually an aphrodisiac; as if you needed one, lol.

We rode the waves of ecstasy that coursed through our unified field, wave after wave washing over us like an ocean of emotion full of love and pleasure. Seriously making love in 5D was like having every chakra orgasm at once.

We were already pregnant with our fist star child. I had no idea what having a child was like in this world and I had never done it before in my previous other world, so I was completely overwhelmed with excitement and anxiousness. I loved it though and I loved my parents doting over me. I loved my crew King, Avatar, Mill Boy, Thomas, Queen, Mercy, and Rebekah's constant cuddling and attention. We were all pregnant all my Queens and I. As my girls and I were retired Valkyries we basically put down the idea of ever having to work and instead played full time, even overtime.

Just then the gong sounded calling us all to the temple as it was time to have our daily devotions and classes. We raced each other as we rocked our mad parkour skills, jumping over rocks flying up trees, skipping over creeks, and giggling all the way. "I am gonna get there first!" I teased Jacob as I disappeared into a network of jungle vines. He leaped high off a tree top and triple flipped as he shot through the air landing perfectly on a bridge that took us over the massive river of life that ran below. The mists of the gushing waterfall just beyond the bridge sprayed us in the face as we were nearly neck and neck racing to see who could get to the Temple first. Jacob then scooped me up saying ..."now now my love you musn't get little star fire in your belly there too excited and we don't want our little cherubim to think for a second Mamma can beat Poppa, now do we!" He chuckled as large wings unfolded from his sides and flew me to Temple right on time for our lessons to begin.

The sounds of a million crystal bowls reverberated as they mixed with the gongs and chimes tied up everywhere in the gardens around the Temple Gates. We could see Zepharo laughing as he made a bet with some other Sasquatches as to who would get there first. He loved our grand entry and gave Jacob a pat on the back.

"Gather around gather around" said Niro and Zepharo as they got ready to teach us our daily classes upon how to use our powers. Our school was like going to Hogwarts minus the whole dark spells class and freaky wizards. Our school was total Magi training 101 and we loved learning it wasn't like high school was where you were like late every day because you hated going no it was like do we get to go to school yet? Can we have another class?

https://ascension.aum.ca/

Printed in the United States
By Bookmasters